K M HAMILTON

Rising Warrior

The Ebun Chronicles book 1

First published by Vieira Publishing 2022

Copyright © 2022 by K M Hamilton

All rights reserved. No part of this publication may be reproduced, stored or transmitted in any form or by any means, electronic, mechanical, photocopying, recording, scanning, or otherwise without written permission from the publisher. It is illegal to copy this book, post it to a website, or distribute it by any other means without permission.

Editor: Kite String Editing

Proofreader: Divas at Work Editing

Cover Art: Julia Bax

Cover Design: Miblart

First edition

This book was professionally typeset on Reedsy. Find out more at reedsy.com

Dedicated to my wonderful husband.

Contents

Acknowledgement	iii
Chapter 1	1
Chapter 2	22
Chapter 3	34
Chapter 4	44
Chapter 5	58
Chapter 6	86
Chapter 7	95
Chapter 8	108
Chapter 9	114
Chapter 10	129
Chapter 11	137
Chapter 12	143
Chapter 13	159
Chapter 14	165
Chapter 15	196
Chapter 16	208
Chapter 17	214
Chapter 18	228
Chapter 19	253
Chapter 20	267
Chapter 21	277
Chapter 22	296
Chapter 23	302

Chapter 24	308
Chapter 25	327
About the Author	345
Also by K M Hamilton	346

Acknowledgement

Many thanks to the following contributors: Jacob Vieira, Sarah Hamilton-Jiang, Ellie Race, Stephanie Francis, Mums Night Out Group, Sarah Sager.

Rising Warrior

THE EBUN
CHRONICLES

K M HAMILTON

Chapter 1

"Cuz, I'm going to be late! Are you ready?"

Marcus Campbell paced his aunt's faded navy carpet in his pearly-white trainers, his stomach flipping with excitement. His hands burned uncomfortably, as they always did when he was nervous, turning an embarrassing red noticeable even on his dark copper skin. He shoved them into his pockets, trying to ignore them.

"Calm down, cuz. You're still gonna be ten minutes early," his cousin yelled back.

In just a few minutes, all Marcus's hard work would pay off. He would be head boy of one of the Stratford gangs in East London: the Q Block crew. The biggest in the area.

His cousin Levi came bounding into the living room, tucking his shirt into his trousers. "I'm ready," he said eagerly.

"Why do you tuck your shirt in like that?" Marcus rubbed his forehead.

"It's comfortable."

"All right, all right, let's just go before we're late."

"You're obsessed with being early." Levi shook his head, following Marcus to the front door. "You think Crazy B cares what time he shows up?"

"The leadership is mine for the taking." Marcus grinned. "No way they're going to give that simp head role."

Crazy B was the other kid up for head position, but it was Marcus who had the brains and the brawn. He was the one who'd brokered the deals to combine the smaller gangs into one.

"Hang on, aren't we waiting for Ben?" Levi paused.

"Nah, he said he'll meet us there."

"This is a big deal for us, bro. He should be here, not running around after people."

"It's all good." Marcus put his hand on Levi's shoulder and guided him out of the door. "Jermaine's going to be waiting for me. Let's go."

The blustery wind whistled through the grey London flats. Marcus inhaled deeply as he pulled his hood over his hair; his attempt at growing dreads made it look as though he had small black stumps rising out of his head. He was tall for fifteen and, according to his cousin Ben, had soul-searching eyes. Perfect for commanding a gang, he'd said.

As they descended the gum-mottled stairs in their block of flats, Marcus's chest swelled with pride at the thought of what this would mean for him and his cousins. He'd finally feel as if he were in control of something in his life. His cousins would be his right-hand people for always sticking with him and trusting him. Maybe he could garner more trust with his aunt Georgie, too. He'd been living with her and the boys for the last eight years, but he ruled the roost. He'd tried to be respectful to his aunt, but it was too easy to get his own way with her; she always backed down. She didn't have the steel or resolve to control three teenage boys.

Now there was another complication: Carnell, her live-in

CHAPTER 1

boyfriend.

Marcus brushed off those thoughts and focused on what he would say to Jermaine. Jermaine had been best friends with Donovan, the previous head boy of Q Block crew, who'd landed in juvie two weeks ago. Marcus had worked closely with Jermaine and Donovan; they'd often asked for his opinions and for him to mediate between other gangs. Crazy B had tried to force his way into their conversations, but he was like a bull in a china shop, throwing his weight around and bragging about his connections. Marcus would keep Jermaine onside, obviously, but Crazy B needed placating.

Once Marcus and Levi emerged from the block of flats, they headed towards their local shop. Despite its proximity to his home, Marcus never went in there. His mum used to take him there for sweets at the end of every week—before she left. His heart still hammered when he got near. He shook his head hard. Even after eight years, he was still trying to dispel those memories.

"Marcus." A gravelly voice knocked him back into the present.

Carnell ambled towards them with one of his lackeys. A plume of smoke spiralled out of his mouth, and his eyes narrowed as the boys got closer. Like some museum painting, Carnell's eyes always followed Marcus, as if to judge him and pick him apart. Avoidance was the best way to deal with those withering looks, he'd found.

"Where you boys going?" Carnell's eyes swept over them.

"Just to meet some mates," Levi responded, trying to avoid Carnell's gaze.

"Hmm." Carnell nodded. "Do me a favour, yeah?"

He reached inside his pocket, and the hairs along Marcus's

spine stood up.

"We can't," Marcus interjected. "We're going to be late."

Carnell paused, his hand not yet out of his pocket, and squinted at him. Marcus held his gaze.

"Late for who?" Carnell straightened up.

"A group of us are meeting at the station." Heat rose in Marcus's neck as he tried to control his temper. He didn't have time to wait around. He wanted to be in a good mood when he met with Jermaine.

"All right," Carnell said slowly. "What time will you be back?"

Levi opened his mouth to reply, but Marcus jumped in. "Late."

Carnell took a long drag of his cigarette and smiled, showing a gleaming yellow tooth. There was nothing friendly about that face.

"Be back before eleven," he said as he brushed past Marcus. "The door will be chained after that."

He walked away with barely a glance backward. Marcus sighed in relief. The last thing he needed was to be held back by him.

"Why did you lie to him?" Levi asked, trying to keep up with Marcus's strides.

"We're not doing his dirty work for him."

"Why is it any different from what we do?"

"We just get small-scale stuff." Marcus stopped to look Levi in the eyes. "He's dangerous. Don't do any jobs for him, you understand?"

"Okay, cuz, relax." Levi broke his gaze.

Marcus continued to walk, slower this time, and placed his hand on Levi's shoulder. "Let's just enjoy this evening."

CHAPTER 1

He smiled. "Me being head boy is about all of us. You guys sticking by me, giving me information and advice. I couldn't have done this without you."

Levi grinned back. "Don't you forget it. I'm not hiding in any more bushes to spy for you, cuz."

Marcus laughed. "Don't worry, cuz. You'll be working for the head boy. No more lackey stuff for you."

Marcus saw his crew farther up the road, and his chest swelled at the sight of his friends. He could feel it all coming together; finally, their loyalty was going to be rewarded.

"Wha gwan?" they all chimed together in greeting, gripping and bumping one another's shoulders.

"What's going on, bro?" Tyler, one of the older members, grinned at him.

"You got something to light me up?" Marcus asked.

"What, right here?" Tyler's eyebrows shot up.

"Come on, man, don't keep me waiting. It's my big night."

Tyler reached into his pocket and pulled out a lighter. Marcus put his roll to his lips and lit up. Inhaling deeply, he momentarily closed his eyes, his cares and worries sliding out of his body.

"Let's go," he said. Everyone fell behind him into their regular spots, Tyler and Levi always the closest to him. His boys always had his back. He straightened, his chin held high.

"Did you speak to Jermaine?" he asked Tyler quietly.

"I tried to call him yesterday and today."

"What did he say?"

"Nothing. He didn't pick up."

Marcus stopped for a moment and stared at Tyler. A cold sensation ran down his spine. He forced himself to keep walking and push away the doubt that had suddenly seized him.

"Has he spoken to Crazy B?" He could barely utter the words.

"Not as far as I know." Tyler put an arm around his shoulder with a look of confidence. "You've got nothing to worry about, bruv. You've put in all the hard work. You put in all the hours and negotiations. The only thing Crazy B has to offer is his older brother. Everyone knows he's good for nothing."

Marcus swallowed. The thing about Crazy B's brother was that he was the leader of one of the adult crews. That was why Crazy B had false swagger. But Tyler was right; Marcus was worrying about nothing. Donovan knew who should be leader, who should protect their gang and reputation, and Marcus would never let him down.

"As long as Crazy B hasn't gotten to Jermaine and forced him to change Donovan's mind, we'll be all right," Tyler said.

"Crazy B is too shifty. We all know it. Donovan's not mad. He knows what he's doing." Marcus's own words comforted him. Crazy B had no backbone. When they'd gotten in a bust-up with another Streatham gang, Crazy B had been the first to run off, leaving Marcus and the others to clean up and sort them out.

"He's spineless." Tyler nodded. "Someone like him can't lead anything."

The streets were an unforgiving place. Marcus could count on both hands the number of times he'd barely escaped with his life. A couple of older guys had taken him under their wing back when his mum was still around. They'd taken pity on him, and he'd committed petty theft to earn a bit of extra money. In exchange, they'd allowed him to hang around for a couple of hours after school. Marcus would watch them

CHAPTER 1

closely: their tone of voice, how they spoke to each other, where they kept weapons, money. What they would reveal to some and not others. He quickly learned how to copy these mannerisms, how to bend people to his will—especially once his mum left. Donovan had been like a big brother, as they hung around the same people, and together, they had started the Q Block crew.

Donovan wouldn't let him down, not like his mum did when he was seven years old, and his dad before that. He could barely remember his dad leaving, but the memories of the day before his mother left threatened to ruin his big night. The look of fear in her eyes as she stood backed against the wall of their shabby flat . . .

Marcus's hands tingled uncomfortably, and again, he shoved them into his pockets. His stomach was tense now, despite the comfort of his smoke.

"We'll sort him out after I speak to Jermaine." Marcus smiled back. "Find a way to make him feel important."

The meeting spot was just a couple of roads away, and adrenaline pumped through his body the closer they got. All the mess he had to deal with growing up would finally be put behind him. He could prove himself; he would matter. It wouldn't just be his cousins Levi and Ben and his friend Tyler. Everyone in the area would know and respect him. His reach would be far and influential. He would have the protection of everyone now. His own man-made family.

Car lights flashed past them as the night descended. Marcus checked the time on his phone. There was still no sign of his other cousin.

"Where is this boy?" He put his phone to his ear. "Boy, where are you?"

"I'm coming, I'm coming," came Ben's voice, audibly out of breath.

"Good!"

Ben suddenly ran around the corner, his arms flailing as if he were dying on his feet. "Ahh, sorry I'm late," he gasped, resting his hand on his forehead. "My legs! And I'm sweating . . . urgh."

"You're late for everything," Levi snapped. "You couldn't be on time once?"

"I like to make an entrance." Ben glowered at his brother.

"Shut up, you two." Marcus gave them the look of silence, and both boys snapped their mouths shut.

Levi and Ben had been at each other's throats since Carnell moved in with them. Ben always seemed to rub Carnell the wrong way, and the man would lash out or make fun of him. Levi tried to make Ben keep quiet and stay out of Carnell's way. Marcus had stepped in once, but Ben had talked him down. Marcus wasn't going to let that happen again.

"Where were you, Ben?" he asked, changing the conversation.

"Oh, you know, I was just meeting up with Rochelle," Ben said.

"Who?"

"You know, I've told you about her before."

Marcus knew he hadn't. "Just be careful, yeah? You need to watch who you're with and what you're saying."

"Yeah, I know." Ben didn't meet his eyes.

Ben had a reputation for being a talker. Most of the time, he was useful in gaining knowledge from neighbouring schools and gangs; he made friends with everyone. But he'd dropped the ball a few weeks ago and caused serious problems for Q

CHAPTER 1

Block. Marcus had had to smooth things over with the older gang and promise it wouldn't happen again.

"Did you speak to that guy I told you about?" Marcus said to Ben.

"Yeah, I spoke to Leroy." Ben moved in closer. "Once you've been made leader, he'll be happy to talk."

"Was he telling the truth?"

"Yeah, I believe him. He had honest eyes."

Marcus nodded. Ben was a real people person. Eager to please and be liked, he knew how to win people in a friendly way. Marcus repeatedly warned him to be careful, though. He was an easy target for bullies and others in the community.

As they approached the corner where Marcus would leave the others to see Jermaine, he turned to his boys and smiled. "See you guys later, yeah?"

The others nodded, returning his smile. Levi gave him a thumbs-up as Marcus walked away.

Marcus took a deep breath, unable to stop his grin from shaping his face. He fiddled briefly with his metal chain necklace around his neck as Jermaine, slim and dressed all in black, rose to take his hand.

"Good to see you, man." Jermaine smiled as they smoothly performed their secret handshake.

"You two, bruv." Marcus sat opposite Jermaine on the concrete wall. "My boy Tyler said he hasn't heard from you for a couple of days."

"You know how it is, bro." Jermaine swooped his hand over his short braids. "Trying to clean things up, organise things now that Donovan's gone." He looked down at the floor and rested his elbows on his thighs. "Look, there's a problem, Marcus."

Marcus froze. "What is it?" he said, barely able to get the words out.

"Things have taken an unexpected turn."

"What do you mean? Is Donovan all right?"

"It's not Donovan. Crazy B is threatening to walk and take half the crew with him."

Marcus's blood ran cold. "What? Why?"

"He wants to be leader."

What was Crazy B doing? He would have to make him pay.

"Don't worry about him," Marcus said as calmly as he could. "Once I speak to him as leader, he'll know he can't pull that stuff."

"Yeah . . . about that . . ."

No, don't do this. Marcus shook his head.

"You're not being made head boy."

Marcus's head crumbled into his hands. He couldn't believe this was being ripped from him.

"I don't believe this." He sprang up and paced in a circle, trying to control the anger stirring inside, his hands burning in rage. "You're not giving it to me?"

Jermaine rubbed his head but kept it down. "I'm sorry, man. It was a tough decision, but Donovan decided it was for the best."

"What do you mean, 'for the best'? I brought everyone together. I'm the one who smoothed out things when he and Crazy B were at each other's throats. You're going to let this scumbag do this?"

"Donovan is grateful for what you've done." Jermaine stood up and tried to approach him. "The crew still needs you. You're vital to keep the group together now that he's gone."

Marcus stopped and stared at him, mouth agape. "You want

CHAPTER 1

me to stay? Nah, man."

"Things could get really dangerous for us now. We could be seen as weak now Donovan isn't here."

"You'd deserve it." Marcus scoffed.

"Marcus, I'm serious. You'd be in danger, too."

"Me? I can take care of myself."

"Against half of the streets? You're not thinking, man. If things break loose, you'll be caught in the crossfire from both sides. If you stay with us, you'll still have protection and clout. Don't forget Crazy B's brother is the head of Oldtown crew. We can't mess with them."

The Oldtown crew was one of the most dangerous gangs in East London. Marcus's crew had some protection because of that affiliation.

Marcus snorted. Everyone thought he was in line to be the next leader, *everyone*. If anyone doubted that fact, it was because they didn't like him. Now that he was being denied the headship, he'd look weak if he stayed in the crew.

But where would he go? There were no other local gangs he could join; he would be a sitting duck. Or if he did defect, he could cause all-out war, which had a certain appeal at this moment.

"Why did Donovan change his mind? Why did he give it to Crazy B?"

"I don't know." Jermaine shrugged. "He said he had a visitor."

"A visitor? Who?"

"He said he'd never met him before. Tallest guy he'd ever seen, skin like the night with a bald shiny head. He said his eyes were red."

Marcus watched Jermaine closely. He was completely still,

with no hint of deception in him. Marcus's mind raced to identify any tall people he knew with red eyes. He'd never seen any man who matched that description. "What did this man say?"

"Donovan was shook. He said Crazy B needed to be in charge. He would keep the peace."

Marcus spat in disgust, then wiped his wet lips. So this total stranger had walked in and ruined his life for no good reason. That was all he needed.

"I'm sorry I can't tell you more, Marcus. I know what you've done, and if it was up to me, you would be the one to lead us. No doubt. At least stay with us for a while."

Marcus looked back at the road he'd come down. Round that corner, all his friends were waiting for him to come back. To lead them. He swallowed hard, pushing his anger down.

"All right . . . yeah," he said quietly.

Jermaine sighed and tried to embrace Marcus, who barely responded.

"Thanks, bro." Jermaine smiled. "This means a lot, you know. We won't forget this, all right?"

For two solid years, Marcus had worked for this. He'd coerced, persuaded, and pressured the neighbouring gang to join with them. When the gangs in the other boroughs had gotten bigger, he'd been the first to sound the alarm. He had traction with the older gangs in the borough, which was more than could be said about Crazy B, who'd spent his whole time sucking up to Donovan. Not a single original thought had ever entered Crazy B's head, and he'd contributed nothing.

Marcus's fists balled, only slightly cooler than they'd been before. His jaw clenched so hard, it ached.

This was how they rewarded his hard work, by allowing some stranger to derail everything. He could've handled Crazy B by himself, or asked Crazy B's brother to control him better.

But he couldn't control someone he'd never met: a tall stranger with red eyes who must have intimidated Donovan. He needed to find out who this stranger was and make them pay for robbing him of what was rightfully his.

How much longer could he wait before he got what he deserved? A place to belong, and some control over his life for once.

As he left Jermaine, Marcus racked his brains, trying to think which adult hated him enough to sabotage him like this. The description didn't match any of the leaders of the adult gangs. Maybe it was one of their subordinates he hadn't met, but the question remained as to why. The only person he could think of was Carnell. Marcus never did his bidding, hardly spoke to him, and had once come close to exchanging fists.

Swallowing what was left of his pride, Marcus went to deliver the bad news to his awaiting friends.

"I can't believe they did this to you." Tyler shook his head in disbelief. "You practically made this crew. Without you, we'd still be tiny, fighting off all the other gangs."

Half an hour later, they were sitting in Tyler's living room. His mum worked late, and they'd taken full advantage, with lots of people milling around and drink flowing to drown their disappointment. Marcus had walked there in a daze, ignoring all attempts from his boys to engage with him. Levi had recognised his fury and diverted everyone's questions.

"Yeah, I know," Marcus muttered. His head was feeling fuzzy, which made it difficult to think clearly. "Are you sure you heard nothing about this, Ben?"

Ben, who was sitting beside him, shook his head. "Nothing. Everyone I spoke to thought you were going to get it. They were looking forward to it."

"You hear everything," Levi interjected, his eyes narrowed as if he didn't trust his brother. "You trying to tell me there wasn't even a whisper of something going on? Are you protecting somebody?"

"No. I'm telling you there was nothing, and from that description, it could be anybody. That man might not even be from around here."

"Why would anyone outside of our crews care about Marcus?" Tyler said. "Are you sure you haven't been running your mouth?"

"No, I haven't." Ben's voice climbed an octave, and his eyes looked hurt. "I only made that mistake once. I've told you all it won't happen again."

"Enough, fam," Marcus cut in. "I need to think."

His head was hurting, and he needed to calm down. He could feel anger beginning to replace his melancholy.

The doorbell rang, and a hush fell across the room.

Tyler and Marcus looked at each other for a moment before standing up to answer it. Marcus's heart raced, but he held up his head as they opened the door.

A chubby freckled kid with bleached-blond hair stood on the other side. He peered up at them from under his dark green hood, flanked by two other hooded boys.

CHAPTER 1

Crazy B.

"Wha gwan?" The guy smirked.

Marcus nodded and forced his hands into his pockets to stop himself from doing anything stupid.

Crazy B looked back at him, waiting for him to speak. Marcus wasn't going to give him the satisfaction.

"You want to come in?" Tyler's hands twitched.

"Marcus," Crazy B said slowly as he stepped to the side. "Let's talk."

"I'm good here," Marcus replied, folding his arms. He wasn't stupid enough to allow them to jump him and teach him to fall in line.

"Fair enough. Look, we don't want no drama. We got to do what's best for the crew, right?"

Marcus wanted to spit. He took a deep breath and looked directly in Crazy B's eyes.

"We could be a good team, you and me. You bring people together. I have the manpower." Crazy B pointed his two thumbs back towards his crew. "We got you, Marcus. We just need to know we're on the same team here."

"What do you want from me?" Marcus shifted his feet.

"We think it's time we do our own thing. Make some serious cash. We need to shift bigger things. I think Donovan was playing it too safe."

Marcus smirked to himself. Donovan was smart. He hadn't trusted Crazy B's lot, and that was why he hadn't expanded into more dangerous territory.

Crazy B's bark was worse than his bite. Marcus wondered if he had an inferiority complex, overcompensating for his lack of brains or tact. The number of times Crazy B had backtracked when he'd been caught bad-mouthing Donovan and other influential gangs was a joke. Marcus had told him on many occasions to stop or he'd be thrown out; it would catch up with him. He'd even bad-mouthed his own brother, to make himself look hard.

"What do you need me to do?" Marcus asked.

"Keep everybody sweet. Tell them something big is coming and to be ready when it does. People are going to know the Q Block crew."

"Who you selling to?"

"Some new guys from Eastern Europe."

Cold washed over Marcus. "Are you mad? We don't know anything about them."

"Exactly." Crazy B smiled, looking back at the two boys flanking him.

Marcus shook his head. The Eastern European gang had moved in only a couple of months ago. "This is a mistake. We need to get to know them first, and who's dealt with them before."

"Make it happen, Marcus. Word on the street is there are deals to be done with them. I want to get in first."

One of Crazy B's boys took out his phone, and after a couple of seconds, Marcus's phone vibrated.

What an idiot, Marcus thought. There was no way adults were going to let small-time kids get rich, especially if they were strangers. Marcus looked at his phone: Dacus.

"Don't contact him until I tell you, yeah?" Crazy B leaned in close, as if to appear menacing.

"Fine. What's the time frame?"

"Two weeks."

Marcus felt sick, but he swallowed and nodded. He couldn't believe he was taking orders from this fool who was actively

CHAPTER 1

trying to get him in trouble straightaway.

"Laters." Crazy B turned around without waiting for a reply.

Tyler shut the door; Marcus licked his parched lips.

The price of being an orphan was that there was no one to save you. No one to tell you to choose otherwise from a place of deep love. No one to give you options. Despite the love his aunt had for him, she didn't treat him exactly the same as her boys.

Tyler put his hand on Marcus's shoulder.

"Two weeks isn't enough time," Tyler said. "Background checks and establishing contact with guys we know nothing about. Is this a death trap?"

"Looks like it." Marcus sighed.

For the rest of that evening, Marcus sat in the corner of Tyler's living room, watching the rest of his close-knit friends laugh and tease one another.

He couldn't do it.

Even the new girls Tyler had tried to introduce to Marcus couldn't lift his mood.

"You're quiet," said a silky-soft voice.

Marcus turned to see a short girl with long black braids and almond-shaped hazel eyes looking up at him. Her skin reminded him of honey.

"Yeah . . . I've got a lot on my mind." Marcus averted his eyes. He needed to think. Should he get behind Crazy B? Or risk subverting his leadership?

"I've been looking forward to seeing you for ages."

"It's been a bad night."

"I'm sorry about that." She positioned herself behind him,

gently placing her hands on his shoulders, and tried to knead out his tension.

Marcus sighed loudly, wanting to find an escape from the room. He reached into his back pocket and got his phone. There was a missed call from his aunt Georgie.

The time was a quarter to eleven. He had to leave.

He quickly exchanged numbers with the braided girl at her insistence, then glanced around to track his cousins. Out of nowhere, Tyler grabbed him by the arm.

"You all right, bruv?" Tyler looked earnestly at Marcus. "Don't do anything stupid. Just keep your head down for a bit. We'll figure this out together."

Marcus tensed at these words. He wouldn't act rashly, but he had every right to. It was his right to show Crazy B who was boss.

"Yo, Marcus." Levi's face appeared from the corridor. "Mum's been calling. We've got to go!"

* * *

Marcus, Levi, and Ben ran at full pelt down the road.

"You didn't hear your phone ring?" Ben asked Levi.

"It was on silent. Didn't she call you?" Levi said in defence. "My phone died!"

Levi glanced at Marcus. "Why didn't you pick up?"

"I didn't hear it," he replied. He just wanted to be left alone.

"She was chewing out my ear, man," Levi complained. "We're going to be in so much trouble."

CHAPTER 1

The boys rounded the corner and sprinted up the stairs, onto their corridor, where loud music boomed from the neighbours' flat. Levi opened the door.

"Hi, Mum," he panted. "Sorry we're late."

"You know what, Levi?" Aunt Georgie came through the door, her arms crossed. "It's eleven o'clock at night. What do you boys think you're doing?"

"It's eleven fifteen," Marcus found himself saying. He instantly regretted it.

Her eyes swivelled towards him. "You think this is a game?"

Her voice had a dangerous edge, her anger close to the surface. Her short brown curly hair was swept up into a small bun. Freckled cheeks and a small frame made her look younger than she was, but whenever she lost her temper, she commanded respect in such a way that everyone paid attention.

"No . . . no, I was just trying to be accurate," Marcus said, his voice becoming quieter.

"There are dangerous people out there." Aunt Georgie's voice grew low, almost threatening. She pointed towards the door. "I can't help you out there. When you're out late at night, you're on your own."

One of those dangerous people is shacked up in here, Marcus thought. His eyes flitted towards the living room, where Carnell's leg stretched out into view.

"I'm so sorry, Mum," Ben quivered. "I would've picked up my phone, but it died. You know I'm normally the sensible one—"

"You can't sweet-talk your way out of this, Ben. The streets are dangerous. I keep telling you boys, yet still, you come home later and later."

"It wasn't our fault—" Marcus started, his cheeks burning.

Her head snapped towards him. "Whose fault is it, then?"

Marcus looked away. He didn't have it in him to argue with her. She had no idea what he was involved in and how everything he had fought for was now hanging in the balance. Honour was everything on the streets. Without respect, you were a walking target, or worse, you were nothing.

"We'll be back earlier in the future, Mum. Promise," Levi said.

"You said that last time. What's it going to take for you boys to get it—"

"Come on," a lazy drawl came from Carnell's direction. "I'm trying to watch TV. Let them go upstairs, man."

There was a collective moment where everyone held their breath, shocked that he was so quick to let them off the hook. Aunt Georgie glanced back at him, a puzzled look on her face. Marcus's mind began to spin. Why was Carnell so eager for her to leave them alone? Why was he so calm? Did he have something to do with Marcus's displacement in the crew?

When Aunt Georgie turned back to them, the anger had fallen from her face.

"All right, boys." She sighed. "Go to your rooms. I don't want to hear another word."

The boys trudged upstairs and split off into their rooms. Marcus was grateful for the concern, but he always wondered if what she was actually concerned about was Levi and Ben following him around.

Marcus threw off his hoodie and collapsed on the bed, sighing deeply as his eyes rested on the window.

He'd known it was late and they should have been back

CHAPTER 1

sooner, but he hadn't cared too much at the time. It was only because of his cousins' insistence that he had started to run home with them. The run had calmed him down—his hands no longer burned, and his anger had dissipated—but he wasn't going to let Crazy B get away with what had happened tonight. Being Crazy B's subordinate was unacceptable. The guy would put everyone down, try to assert his power, make risky deals, and lead the crew to ruin.

As the evening wore on and sleep crept into his body, Marcus concluded someone would have to pay, and whatever the cost, he was going to be head boy.

Chapter 2

The blazing morning sun streamed in through Marcus's window and shone brightly on his closed eyelids. He'd fallen asleep on his bed without showering, and he stank. He got up and headed to the bathroom to clean himself off. He'd slept well, and the beginnings of a plan were formulating in his mind.

After a hot shower and a change of clothes, he headed downstairs.

"Afternoon," Ben chirped, eating cereal on the sofa.

"What do you mean 'afternoon'?" Marcus asked, stretching the last of his negative thoughts away.

"It's late, boy." Ben snickered.

"Who are you calling 'boy'?" Marcus laughed, playfully kicking Ben's foot.

"Don't do that. I bruise easily!" Ben squealed.

Marcus walked into the kitchen. "Is there anything to eat?"

"Mum left some cornmeal before she went out," Levi cut in as he entered the living room. "We got any plans for today?"

"Nah." As Marcus lifted the lid of a pot on the stove, the smell of creamy corn, cinnamon, and nutmeg hit his nostrils. He inhaled deeply, and his stomach rumbled. Memories of

CHAPTER 2

Saturday mornings spent eating cornmeal porridge with his mum and Aunt Georgie intruded on his mind. Forcing the thought away, he served himself a heaping bowl of the steamy yellow porridge.

"Don't eat all of that, you hear?"

Marcus spun round to see Carnell's silhouette in the doorway.

"I'm not here just so you can stuff your face." Carnell was so still, he looked frozen, yet his stare burned through Marcus's eyes, as if to destroy him right there on the spot. Marcus wanted to punch right through his face, break the hold of fear his presence seemed to inflict on the house.

"There's plenty left." Marcus turned away, grabbing his spoon and looking out the window.

"Good."

Marcus quickly made his escape as Carnell advanced into the kitchen. The man's unpredictable nature was the last thing he wanted to experience right now.

Some days, Carnell tolerated Marcus. Other days, he looked at him like something nasty on his shoe. He didn't treat Levi much better, but he was particularly mean to Ben. Carnell was a man of the streets, as was Marcus, and even more protective of his reputation. He constantly smirked and laughed at Ben's flamboyance, which made Ben more and more uncomfortable in his own home.

In the beginning, Marcus had thought of getting into Carnell's good books, maybe putting himself in a good position for another time. But when he saw how the man belittled and talked down to his cousins, he couldn't stomach it. He'd seen him throw the TV remote at Levi's head once. At first, Marcus hadn't understood how Aunt Georgie could stand Carnell's presence, but one evening, he'd overheard a conversation in their living room when he went to get a glass of water. Carnell had been saying how he'd take care of her; she wouldn't need to worry about her boys. His voice had been soft as butter as she giggled.

Protection was what mattered round here. If you weren't covered, you were liable to get picked off. She gave him shelter and a bed; he promised her and her boys protection outside the door, and other more intimate privileges. Any of his own acts of violence or intimidation he explained away as being "discipline" or as commanding respect. Marcus guessed his aunt believed she couldn't do any better.

He'd often wondered what Carnell dealt in. As Marcus tried not to burn his mouth with the cornmeal, he scrolled through the contacts on his phone, trying to figure out if there was any crossover between his gang and Carnell's. Q Block dealt in petty crime. Was it possible Carnell's crew, Silent Death, wanted to expand into the younger gangs? Carnell would know there was more chance of Hell freezing over than Marcus bringing the crews together. Crazy B, however, was power -hungry. If his brother wasn't encouraging him to expand—which would've been the logical conclusion—he was mad enough to look elsewhere for allies. Like Carnell's Silent Death.

Marcus's finger hovered over Shaun's name. He wanted more information about Crazy B's next moves, but he needed something solid to link Crazy B with Silent Death before he called in favours to Shaun.

After devouring his breakfast, Marcus headed towards Grandma Maisey's house with his cousins.

"I just need to visit Dwayne," he said as they walked along

the pavement.

"Do we have to?" Ben rolled his eyes. "That woman he's with scares me."

Marcus chuckled. "Fine, you guys can wait by the wall for me."

Ben wasn't wrong about Dwayne's right-hand woman, Cherry. She was built for the army, had piercings all over her face, and looked as though she just wanted an excuse to punch someone's lights out. But Marcus needed money, and he couldn't rely on Q Block with Crazy B in charge. Dwayne, a small-time "trader," had looked out for Marcus ever since he first moved in with Aunt Georgie. In exchange for small stolen goods, Dwayne would give Marcus some money, which took the pressure off his aunt. He never had to ask her for anything, and she never asked where he got his new trainers or how he could afford the cinema. He suspected she knew, hence why she kept someone like Carnell around.

Marcus had brought a backpack of stash with him, a few things he'd collected over the last couple of months from nearby electrical shops. His cousins or friends would distract the shopkeeper so he could slip things into his coat or pockets. Security barriers didn't seem to work around him; his hands always burned as he willed the alarm to keep silent, which it always did. Even the cameras didn't catch him: a secret skill he seemed to possess, although he tried not to think about it too much. He was tired of being different, an outsider. No one understood how he dodged the cameras and alarms. Marcus was just grateful for a bit of good luck in his life.

They approached a familiar narrow footpath with high redbrick walls on either side. This pathway always filled him with dread. It felt more like an enclosure than a path.

He'd managed to swipe only a few expensive earphones to trade. The security tags had come off easily in his hands.

"Just wait here, yeah?" he said.

"We'll keep watch." Levi nodded.

Marcus crossed the road towards the narrow alleyway. It felt like the longest walk of his life. If you got jumped, there was no way to escape.

Two hooded figures sat on the wall straight ahead, and a third leaned next to them, their faces obscured. Marcus swallowed as the shorter one walked with a swagger towards him, lowering the hoodie to reveal a shock of blond locks and a glistening nose ring.

"What's up?" Cherry's gruff voice asked, her eyes fixed on him. "What you got for us?"

Marcus swung his bag off his shoulder and revealed the five wireless earbuds he had. She swiped them quickly and turned back to the others. Marcus stepped back, slightly unnerved by her swiftness.

The three slowly turned the loot in their hands, the other two faces still shrouded in darkness.

"Seems legit," the male voice in the middle said to Cherry. Dwayne's voice was deep and penetrating. Unnaturally tall and dark like the night, he was an intimidating presence. He knew everyone in the area, one of the few able to navigate each of the gangs and retain his position as a provider of resources.

Was it him who'd sabotaged Marcus, despite all the things Marcus had provided for him? What would he have to gain? Marcus tried to swallow down these questions until he was away from them.

Dwayne pocketed the treasures with one hand, drawing on

a roll with his other, and nodded towards Cherry. A plume of smoke drifted from the shadow of his hood.

Cherry turned around, flicking through a wad of notes in her hands. "There you go," she said, slapping the money into Marcus's palm.

He did a quick count. Only ninety pounds.

"Only ninety?" he asked, shocked. "Those are worth a hundred each, and I got you five."

"Yeah? What you gonna do about it?" she said, squaring up her shoulders.

Marcus's face burned, and he clenched his fists. "Those were really hard to get. I'm worth more than that, bruv." Was everyone trying to make him mad?

"You being ungrateful?" Cherry asked, pulling her hands out of her pockets.

"No, I just deserve more than that." Marcus glared back.

"Cherry," Dwyane's deep voice cut in. "Give him another twenty."

Marcus nodded in his direction, unsettled that Dwayne hadn't removed his hood. What was he hiding from?

Cherry narrowed her eyes, kissed her teeth, and dug into her pocket for an extra twenty. She pressed it hard into his hand.

"Thanks," Marcus forced out. With one last glance at the three suspicious characters, he turned and headed back towards his cousins, putting the money in different pockets. His face cooled, and his shoulders began to relax as he walked away.

When he approached the entrance of the alleyway, a police car crawled across the road, the officer's eyes following Marcus's path. His blood ran cold as it passed him. With his heart in his throat, he fixed his eyes straight ahead, hands firmly in his pockets. If he was pulled aside, although he wasn't carrying any loot, they'd question why a Black fifteen-year-old was walking around with over a hundred pounds on him.

The police car rolled on. Marcus sighed in relief and crossed the road to his cousins.

"That was close," Levi said, fear still etched into his face.

"I know." Marcus breathed heavily, rubbing the stubby locks on his head.

"How much did they give you?" Ben asked.

"Not as much as I deserved." Marcus shrugged. At least, he'd squeezed a bit extra. "Let's go to Gran's. We can share it there."

His heart began to steady as they headed towards his gran's house, the only place on Earth he truly felt safe and sheltered from his reality. He needed a place to relax and gather his thoughts. It was too risky to get stoned outside when he had been so publicly humiliated by being denied leadership of Q Block. Seen as a liability, he'd be easy pickings. What he needed was to lay low.

They rounded a corner onto his gran's street. Hers was a small grey-and-white house—one of many lifeless 1960s buildings from the outside, but the inside was full of colour and the smells of spiced curries and beans. Memories of family and laughter, reggae, and stories of back home in Jamaica, his gran's origin, began to filter through his malaise.

A woman with long white locks swept up into a bun and a tasselled shawl around her shoulders stood on his grandma's doorstep. She turned to face them, and her eyes instantly locked with Marcus's. She was a little younger than his

CHAPTER 2

grandma. Her eyes sparkled, and a smile spread across her freckled cheeks.

Just as the boys approached, the front door swung open.

"Amala." His grandma beamed, embracing her friend. Her eyes opened to see her grandchildren watching awkwardly. "What a surprise, boys." Her smile widened as she released the woman. "What have I done to be so popular today?"

"We just wanted to see you." Levi stepped forward and hugged his grandma tight.

"Come, come! I'll fix you all something to eat." Grandma Maisey tried to usher everyone in.

"Maisey, let me go. You spend some time with your grandsons," the lady called Amala said, stepping away from the door.

"Stay, Amala. I'll put on some tea."

"I'll come back later. Spend some time with your boys." With a wink at Marcus, Amala twirled round and swirled off. Marcus watched her stride down the road.

Ben took Grandma Maisey's arm. "She's very regal, Grandma," he said, nodding at Amala's disappearing frame. "You have great taste in friends."

Ben was right; she'd had an aura of importance. Even her speech suggested she was highly educated. Why had she paid Marcus any attention? As he walked into Grandma Maisey's house, he wondered if his gran had been talking to this stranger about him and his life.

"Marcus," his grandma said, holding him tight. The smell of flowers and her soft, pillowy skin next to his cheek began to melt his rigid body. Her hair was dyed a dark red-brown, and she wore a delicate silk scarf around her neck and a smidge of plum lipstick. She was the complete opposite of his stressed and dishevelled aunt.

"It's so nice to see you boys." Grandma Maisey pulled away and rubbed his back. "It's been too long. Sit down and let me fix you all something to eat." She squeezed Levi's cheek before she left the room.

Marcus felt a pang of guilt in the pit of his stomach for not coming to see her more often. When they were younger, he and his cousins would visit every week with Aunt Georgie, but as they got older, that had gone down to barely once a month. Yet, whenever he felt lonely or insecure, Grandma Maisey's home was a haven. It was quiet, no drama, and plenty of soul-filling food. Time seemed to stand still, and happy memories of his aunt and his mum warmed his soul.

Marcus shook his head, trying to stop any memories of his mum from penetrating his thoughts. He took the money out of his pocket and split it up, retaining more for himself, since he'd done the deal.

Grandma appeared from the kitchen with fruit juice and biscuits. Just like old times.

"Thank you, Grandma." Ben smiled, his hand launching for the biscuits.

"You're welcome, darling," she said and sat opposite them on her floral sofa. "Now tell me, what brings you boys over today?"

Marcus shifted in his seat. "We just wanted to spend some time with you, Grandma." He took a large gulp of juice.

"You sure you're not getting into any trouble?" she said, her eyebrow arching as she lifted her cup of tea to her mouth. Her eyes watched the boys closely.

"No, Grandma." Levi smiled. "We're being good."

"Very well." She placed the teacup back on the dish. "How

CHAPTER 2

are you all doing at school? Ben, I hope you are still getting top marks?"

"Of course, Grandma," Ben said, devouring another biscuit.

"Good, and how about you, Levi?"

"I'm doing all right, Grandma." He nodded, tentatively nibbling a biscuit.

"Does that mean top marks?"

"I'm trying."

"I hope so. You can do great things, Levi." She turned to Marcus. "You, Marcus? Are you making me proud?"

Marcus blinked at her for a moment, surprised at the word "proud." No one had ever used that word with him.

"He always gets top marks, Grandma," Levi interjected.

"Good." She beamed. "Don't squander your gifts, boys. You are bright. Apply yourselves and change the world."

Marcus couldn't help but smile at his grandma's optimism. He was smart, but he had to survive on the streets first if he was ever going to get anywhere in life. He didn't always apply himself, but he always seemed to get away with it in class. He had his final exams next year, so he knew he would have to work harder at some point.

They exchanged pleasantries for an hour. Marcus's whole body had finally relaxed, and his mind was clearer than it had been in days.

"You boys are such a blessing." Grandma Maisey smiled benevolently at her grandsons. "You have such flair, Ben, the joy you could bring to people's lives! Levi, you are the most loyal person I have ever met. Make sure you align yourself with someone who is worthy. Marcus . . . you are the most curious. You could be great . . . Make sure the path you are on is a noble one, my boy. Your mother isn't here to set you straight, but I sure will."

The peace Marcus had felt imploded. What did she know?

"What do you mean, Grandma?" He swallowed, trying to feign a smile. Why would she bring up his mother like this?

"Your mother is a good woman, but she never took charge of her life. The prettiest girl in the neighbourhood, smart like you too, and yet, she could never make things work for her."

She leaned in then, an intensity in her eyes Marcus had only seen once in his life: the time she had asked Aunt Georgie if she could really take care of Marcus. Aunt Georgie had insisted that being with family his own age would be best. He'd enjoyed every minute with his cousins.

"Life will be much harder on you, Marcus. Use all of your powers to be a success. But remember to trust others and help those who love you the most."

Why was she talking like this? There was no way she could know what his life involved, what it was like. How he constantly had to prove himself and stand on his own.

A loud ringtone snapped the tension that had been gripping Marcus's stomach. It took him a moment to realise it was his cell.

Crazy B's number popped on his screen. His hands gripped the phone.

"Hello?" Marcus kept his voice level.

"It's B."

Marcus stood, mouthing the word "sorry" to his grandma before exiting the room. Ordinarily he would have never interrupted his grandma's conversation, but he didn't want to hear what she had to say next. What would she know about being alone on the streets?

"What's up?" Marcus said, shutting the door behind him.

"You started making any moves yet?"

"On what?"

"The deal I need you to close," Crazy B huffed.

Marcus scrunched his eyes. "Yeah, I'm making some plans." He needed to buy himself time.

"Good. People need to know I'm in charge. I'm going to make moves."

"I got it covered." Marcus sighed. "You don't need to worry about a thing, bro."

Chapter 3

It was a long walk home. The streets were deserted, the shadows long and threatening. Ordinarily, Marcus would have been on high alert, but he could think of nothing other than removing Crazy B from his life.

The time was nine o'clock when Marcus and Levi left Grandma Maisey's. Ben had left earlier to meet some school friends. Marcus encouraged him to dig around, see how people really felt about Crazy B leading Q Block. Ben was eager to help, as always. He was proud to be connected to his cousin, not only for prestige but also for protection. No one would mess with him with Marcus around. Marcus had even overheard him brag about it once, much to his embarrassment.

Levi never bragged. Marcus had always thought he was just a quiet supporter, but lately he'd noticed Levi seemed withdrawn and would sometimes shoot him resentful glances. The unspoken tension made Marcus deflect any praise. In his heart he begged for it to disappear.

When Marcus and Levi arrived home, the television was blaring. They walked into the living room, furtively glancing at Carnell slumped on the sofa. Marcus hurried into the

CHAPTER 3

kitchen to get a glass of water.

"All right, Carnell?" Levi said, trying to make conversation. "Is Mum in?"

"She's upstairs, man," Carnell slurred. A can of beer dangled from his fingertips, and two lay crumpled at his feet. Marcus hadn't known him to be a big drinker; it was too early for him to be drunk. Every muscle in Marcus's body tensed.

"Where's your brother, Levi?" Carnell asked slowly.

"Umm . . . he's out with friends. He'll be back soon."

Carnell didn't respond. His eyes stayed fixed on some violent movie, someone's brains being blown out. Marcus couldn't stand the tension and walked past the screen to get to his room. Carnell didn't flinch.

Tiredness dragged Marcus down like a weight tied around his shoulders. The walk home had led to a plan emerging; he knew what action to take. Tomorrow was Sunday. He'd pick through some electrical stores on the other side of London and be back in time to go see Dwayne and Cherry—find out how to get in their good books and get money and protection from them. Getting closer to the adult gangs was key. Maybe he could even find Crazy B's older brother and usurp his authority.

Marcus lay down on the bed. He'd barely finished scrolling through his social media before he was fast asleep.

A loud cry startled Marcus awake, every fibre of his being frozen. His eyes darted around as he tried to figure out where he was. It took him a moment to recognise the shapes of his room.

He heard another loud cry and leapt out of bed.

Dashing to the hallway, he headed straight to the living

room, pushing the door wide open.

Ben was on the floor, cowering at the feet of Carnell.

Carnell looked so angry it was evil.

"What did you say to him?" shouted Carnell over the huddled form.

"I don't remember . . . I swear!"

Carnell punched Ben so hard in the back that his spine arched at the impact. The cry sent shockwaves through Marcus, and his face began to burn. Heat rose in his chest. Levi and Aunt Georgie burst past him, almost knocking him out of the way.

"What's going on? Carnell, what are you doing?" His aunt's face slacked in horror as she reached down to her youngest son.

Carnell grabbed her by her collar and threw her onto the other side of the room.

"He needs to answer me," Carnell slurred. "He's been running his mouth."

"Leave him alone! He's a kid! What's wrong with you?" Aunt Georgie cried as she scrambled to her feet, Levi heaving her up.

"He thinks he's smart. He thinks it doesn't matter what he does. Actions have consequences. He's messed up big time." Carnell began to undo his belt. "I'm going to show him who's smart now."

"Stop!" Marcus shouted. Red-hot anger raged through his blood as he barrelled towards Carnell.

But tonight Carnell had superhuman strength. In one push, he dashed Aunt Georgie into the TV. He knocked Levi over his brother, smashing his face on the table.

Marcus's knuckles felt as if they would split as his fist col-

CHAPTER 3

lided with Carnell's eye socket. Carnell stumbled backwards but regained his footing, then lunged at Marcus. His face twisted in rage, his teeth bared.

Carnell moved swiftly, cracking a punch into Marcus's forehead. Marcus's knees buckled. Water sprang to his eyes, and pain washed over his face.

He couldn't think or see for a moment. Everything went dull before it came back into sharp focus. Levi was trying to drag a crying Ben out of the room. Aunt Georgie yanked at Carnell, who was advancing towards Ben. Carnell shoved her off.

Anger exploded in Marcus with such force he felt as if he were on fire. All he could see was blood red as he ran straight at Carnell.

Carnell abruptly spun round to point a gun an inch from Marcus's face.

Marcus froze. He could barely breathe, the rage dissipating slightly. Every bone in his body felt like lead. Fear gripped his stomach. He tried to swallow and clawed at the rage to hold on to it longer.

"Step away," Carnell said through gritted teeth. His eyes looked dead. "I'm handling business."

In a split second, Marcus reached for the weapon. As he ducked to the side, a loud bang escaped the gun. Terror coursed through his body, but he couldn't lose focus.

He tried to pry the gun out of Carnell's hands, but Carnell started to overwhelm him, turning the gun to point at him. Marcus's hands shook with the strain to keep it away. He closed his eyes, reaching for that rage to give him strength.

Carnell was now pulling him close by the scruff of his neck, while Marcus held on to the gun in one hand and Carnell's wrist with the other. Marcus's hands seemed to become fire, his whole body consumed in heat and his ears pounding.

The gun began to turn by itself.

It turned all the way round.

Carnell's face changed from madness to fear. His mouth slacked, eyes widening. Marcus focused all his mental effort to force the gun down. It was light in his hands, moving by itself.

Sweat ran down Carnell's terror-etched face. "No . . . ," he gasped.

A bang shattered the silence, and Carnell and Marcus crumpled to the floor.

Marcus sat up, looking over at where Carnell sat gripping his thigh. The man hollered like some kind of animal as blood began to bubble through his trouser leg. Ben was screaming, Aunt crying. Levi came over and shouted something. Marcus couldn't hear. He couldn't think. He felt as if he'd fallen into a river of ice. Numb and freezing. All heat had left him; his eyes and forehead throbbed.

"Call the ambulance! Call the ambulance!" someone shouted.

Someone pushed him out of the way. Marcus observed this slow-motion event before time suddenly sped up with sharp, piercing clarity. He got up and ran to get towels, passing Levi on his phone. By the time he ran back to put a towel on Carnell's leg, Marcus was starting to sweat.

"You shot me!" Carnell repeated over and over again.

CHAPTER 3

The ambulance came quicker than he anticipated.

Marcus was panicked, frightened. He felt as though he wanted to crawl out of his body—leave this place and his existence.

Bad things always happened around him. People always left.

He really was the cause.

The three boys sat in the hospital corridor, drained and frightened.

"Do you think he's going to die?" Levi whispered, the first one to speak for hours.

"I hope he does," Ben said, his voice croaky from crying and his face still swollen from his beating. He turned to Marcus. "You saved us."

"No, I didn't," Marcus replied. His skin felt clammy and cold. He thought he was going to be sick.

"You stopped him, cuz." Levi's voice was barely above a whisper. "You did what had to be done."

"I'm not like that though." Marcus tried to swallow. "I don't . . . shoot people."

"It was either going to be him or us." Levi held his gaze.

For a moment, Marcus believed him. Maybe he had saved them. Maybe he had done what needed to be done. He'd protected his family.

The double doors next to the boys swung open.

Two police officers walked through, locking eyes with the boys. Marcus's stomach dropped.

"It's all over now," he said to himself.

Marcus had always felt he was on borrowed time. He'd

never seemed to belong anywhere. His aunt had tried her best, and this was how he'd thanked her—by shooting her boyfriend. Maybe Carnell did deserve it, but the cops wouldn't see it that way. They'd send him to juvie. Everything he'd hoped for was now up in flames.

"All right, boys?" said the policewoman who walked in front. She turned straight to Marcus. "Could we have a quick word with you?"

Marcus looked at his cousins, and for an uncomfortable few seconds, he thought about running with all his might. He was fast, but not that fast. They'd catch him.

He stood up as slowly as he could and followed the officers to a nearby room. His cousins watched, eyes wide.

"It's okay, boys. You wait here with these officers," said the male officer, who indicated two other cops entering the corridor. Ben and Levi exchanged a look of fear.

The first two officers led Marcus into a small cubicle. While the female officer shut the door, the male one showed Marcus a chair to sit down at; he sat opposite.

"Okay, is your name Marcus?"

Marcus nodded.

"Okay, Marcus. My name is Inspector Blake. I just want to ask you a few questions about what happened tonight. I understand a man named Carnell Anderson was shot in the house you reside in?"

Marcus nodded again.

"Is he any relation to you?"

Marcus shook his head.

"Can I ask you what you were doing at the property?"

Marcus cleared his throat. "I live there." His voice still sounded hoarse.

CHAPTER 3

"Is he your stepdad?"

"No, he's my aunt's boyfriend."

"So you live with your cousins?"

He nodded.

"And the lady at the property, is that your Aunt Georgina?"

"Yep."

"Okay, Marcus. Can you walk us through what happened tonight?"

Marcus faltered. How could he tell him the gun seemed to move of its own accord? That he had simply willed it to turn and overpower this big man, and that he had pulled the trigger without actually having his finger on the trigger? It had been like magic.

Except it wasn't like magic. Carnell was now fighting for his life. Maybe black magic. Or maybe he was cursed.

"Well, I was in my bedroom. I heard a noise, and I came out."

"What kind of noise was it?"

"Um . . . like pain, I guess? Crying."

The inspector wrote down notes while the policewoman looked outside the door.

"Was it loud?"

"Kinda."

"What happened then?"

Marcus swallowed hard. He felt cold again and sweaty—dizzy. How much should he reveal?

"Carnell was standing over Ben. He was on the floor. He was really hurt."

"Did you see him hit Ben?"

"Later, yeah. He hit all of us."

"Even your aunt?"

Marcus tried to think. Had he hit her or pushed her? "Um . . . I can't remember, but he did push her into the TV."

The officer was silent as he took the notes.

"Can you tell me how Carnell got shot?" Inspector Blake looked Marcus right in the eye.

Marcus forced himself to return the policeman's gaze. He couldn't feel anything, not even his foot shaking. He felt so numb. "Him and I . . . we got into a fight. Suddenly he had this gun. I didn't even know he had one. Then he pointed it at me. I tried to get it off him, and somehow it just went off."

The officer's eyes, still fixed on Marcus, narrowed slightly before he took more notes. "Did you shoot Carnell?"

"No." Every muscle in Marcus's body ached as he tried to keep his nerve.

The officer made notes for what felt like an eternity before he picked up the notebook and slotted it into his pocket. "Are you saying he shot himself?"

"I . . . I don't know . . . I was just trying to get him to stop pointing it at me." Marcus felt as if his insides were breaking.

"Thank you for your time, Marcus. Let's go and join your cousins."

Marcus stood up, his body stiff. When he went outside, Levi and Ben were still sitting in the same seats. The inspector went into the corner to discuss with the other officers—who threw a couple of glances Marcus's way—then spoke into his radio, but Marcus couldn't hear what was said. For a moment he wondered if he could interfere with the radio itself somehow, stop the police from talking and conniving against him. But now wasn't the time to see if he really could do what he thought he had done.

"We'll be in touch," Inspector Blake said before all four

CHAPTER 3

officers disappeared down the corridor.

Marcus sat down heavily on the cold chairs. He'd been fortunate to avoid run-ins with the police up until now. Donovan hadn't been so lucky, and look where he'd ended up. Marcus had little doubt they would be all too ready to throw him in too.

"What did you say to them?" Levi whispered in his ear.

"The truth." But he wasn't even sure about that.

"We covered for you," Ben piped up. "We told them he shot himself while you were struggling."

Marcus wanted to run away, escape this life of abandonment and violence, but he forced those feelings down with a hard swallow. There was no escape for him. He had protected his family; that was all that mattered.

"Thanks," he said. "But, Ben, what was Carnell upset about?"

Ben's bruised face somehow drained of colour. He looked away. "Don't worry, I'm not going to snitch."

Chapter 4

The morning light burned Marcus's eyes.

They'd been in the hospital all night. Someone had looked at Ben's face and given him an ice pack to stem the swelling. Getting any sleep in the stiff plastic chairs was impossible. Marcus was completely drained, but there had been no sign of Aunt Georgie, and he had no idea where they were supposed to go.

Finally, his aunt walked through the doors. Her arms hugged herself tight, and her eyes were red as she approached the boys. Gently, she touched Ben's head. All three of them looked up at her.

"You boys okay?" she said. Her mouth twitched, unable to smile.

"Yeah, Mum. You?" asked Levi.

She nodded but looked away from him. "You, Marcus?"

"Yeah." He nodded.

"Come. Let's go home."

"What about Carnell?" Marcus asked. "Is he going to be okay?"

"He'll make it," she said, and walked ahead of them without looking back.

CHAPTER 4

The taxi was deathly silent. Marcus felt as if he was in a daze, exhausted yet on edge. He watched the houses and buildings whizz by his window and wondered what it would be like to live a normal life: two parents who worked normal jobs, with 2.5 children.

The buildings suddenly looked unfamiliar; they were going in the opposite direction of home. Panic began to trickle through him.

"Where are we going?" he piped up.

His cousins' eyes flew open, and they looked out of their windows.

"Your grandma's," Aunt Georgie responded quietly.

Despite sleep threatening to overcome him, the hollow fear in his stomach forced his eyes to remain open. What was Aunt Georgie thinking? Was she grateful? Did she hate him? Was she scared? Would she leave like his mum? Did she see what his mum saw: a feral, violent, unlovable child?

The thoughts crowded his mind. If only he could escape this life, just for a moment . . .

The taxi slowed to a stop outside Grandma Maisey's house, and Levi opened the door and stepped out. Every muscle in Marcus's body ached.

The front door swung open before they could knock.

"Thank God you're okay!" Grandma Maisey said, pulling Aunt Georgie into her arms. "My poor babies! Come, come." She ushered them inside, eyes darting around the neighbourhood before she shut the door firmly behind them.

She cupped her daughter's face in her hand. "Are you all right, darling? Did the doctors look at you?"

"Yes, Mum." Aunt Georgie's voice was barely a whisper.

Grandma winced at the sight of Ben's shiny purple bruise.

"My poor baby," she said, touching his cheek. "Boys, go into the spare bedroom. Get yourselves cleaned up, and I'll have some food for you in half an hour. I just need to chat to Georgie." Her eyes were fixed on her daughter.

The boys trudged upstairs. It was a small house, only two bedrooms, but Grandma always kept the spare room impeccable—just in case she had any surprise visitors, she used to say. Levi lay down on the bed, and all of Marcus's remaining energy drained out of his body as he slumped down next to his cousin.

"Do you mind if I clean up first?" Ben asked.

"Go ahead," Marcus replied, closing his eyes. Ben quickly left the room.

"This is a nightmare," Levi muttered, his eyes closed and his voice thick with tiredness.

"We survived though. That's the main thing," Marcus said, trying to reassure him.

"Yeah, but for how long? And why is Ben running around with people from the Silent Death crew?"

"Shhh!" Marcus said, his eyes darting towards the door. "You don't want your mum to hear. Anyway, it happened. You know how life is on the streets."

"No, I don't. Carnell is a top dog in the Silent Death crew. Ben knows better than to go chasing someone from another gang. The boy needs to control himself."

"Look, it's done now. We've just got to suck it up and keep low for a while."

Levi went quiet and turned away from Marcus. "I don't know if I want this life, bro."

Marcus stared at his back. "What do you mean?"

"I mean . . . all this violence. Constantly looking over your

CHAPTER 4

shoulder. Watching what you say, being careful where you go . . . even how you look. It's exhausting."

Marcus sighed. "Look, Levi, I don't think we have much of a choice. This is our life. Our crew, Q Block, they've always been there for us. Whatever dumb thing Ben said probably just embarrassed Carnell. Nothing more. Maybe he lost out on a deal or something. Let's just stay close to the Qs."

"Why can't we just look out for ourselves? At least for a bit."

"The streets don't work like that. It's all about who you know."

"You *know* people. Loads of gangs respect you—"

"Yeah, but the right people? Would they cover our backs if anything happened to us? I don't think so. Look what just happened to me with Crazy B. They threw me under the bus. I didn't matter." Marcus's face was burning, his stomach churned, and his eyes were stinging. He turned away.

"All right."

"Cool." Marcus swallowed back the tears that threatened to spill. He was barely keeping it together. "I'll make some later, see what's being said."

His phone hadn't blown up yet, so clearly the word hadn't gotten out. What would everyone say if they heard he shot his sort-of stepdad? Would he get more respect or become a target? The latter seemed most probable, and the thought made him feel as though he'd been dunked in ice.

An hour later, they were all seated at Grandma's table, eating fried Johnnycake dumplings with doughy centres, ackee and saltfish on the side, and bright green callaloo cabbage mixed with onions and garlic. They rarely had such a big traditional Jamaican meal, but it boosted Marcus. Warmth and strength began to melt the icy block that had lodged in his stomach.

The smells of the salty spiced fish, the slight sweetness of the dumplings, and the freshness of the greens warmed him from the inside out.

"All right, boys. We need to head home and grab some of our stuff," Aunt Georgie said as she rose from the table with her plate.

The three boys stood up, but Grandma gripped Marcus's arm.

"Marcus, why don't you stay for a moment," she said.

Marcus glanced at his cousins, his stomach tense. His aunt avoided his gaze as she put on her coat. His cousins paused in confusion.

"Umm . . . okay." Marcus sat down carefully.

"I'll see you boys later." Grandma smiled decisively.

"Laters," Ben said. Levi nodded, his eyes flicking between Marcus and his grandma. The door slammed behind them.

"Now, Marcus. I wanted to see how you were doing. Georgie told me it was you who got in the middle of things."

"Just tried to protect them," Marcus said, shrugging. "He was beating Ben. I mean, the man was out of control, Grandma. I've never seen him like that—"

She gripped his shoulder, tears brimming in her eyes. "I want to thank you for what you did." Her voice cracked. "She should never have gotten with that devil. I told her from the very beginning, but she insisted he was getting better. But you . . . you are probably one of the bravest boys I've ever met. You saved them."

Her eyes shone as a tear trickled down her cheek.

"No boy should have to defend his family like that. But you did." She sighed and looked away into the distance. "I always wanted better for Georgie, but she is headstrong. She made

CHAPTER 4

excuses for him. Said he helped with the bills, made her feel safe, happy. But I always knew . . . It was the same with your mother."

Marcus froze. He didn't know if he wanted to hear this, but his tongue felt thick in his mouth, and he couldn't speak.

"She was a gentle person . . . fragile even. In every way possible. Then she fell in love . . . with a man who couldn't love her back. And it broke her. She had no strength in her after that. You are not to blame for her either, but she wasn't strong enough to raise a boy like you."

Marcus's throat ached. He lowered his eyes so she couldn't look at him directly, then uttered the words as best he could. "You mean violent like me?"

He stared at the table, unable to stop the silent tears.

"You are strong willed, Marcus. That was only one time you ever did something like that. There is something powerful within you, fighting to get out and make its mark on the world. You need to harness it, not be afraid of it."

"Yeah . . ." Marcus nodded. The awful memory was branded into his consciousness.

He'd been upset with his mum that night. She hadn't been listening to him, which wasn't unusual for her. She'd always seemed to be emotionally vacant, despite her body's presence. He'd begged her to look at the small toy he'd made, just once. He shook her arm; she continued to gaze outside. He called her name. Finally, with all the rage of a seven-year-old, he pushed her to get her to look. But she tripped over a basket of laundry that had been there for days and fell into the wall two feet away. She'd looked at him with such horror he'd immediately burst into tears and said sorry.

She took him to his grandma's the next day and never came

back.

Grandma Maisey took a deep breath. "So now you have a decision to make, Marcus. This path you are on . . . is incredibly dangerous. Now, I've discussed it with Georgie, and we both think it best you come live here with me."

Marcus's eyes widened. "What?"

"You need a clean break, Marcus. Living with Georgie and the boys will put you all at risk."

"What are you talking about?" Marcus was almost breathless. "She's not taking him back, is she? After what he did?"

"No, no, she isn't. But this is about everybody's safety, not just your own."

The penny dropped. If he stayed with them, they would be targets. If he stayed away, the only target would be him. "She doesn't want me there anymore, does she?"

"It's not that." His grandma shook her head.

It was that.

"We all know what you did was in self-defence, and we don't think he'll press charges. But Georgie is thinking of going into hiding. She wants a clean break for her and the boys."

Not me, Marcus noted. Aunt Georgie may as well have punched a hole through his chest.

"You will be safest with me." His grandma smiled. "A new school, new area could be the beginning of something really great for you."

So this is what it feels like when your world comes to an end, Marcus thought, *everything crashing in all at once.* He swallowed his remaining tears. "Okay, but there's no need to split Levi and me up. Or Ben. We look out for each other."

"I know you do," she said intently. "Marcus, I know you'll defend those boys to your last breath. But it's obvious it's too much for Georgie to look after the three of you. She took her eye off the ball, and this is the result. I think she needs to concentrate on raising those boys right. I can focus on you."

Marcus couldn't believe what he'd just heard. Yes, he'd given Aunt Georgie a hard time on occasion, but he'd never realised she thought of him as a burden. But as he looked back, he conceded he was more combative. He was the one who'd often do the opposite of what she asked. She was even lenient with him on their nightly curfew; he'd known how to work around her.

"Marcus, I want you to give this some serious thought. If you insist on staying with them, I won't split you and the boys up. But I have good connections in this community. There is so much good that needs doing. You could do that here."

She stood up and started gathering the remaining plates on the table.

"Would it be all right if I went for a walk?" Marcus asked, desperate to escape the suffocating future he was being offered.

"Yes, darling. But don't go back to your old place. Not yet, you hear?"

He nodded and rose to help her with the table.

"You go," she said, waving him away with her hand.

Marcus left without another word.

A gust of wind blasted Marcus's face as he approached the walkway. He flicked up his hood, shoved his hands deep into his pockets, and kept his eyes fixed to the ground, walking in the opposite direction of his old home. If that ever really was his home.

In twenty-four hours, everything had been taken from him. His role as leader of Q Block, his home, and now his cousins. The closest he'd ever had to blood brothers. His whole body burned with anger.

A tree branch brushed his cheek. Marcus swatted it away but then paused to look at it. He'd never noticed how green this area was. Trees swayed gently among the grey buildings. Some people had pots of flowers and shrubs around their front gardens, a hint of beauty and calm within this drab existence. This area was quiet, the houses a little bigger. A couple of girls walked by, engrossed in their conversation. He wouldn't need to worry about his status around them; they didn't know him.

The sun peeked through the clouds, and for a moment everything felt a bit brighter and less bleak. But the sun soon hid its rays, removing that small sliver of hope in Marcus. His thoughts returned to last night.

How involved would the authorities be? They'd monitored him for a couple of years after his mum left. They'd considered putting him in foster care, but Aunt Georgie had insisted he stay with her. Look how well that had turned out.

The police were different. He could do prison time. How long would it be until they stopped by?

He wanted the ground to swallow him up.

A small well-kept park with a freshly painted black gate appeared to his left. Marcus veered towards it and sat down heavily on a nearby bench.

Leaning forward, he rested his forehead on his weary hands. He was tired and drained. Where could he go? His grandma had no idea who he really was. How could she possibly protect him if he got in trouble? Their saving grace was that Carnell

CHAPTER 4

didn't know where Grandma Maisey lived.

And what on earth was he going to do about this deal with Crazy B?

He kicked an empty can towards a rubbish bin just ahead of him, and it rattled against some beer cans round the bottom.

Like a bolt of lightning, a memory struck him right in his chest.

He'd moved the gun that shot Carnell, with just his thoughts.

Marcus held his breath and slowly looked down at his hands, turning them over. He remembered how much they'd burned—how every cell in his body had willed the gun to turn, and it had.

Fear tried to grip his stomach, but he closed his eyes for a moment, then opened them slowly. He pointed his finger at one of the cans and swiped his hand to the right.

Nothing happened.

Confused, he thought for a moment. Every time something strange had happened around him—even when the security alarms mysteriously stopped working in the electrical shops—he'd been feeling angry or anxious, and his hands had grown hot.

He closed his eyes and thought about Carnell standing over Ben with his belt. The burn came through strongly, and Marcus once again swiped his hand to the right.

The whole rubbish bin flew to the side, crashing into the tree a few feet away.

He bolted upright, his hood falling off.

It was true. He could control metal.

A shiver of excitement ran down his spine. He concentrated harder and this time focused on three cans in front of him, moving his hand back and forth. The cans mimicked his actions as if attached to string.

He rubbed his eyes and quickly checked his surroundings. Maybe this was just sleep deprivation and his mind was playing tricks?

Over and over again, he played with the tins. He lifted the cans in mid-air, made circles and figures of eight with them. Adrenaline pumped through his veins.

He moved closer and spun his hands round and round to create a tornado of cans around the rubbish bin. He lifted the cans right up to his face, then glanced ahead and shot them forward into a tree. One hit the tree, one flew off into the distance, and one hit a man in the back of the neck.

Marcus dived behind the dust bin and held his breath. Sweat prickled every part of his body.

After a few seconds, he carefully peered around the filthy bin. The man walked away, cursing and rubbing the back of his neck.

He would have to be more careful.

Marcus laughed out loud, holding his forehead and quickly checking no one was around. He walked over to the tin can in the tree and pulled it out of the bark. After gathering the others as well, he threw all but one into the bin, then sat down with the last tin at the bench. He imagined pushing down on the tin, trying to crush it. Nothing happened at first. He tried harder, imagining a force piercing through the tin. His hands ached now, and the effort to generate the heat made him tired.

With a small clang, the can crumpled in his hands.

"Yo . . . this is madness," he whispered. He checked his surroundings again and saw a couple with a dog walking towards him. Marcus replaced his hood and searched the park

CHAPTER 4

for anything else that was metal, away from any onlookers.

He had magic. Disbelief still coursed through his mind. How had he not noticed before? Was he born with this? He knew security barriers never worked around him, but he'd dismissed them as being faulty, despite them catching others. How could he have ignored what he could do?

The playground up ahead was vacant. His brain lit up at every metal apparatus his eyes fell on, and he made his way quickly to the climbing frame, the biggest structure.

Marcus gripped the cold metal in his hot hands and pulled the metal pole towards him. He made just a dent at first, but after some effort, the pole began to give, lifting from the cemented base.

He wanted to shout with excitement; wonder had replaced any fear he'd had. He pushed the metal back into place, but the once smooth pole now looked deformed. He tried to pull out the dent to make it smooth again, but before he could, he heard the laughter and screams of children approaching. Pulling the hood farther down his face, he walked swiftly in the other direction. He looked around for something else to manipulate, but now other people were starting to appear.

Grinning to himself as he left the park, Marcus was amazed by how much metal surrounded him. Cars, lampposts, signs, vans, buses, fencing. Suddenly the whole world felt like his playground. He could move this world around.

His hands had a deep ache now, heavy and prickly, but he felt charged up. Adrenaline surged through his veins, all fatigue gone from his body.

He'd never felt like this before.

He felt invincible.

If he could control metal, even stop guns from shooting

at him from close range, there was literally nothing anyone could do to stop him.

When he arrived at his grandma's house, he knew exactly what he was going to do.

"All right, Grandma. I'll stay with you."

"I'm so glad." She beamed back; her arms spread out to give him a hug.

Despite all his flaws, she always had an endless reserve of acceptance for him. She didn't look at him as an inconvenience. She looked at him with love, and he regretted how quick he'd been to dismiss her earlier.

"In fact, there is someone I would like you to meet later today," his grandma said, breaking away from the hug.

"Who?"

"She is a good friend of mine. You met her the other day on my doorstep. She knows everyone in this area. She may even have a mentor for you."

Marcus's stomach tensed. This wasn't the deal. He thought there'd be no strings attached to him staying here. "A mentor? Why?"

"Nothing serious. Just someone who works with gifted youths in the area."

"Gifted youths?" Was she trying to get him on board?

"Very bright kids, kids with promise, those who could become leaders. Amala told me about it. I think it would be a great idea to get your mind off things."

Marcus stiffened as the memories of last night bombarded his mind. The euphoria of the previous minutes evaporated.

"It's going to be okay, my boy." His grandma put her arm around his shoulder and gently squeezed. "Your aunt called and asked if you could pick up your belongings. Do you want

CHAPTER 4

me to come with you?"

"No, it's okay, Grandma. I'll get it sorted." His heart sank to his stomach.

Despite his previous joy in discovering his powers, the absence of his cousins was palpable. A painful reminder that everyone would abandon him.

Chapter 5

What a difference twenty-four hours made.

Marcus stood in his old bedroom surrounded by his old books, clothes, and games. Before, his life had only been about becoming a leader. He'd had a crew and his cousins; he'd been a well-known peacekeeper. Now he was a different person: alone, violent, and powerful.

This room had been his sanctuary; this flat housed those dearest to him. Now they were all being wrenched away. A deep ache pulled at his chest.

He yanked a suitcase down from the top of his wardrobe and threw in his clothes and a myriad of trainers. The few books he owned, his ear pods, and his toiletries went into his rucksack. It surprised him how quickly he finished. Nothing really seemed that important to him now. The most important things he wanted he couldn't keep.

In the hall, his aunt's and cousins' boxes and suitcases were piling high. Heavy feet approached from behind. He swallowed hard before he turned to face another family member who would abandon him.

"Marcus, man . . ." Levi embraced him hard. "You really going to stay with Grandma Maisey?"

CHAPTER 5

"Yeah." Marcus lowered his head and kicked at the skirt board. "It's better this way. Fresh start for everyone."

"What are you talking about? We're blood, bro. We stick together through thick and thin."

"You know I'm always there for you, cuz . . . but I think Grandma and Aunty are right. I might have a target on my back from now on. This'll keep you safe."

"Is that what Mum said? Is this her idea?" Levi's eyebrows pressed together.

Marcus wished he hadn't said anything. "Nah, bro, it's not like that. Just a sense I'm getting. She always found me more difficult than you two."

"Yeah, well, it's because you've got a thick head. People can't get through to you!"

"Shut up, man," Marcus said, playfully punching him in the arm.

"What about Crazy B?"

"You know I can manage him," Marcus said. *I have an edge now. I have genuine power.*

"You're going to turn into an old man, you know. Living with Grandma and all her old friends, having tea parties!"

A laugh escaped Marcus's mouth. It felt alien and sad. "At least I'll have decent food to eat instead of the crap Aunty makes!"

"Nah, bruv." Levi laughed. "Don't let her hear you say that."

Marcus turned serious. "Do you know where you're going yet?"

"Nah, the social worker will be around soon to give us instructions. I think it'll be North London though."

"Hope so."

"You had a visit yet?" Levi asked.

"From the social worker? Nah, not yet. I think Grandma's already making plans for me though, so I'll be all right."

Levi grabbed Marcus's shoulder, his eyes full and earnest. "It's not too late. You can change your mind, you know."

For a split second, Marcus wavered. A fresh start with them, free of Carnell and the old way of doing things? They could start their own crew. He would show his cousins what he could do. But would they trust him? Would they become afraid of him? Carnell wasn't pressing charges, but did that mean he wanted to take Marcus out himself? If that was a possibility, Marcus knew he couldn't put them in danger.

"I've made up my mind," he said as he hoisted his rucksack on his shoulder. Right to his core, he ached, and his eyes burned with the tears he was afraid to spill.

"Marcus, I'm going to miss you!" Ben came around the corner and squeezed him into a hug. "Why can't you come with us?"

"Trust me, it's better this way," Marcus said, trying to straighten up. It felt as if the world was on his shoulders.

"You're the one who looks out for us though. You're like a big brother to us."

Levi looked down, and Marcus looked away guiltily. He'd outshone Levi. Even though Levi was a couple of months older, Marcus had always taken charge. His cousins followed him, listened to him, waited for his consent in most things. Maybe this split would give Levi the chance to be the true older brother he was. Marcus sighed.

Aunt Georgie entered the corridor. "You ready to go, boys?"

Levi shot her a look.

Ben collapsed in her arms. "Yeah."

"Come here," she said, letting go of Ben and reaching for

CHAPTER 5

Marcus. A brief hug, and then she pulled back to look him level in the eyes. She and Marcus were the same height.

"I'm sorry I couldn't protect you . . . ," she whispered, her brimming eyes locked with his. "I should've seen what he really was. Carnell said he doesn't want an investigation. You need to keep your head down though, all right? Don't get into trouble. Grandma can give you all the attention I couldn't. But none of this is your fault. Don't blame yourself. Once I've sorted myself out, maybe you can even come back and live with us."

Marcus nodded, but he heard the lie between her words. She would never ask him to return, just like his mum had never returned. Funny how he was always told things weren't his fault, yet he was always the one left behind. He was the common denominator.

All three walked him down to the awaiting taxi at the bottom of the stairs. He nodded at them as he opened the door and slid into the seat. As the taxi pulled off, he allowed himself one last look at the block of flats that had been his home for the last eight years, and at the three figures he once thought he'd always be with. For the second time in his life, Marcus learned that no one really wanted to be around a kid like him.

* * *

Crazy B must have found out what happened.

Marcus had tried to call him repeatedly, and every call had

gone straight to voicemail. Maybe he was about to cut ties with Marcus and freeze him out. Marcus clenched his jaw at Crazy B's cowardice. That kid always was an entitled brat.

The aroma of curried goat drifted into the dining room, where Marcus sat waiting for his new mentors to come to dinner. Hunger gnawed at his stomach, and it growled loudly in protest.

The doorbell rang, and relief spread through his ravenous body.

"That must be Leonard and Amala," Grandma said. "Let me go and get that. Did you set the table?"

"Yes, Grandma," he replied as he stood up.

"Don't look so serious. You'll like him." She smiled broadly, hung up her apron, and went to let the guests in.

Marcus's muscles stiffened. He just wanted to be left alone with this new ability, or at least make some plans to meet the European guys, but his grandma hadn't given him any peace since he'd stepped back into the house. He knew she was worried about him. Levi and he were tight; he'd loved being with his cousins. He wondered what they were doing now as he pushed down the dark emptiness inside.

He'd gotten a couple of calls from his old crew: Were the rumours true? Did he shoot Carnell? He'd told them he'd speak with them tomorrow, that he'd moved away and couldn't see them for a while. His social worker had called too but had only spoken to his grandma in hushed tones, checking in to see if he was okay and to discuss schools.

Marcus wandered into the kitchen and watched the frying plantain caramelise. He preferred to be in here with the food than under the guests' scrutinising gaze. He inhaled the aromas of the curried goat, and the rich garlic, ginger,

CHAPTER 5

and curry smell made his mouth water. With the rice and peas, fried plantain, and salad, this was his favourite meal. Grandma had pulled out all the stops tonight.

Heartfelt laughter pierced through his thoughts. He watched through the corner of his eye as Grandma Maisey and her friends moved into the dining room.

"Marcus, come here and say hello," his grandma called.

He turned off the stove and walked towards the man and woman next to his smiling grandma.

"This is Amala," Grandma said. "You met before at my doorstep."

"Hello, Marcus." Amala beamed up at him, offering her hand. Her tight curls framed her freckled caramel face, and a radiance he had never felt before emanated from her, seeming to bathe him in light.

He shook her hand. "Nice to meet you."

"And this is Leonard. He was the mentor I told you about."

"Good to meet you, Marcus." A broad smile spread across the man's face, and he enthusiastically shook Marcus's hand. He was a big man, with eager eyes. His ears stuck out, made worse by his very short haircut.

Marcus wasn't interested in a dad figure, so he'd have to keep him at a distance. He nodded in response.

"Sit down." Grandma Maisey beckoned to her guests. "Marcus, come help me get everything served."

Soon everyone's plate was piled high, and bright tropical pink drinks were shared. The adults relaxed in their chairs and let the conversation flow comfortably. Marcus only half listened. He didn't recognise any of the names mentioned, but you never knew what you could pick up from conversations. He had a knack for gathering bits of information that could prove useful at some point in the future.

Once everyone's stomachs were uncomfortably full, Leonard shifted in his seat and turned to Marcus.

"So, Marcus, how are you?" he said, dabbing at his beading face with a napkin.

"Okay," Marcus replied.

"Good." He nodded slowly. "The last couple of days must have been pretty hard on you."

Marcus shrugged and wiped his mouth with a napkin. He kept his eyes fixed on his empty plate.

"You'll be safe here. Gangs aren't an issue round here," Leonard said too confidently. Marcus didn't believe him. "We've worked hard to make the streets safer and drive some of them out."

Marcus's muscles relaxed slightly. Maybe he could do his own thing here, build his own crew.

"Your grandma said you're pretty smart. How are your grades at school?"

"They're okay."

"What school groups were you in?"

"Top."

"For which ones?"

"All of them."

Leonard nodded in approval. "This is going to be a strange time for you, but we're here to help. Your grandma has told us a lot about you, and Amala and I think we could use some of your talents to help others."

"In what way?" Marcus asked, meeting Leonard's eyes for the first time.

"There are a lot of kids around here that could use someone like you. Someone with street smarts and book smarts. Tell

CHAPTER 5

me, what do you want to be when you grow up?"

Marcus recoiled. He hated that question. He'd never had time to give it any serious thought—too busy making deals and pacts for the Q Block crew. He shrugged.

"No ideas?"

"Not really."

"That's not a problem," Amala said, speaking up for the first time. "We're in this together, to help you develop your talents. It'll come to you."

"We want you to aim high though, Marcus," Leonard interjected. "No playing small. We want our kids to become the best in any field they choose. Medicine, law, business. Nothing should be off-limits."

Marcus smirked. He was sure some things were off-limits. Were drug dealers included?

"Any support you need we will explore," Amala said, looking intently at him. "This is a sizeable piece of helping you gain confidence."

"What makes you think those kids will listen to me?" Marcus piped up. "They don't even know me."

"You are a natural leader, Marcus," his grandma said, patting him on the shoulder. "Look at the way Levi would follow you around, and he was older than you."

Lots of other people listen to me too, because they know I mean business, Marcus thought.

"What do you say, Marcus? Want to give us a shot?" Amala smiled.

There was hope in that smile. He'd seen that hope before in Aunt Georgie's eyes years ago. The memory made his chest tighten.

He looked straight at Leonard. "What's in it for you?"

"Marcus!" his grandma exclaimed.

"No, it's all right." Leonard held up his hand to calm her. "It's a good question."

He leaned forward—elbows resting on the table, hands clasped together—and looked at Marcus directly. "I had a rough background too, Marcus. No one was there to stop me from falling through the cracks. So I fell. Petty stuff, being in the wrong place at the wrong time. The blame was pinned on me, and I ended up doing time. I vowed I'd never make that mistake again. I would take control of my own life. After a while I met Amala, who was a social worker at the time, having just finished being a nurse. She was working with a lot of youths in the area. I was tired of seeing all these kids just hanging around on the streets, wasting their time and their lives. We both started up a youth group for kids who had promise."

"So it's exclusive? Only smart people can join?"

"Not just them," Amala said. "It's for anyone who wants to come and achieve great things, escape their environments. You know what the streets are like, Marcus. It's a cold place, and talent more often than not goes to waste. We need kids like you who know how to carve their own path. Or at least have the potential to."

He didn't know how they knew this about him. His grandma must have hyped him up to these strangers. The idea of spending more time with others, though, made him angry. He had his own things he wanted to do, but he needed to keep his grandma sweet so she wouldn't ask questions and would give him some space when he needed it.

"Okay. I'll join." He smiled slightly, just enough to make them believe he was all in. A new idea sparked in his mind.

CHAPTER 5

"I'm glad to hear that." A big smile spread across Leonard's face. "You're going to be such an asset to this group."

Yes, thought Marcus, *my own crew of smart, ambitious kids.*

* * *

Tuesday came round quickly. The social worker had visited and set the terms of him staying with Grandma Maisey: staying out of trouble.

When asked to recall the events of that night with Carnell, he'd felt so stressed and drained he wanted to lie down afterwards. A dark cloud inhabited his thoughts, and his head pounded. He slept badly, every action of that night playing on repeat in his mind. He knew he'd pointed the gun, but had he pulled the trigger?

After all his experimentations over the last few days on every piece of metal he could get his hands on—from cutlery to his grandma's cooking pots—he wanted to move on to bigger, heavier things. He wanted to push his limits and really see what he could do. But this new discovery was making him nervous. What exactly was he? What did having these powers mean?

Manipulating metal with your bare hands was not normal. Sure, it gave him an added layer of protection; he wouldn't have to rely solely on his brawn. But what would happen if someone discovered what he could do?

Days passed by, and Grandma Maisey gave him a wide berth, only asking him to come for the occasional walk, help with carrying bags, and help her with dinner in the evening. He kept his belongings neat and sprayed his cologne around his room so it no longer smelled like lavender and peonies.

He still hadn't heard from Crazy B. Tyler had messaged him to say there was a ban on speaking to Marcus. The excuse was that Q Block needed protecting.

Disbelief hung around Marcus's mind like a dark cloud, making it difficult to think straight as he drowned in his own isolation. He returned to the park daily to practise his powers of bending and shaping metal, the only thing keeping him sane and hopeful.

That afternoon he got a message from Leonard with the time and place to meet the others in the club. Marcus decided to leave early so he wouldn't be late and so he could familiarise himself with the new roads, carefully observing everyone he passed. Were they spies for Carnell? Friends of his grandma who knew his tragic story? He pulled his hood farther down his face.

His phone buzzed suddenly in his pocket, and he pulled it out to see Crazy B's name. He swallowed hard.

"You all right, bruv?" Crazy B asked.

"Yeah, you?" Marcus answered stiffly.

"Yeah." He paused, as if considering what to say next. "I think you should lay low for a while. We don't need any attention. Let's talk in a week. I still want you to talk to Dacus, but wait for my say so. You understand?"

"No problem." Marcus kept his voice smooth, relief spreading through his body.

"Stay safe," Crazy B said and promptly rung off.

Marcus immediately called Tyler.

"Yo?" Tyler sounded surprised.

CHAPTER 5

"Where are you?" Marcus asked.

Tyler's voice dropped to a whisper. "Heading to the garages with Crazy B."

"Good. Listen in for me, yeah? I want to know what he's planning with these Eastern guys. He's giving me an extra week. He wants to keep me in the dark."

"No problem, bruv."

"Laters."

Marcus sighed loudly, looking up at the dull, cloudy skies. At least Crazy B was talking to him now, though why no one else was allowed to speak to him was confusing.

He arrived at a cream-coloured building with a tattered banner that said BAME CENTRE on the front. Out of habit, he looked around the rather large building before going inside. The paint was peeling and discoloured, anything but inspiring.

He pushed the creaky door open to find a bespectacled receptionist staring at him through a thick glass window.

"Can I help you?" she asked.

"Hi." Marcus flashed his most charming smile to the girl. She had dark, penetrating eyes and wore her hair in a simple bun, highlighting her high cheekbones and doll-like eyes. "I'm looking for Leonard."

"Your name?"

"Marcus."

"Okay, wait there." She got up and disappeared behind the wall.

The place was bleak. The walls were a dirty peach colour, the floor a dirty moss green. If this was where they were hoping to embolden kids, they had a lot more work to do.

Leonard appeared in the doorway straight ahead. "Marcus,

good to see you, man." He walked forward and grabbed Marcus's hand. "How's it going?"

"Good." Marcus nodded, quickly withdrawing his hand and shoving it into his pocket.

"You sure?" Leonard folded his arms as if awaiting more details.

"Yeah."

"Do you know which school they want to transfer you to?"

"They said either Forest Park School or Hightops, but she wasn't sure if they had any places there."

"Hmm . . . well, let's hope for Hightops. That's the better school by far. How you feeling at your grandma's house?"

"Good."

"Boring?"

"Well . . . that would seem ungrateful, wouldn't it?" Marcus smiled.

Leonard grinned. "She's a good woman, your grandma. Come. Let's meet some of the others." He punched in a code on the side of the door, waited for the click, and then pushed it open. "There are about four kids here, around your age. The others will come later. We have about ten younger ones who all need to be mentored. Good kids, some really bright. Some just want a safe place to be and not get into trouble. Have some peace."

As they made their way through the corridors, Marcus noticed the heart of the building was just as dull as the entrance. He couldn't imagine spending any time here.

"You're a bit early," Leonard said as he punched in another code, releasing another door that opened into a large classroom. "I was going to chat to you first, but you can sit in and watch."

CHAPTER 5

Amala stood at the front, a teacher surveying her pupils. Eight smaller teens sat at cramped desks with their heads down while three older kids—two boys and a girl—peered over their shoulders or sat next to them.

"Do you just want to watch for a bit? Or do you want to get stuck right in?"

Marcus shrugged. He just wanted to watch and be left alone with his thoughts.

Leonard looked at him, stroking his chin. "All right, I'm going to place you with someone. Follow me."

They walked to the other side of the room, where a small white boy with a shaved head sat with his head down, pen suspended in the air. Marcus couldn't tell if he was thinking or pretending to write.

"Hi, Sean." Leonard kneeled to match the boy's height. "You okay, bud?"

Sean smiled briefly, with a curt nod.

"Are you finding this okay?"

Sean nodded again, still avoiding eye contact.

"I have someone new here today." Leonard moved so the kid could see Marcus. "This is Marcus. Do you think it'd be okay if he sat by you for a while? He'd like to help out here sometimes."

Sean smiled and nodded again, risking a quick glance at Marcus before he turned back to his work.

Leonard pulled up a chair next to the boy. "Thank you, Sean. If you need some help, let us know, okay? I'm sure Marcus will help you."

Sean nodded.

Leonard patted Marcus on the back. "Take a seat next to him. See what you can do to offer him some help if he needs it."

Just like that, Marcus was left in charge. A flash of anger rippled through him. This seemed like a babysitter's job.

He sat down on the rickety plastic chair and leaned back. How long was he supposed to stay here? He looked at each of the older teens carefully. Could they possibly already be part of a crew? Or would they take some persuading to get behind him?

His phone buzzed again. Dacus's details.

Already Marcus's mind was conjuring plans. He could do one of two things: establish contact with Dacus now on his terms, or sit on this bit of information and wait for Crazy B to give him the go-ahead.

Any advantage he could get over Crazy B was worth it. As soon as this class was over, he'd sneak out and make a call.

Suddenly remembering Sean, he glanced at the boy's paper. He'd only written two sentences.

"You need some help?" Marcus asked.

Sean shook his head and turned away.

Marcus read through the question. "Do you know what it's asking you to do?"

Sean shrugged, still silent.

Marcus tried to guess how old he was. Possibly two years younger, but his wide eyes and oversized clothes made it hard to know. In any case, the kid clearly didn't want his help. Marcus sat back and returned to his phone.

He had yet to figure out what Dacus specialised in and why Crazy B wanted him specifically. Had he been listening to his brother in the Oldtown crew? Were they planning on merging the two crews together? There would be no chance of Marcus being able to rival them if that happened.

CHAPTER 5

A quick maps search revealed where Dacus was located. Only forty minutes from here. If he paid the man a visit, use of his powers would have to be limited; it wouldn't be an advantage yet.

Aware someone was approaching, he quickly put his phone away and watched as one of the older boys crouched down on the other side of Sean's desk.

"You okay, Sean?" the other teen asked quietly.

"Yeah," Sean said.

"You're looking at poems? That's awesome. You know they're just like songs. There are always patterns to them." The boy pointed to different sections of the poem. "See?"

"Yeah." Sean nodded.

"Would you like me to stay with you while you write the answers?"

Sean nodded again and finally started writing. The older boy threw a look of disapproval at Marcus before he returned to Sean's work. After a little while, Sean sat up straight.

"That's really good, Sean. You didn't need any help after all. Good job." The teen stood up and threw one more dirty glance at Marcus before going to the next table.

Marcus rolled his eyes. That boy wouldn't be in his crew. The guy clearly thought he was above him.

A small smile crept over his face. If only he knew what Marcus could do.

After what seemed like an eternity, Amala spoke up. "Pencils down. It's time for a break."

Everyone put their pencils down and collectively stretched their stiff limbs. Marcus stood up and shook his own legs out. He turned to the small pale kid, who stuffed his things into a tatty backpack.

"How old are you?" Marcus asked.

"Thirteen."

"Oh, year nine."

"No, year eight."

So he must be one of the oldest in the class, Marcus thought. The other students all seemed to be around the same age. "How about you let me help you next time, yeah?"

Sean kept his head down and bolted for the door. Marcus knew he could win that kid over; it was just a matter of time.

Marcus followed the older teens outside until he got to the entrance he'd come through. He turned to the receptionist. "Could I go out for some fresh air?"

The girl looked around. "Yeah, sure."

He leaned a little closer to her. "You got a smoke?"

She furrowed her eyebrows, confused.

"Come on, I'll pay you back."

She looked at him out of the corner of her eye before reaching into her handbag and passing him a cigarette. "I don't smoke," she said, and winked at him with a slight smile.

"My lips are sealed." He winked in return and left through the front door.

Outside, Marcus leaned over the metal railings by the road. He took a drag from the cigarette and looked up into the darkening skies.

This group could be a challenge. He needed to offer these kids something the centre wasn't already offering. The kids on the street needed friendship, protection, and sometimes money. That was what Q Block offered. The Bame Centre offered those things and space for ambition—a long-term goal. He could work with that. His focus would have to be on the here and now to get anyone interested in joining his

CHAPTER 5

crew. He had powers, and he was going to use them to get what was taken from him.

His thoughts wandered to his cousins: what they could be doing now, if they finally had their own bedrooms without him there, if they still ate cereal at night because they didn't want any more of their mum's cooking. He hoped Levi was looking out for Ben, despite him finding his little brother annoying. He wondered if Levi was following someone else or if he had finally stepped into his own without Marcus in the way.

His stomach twisted, his eyes burned, and a deep sadness welled up inside.

He pulled and tugged on the metal railing he leaned on, twisting and contorting it around his wrists, focusing on anything but the pain that welled up within him.

"What are you doing?" Leonard's voice pierced the darkness.

Marcus spun round. Leonard stood just a metre behind him, his eyes enlarged, fixed on the twisted metal in Marcus's hands.

The cigarette dropped out of Marcus's mouth, and he tried to push the metal back down while obscuring it with his body. How could he have been so careless? Leonard began to advance, still staring at the fence.

"It's nothing," Marcus faltered.

Leonard strode over and moved Marcus out of the way, still looking at the metal that was twisted and coiled around itself. "Did you do this?" he asked, his eyebrows furrowed.

Marcus said nothing.

"Answer me, Marcus. Did you break this fence?"

Marcus nodded, avoiding his eyes.

"How?"

"The metal is cheap." Marcus shrugged, his mind racing to find an excuse. Sweat broke out across his face.

Leonard tried to pry the metal in different directions and straighten it out, but it wouldn't move an inch. He looked at Marcus and then back at the fence. "How . . . how did you do this?"

Marcus's mind frantically searched for an answer.

"Marcus."

"Leonard," a female voice interrupted.

Leonard startled at the sight of the beauty who appeared at his elbow. He sighed. "Charlene."

"How are you?" she soothed.

Marcus's eyes connected with the most stunning human he had ever seen: ebony skin; deep, dark brown almond-shaped eyes that pulled him in; and red lipstick slicked onto her perfectly pouty lips. Her small Afro accentuated her sublime features. Her skin glowed in the setting sun. A brief smile flickered across her lips as her eyes scanned the metal behind him, then she turned her attention back to Leonard. She put a cigarette to her lips.

"I'm okay, thanks," Leonard said, his eyes suddenly glazing over. "Just talking to—"

"You seem a little agitated," she purred. "Is there something wrong inside the centre?"

Is she stalling for me? Marcus wondered. He quickly tried to fix the distorted metal with the heat from his hands.

The girl's eyes flicked up and down as smoke coiled from her lips.

"Um . . . well . . ." Leonard shook his head, squinting, as if he was confused. He glanced at Marcus, then peered down at the railing again.

Marcus began to sweat, hoping the man wouldn't look closely enough to see the dents he had made.

"I thought I saw . . . Something looked . . ." Confusion darkened Leonard's face.

"Do you need to prepare for the next class?" Charlene cocked her head to the side.

Leonard checked his watch, his eyes barely focused. "Yes, you're right." He smiled kindly at her, then paused to look at Marcus before heading back into the centre.

Charlene turned, winked over her shoulder at Marcus, and strode off after Leonard.

Marcus finally released his breath, unaware he had been holding it in.

What had he just seen?

Had that girl changed Leonard's mind? Had she cast a spell on him?

That wink meant she was covering for him, but why?

He had a sinking feeling she knew what he'd done. Even if she hadn't seen him do it, she at least knew he was different.

He swallowed hard, despite his dry mouth, and walked back to the centre.

Marcus sat next to Sean again, his foot bouncing up and down in agitation.

He knew Leonard had seen something, but what would his mentor do with this information? Marcus's nerves were a complete mess. This new life would be over before it even started if he was exposed. What would happen to him? Leonard wasn't in the room, but Amala's eyes flitted to him sporadically.

Rubbing his head under his hood, he thought of excuses to get out. He wasn't feeling well and should go home. He'd create his crew elsewhere, away from these suspicious eyes and that girl . . . run away if he had to. He could look after himself. He was fifteen, after all.

"You all right?" a quiet voice asked.

Marcus looked over to meet Sean's large eyes. "What?"

"Are you all right?"

Marcus was taken aback. "Umm . . . yeah, just got some things on my mind."

"These guys are nice. They won't judge you." Sean returned to his slumped position over his work.

So now he wants to talk, Marcus thought with a smile. He leaned in a little closer. "You know these guys well?"

"Kind of."

"How long you been coming here?"

"A few months," Sean said and turned to him slightly.

"It's my first day. Maybe you could show me the ropes?"

Sean smiled, delighted by Marcus's attention. "Who do you know?"

"Just Leonard and Amala."

Sean rattled off everyone's names and ages in the room.

"Thanks." Marcus grinned, surprised at Sean's sudden open nature. "Think I better start making a good impression. Could you help me out with that?"

Sean beamed, and for the next twenty minutes, Marcus walked him through algebra formulas.

Sweat beaded across Marcus's body when he glanced at the time. In a few minutes the class would finish, and Leonard would want to talk or, worse, report him to the authorities as

CHAPTER 5

being a freak.

There was no reasonable way for him to explain what he'd done. Would they tell his grandma or go straight to the police? This would be the last straw for Grandma Maisey. There was no way she'd want a strange, superhuman thug in her house.

Marcus was desperate to leave as soon as possible. He'd need to get to his grandma before Leonard did, remind her that moving metal with your bare hands—or with your mind—was impossible. He would lightly imply Leonard was seeing things, maybe losing his mind because of all the things he'd witnessed at the centre. She wouldn't know Marcus was lying.

If none of this worked, he'd need to bolt before things got worse. The thought made his throat tighten. His grandma was the only stability left in his life.

The lesson finished, and Sean packed up his bag.

"You did well, little man," Marcus said, encouraged by Sean's transformation. He seemed like a nice kid and eager to please.

"Bye," Sean said. His smile faded quickly as he walked past.

Marcus stood up and headed straight for the exit, averting his eyes from Amala. But when the door swung open, he found Leonard leaning against the wall.

"Going so soon?"

"Umm, I thought it had finished," Marcus said, stumbling.

"It has. I want to know what you thought. Let me speak to Amala, and I'll be right back."

Marcus nodded.

Leonard went into the room as the students piled out. The door closed firmly behind the last kid. Marcus waited a moment and then reached for the handle, opened the door slightly, and leaned in close.

"I saw him, Amala. That kid twisted up that metal fence."

"Are you sure?" Amala replied. "Are you absolutely sure? Because if this is true, there's been an explosion of kids with these abilities."

"I saw it. He pretended not to know what I was talking about. He tried to cover, and if I hadn't seen it with my own eyes, I would've believed him. He's very convincing."

"Can you blame him?"

"No, not at all."

"What are we going to do, Leonard? He's the fourth person we've found in as many months. Before that, it was only three or so in a generation. How many more can there be?"

Marcus stopped breathing. *The fourth person in months?* He wasn't alone!

"I have no idea," Leonard mumbled.

"I think we need to speak to Ezra and the Elders."

The Elders? That sounded ominous. Were they like school governors? His whole body went rigid. Were they going to turn him in to the *supernatural* authorities?

Leonard exhaled loudly. "Do we need to get Ezra involved?"

"Don't worry, I'll speak to Ezra," Amala said. "But this place isn't safe. We need somewhere else. If they're exposed, who knows what will happen to them."

Marcus's muscles relaxed slightly. Amala's soft voice implied she wanted him safe, but safe from what?

Leonard sighed heavily. "You're right. We need somewhere away from prying eyes. I might know a place."

There was silence. Marcus stepped away from the door, afraid they knew he was listening.

"I'll talk to him." Leonard's voice was closer to the door now. "See how receptive he is."

CHAPTER 5

As the door opened, Marcus whipped out his phone and pretended to scroll.

"Ready to go?" Leonard's smile was wary, his eyes perfectly clear again.

"Where are we going?"

"Just into one of these rooms." His smile faded, and worry lines creased his forehead.

As they got to the front of the building, the memory of Charlene flashed into Marcus's mind, accompanied by an ache in his lower abdomen. He hadn't seen her in the building or in the class.

"So how did you find it?" Leonard asked, avoiding Marcus's eyes.

"Fine." He shrugged. He just wanted to bolt to get to his grandma first.

"What did you think of Sean?"

"He's nice." Marcus nodded.

"Think you'd like to come back?"

"Depends."

"On what?"

"On what you want from me."

Leonard halted and looked at Marcus, who stared off into the distance for a good while before returning his gaze.

"Do you trust me, Marcus?"

"I don't know. I don't know you."

"I guess I don't have much of a choice," Leonard muttered, rubbing his cropped hair. "Let's pop into this room for a minute."

Marcus stiffened. Being alone in a room with someone who knew his secret was dangerous.

"You can trust me," Leonard promised.

Sean's words, Marcus thought, and moved forward to follow him. They walked into a small classroom with peeling wallpaper.

"Sorry about the walls. We're looking at redecorating. Take a seat."

Marcus sat down at the table, having flashbacks of being in the hospital in front of the police just a few days prior. He took a deep breath.

"All right. I'm just going to lay it out for you," Leonard said, taking a seat opposite him. "I saw what you did outside."

"What did you see?" Marcus asked. His heart kicked at his chest.

"I saw you pull up . . . part of the metal railing with your hands and move it around."

"You sure you saw that?" Marcus wasn't giving in that easily. That girl Charlene's distraction hadn't worked.

"I inspect these surroundings twice a day. I would've noticed anything amiss before."

Why would he inspect it twice? Marcus thought. *Is someone after them?* "Doesn't mean it was me. I was trying to fix it."

Leonard grunted, his eyes fixed on Marcus. "All right." He reclined back in the small plastic chair. Marcus was surprised it didn't crack under his weight. "Let's say I'm right and I really saw you move metal. What would you say if I told you there are others like you?"

A rush of excitement raced through Marcus's body, and his foot bounced to relieve the tension building inside. "I'd say that's not possible." He swallowed; his throat remained uncomfortably dry. Were there others like him? Were they the older kids he saw earlier?

"Look, I know opening up like this isn't . . . what you're

used to. That's understandable. You've had it hard. But you're gifted with something . . . incredible. And you're not alone. There are more gifted kids like you. If you're interested, come and see me on Friday. Here at eight thirty in the evening. I can speak to your grandma if she's worried about you being out late."

Marcus looked back at him, but his lips refused to open. His brain tried to make sense of what was being said.

"You can think about it. Send me a text if you want to know more, yeah?"

Leonard led him to the outside of the building, where they said their goodbyes. Marcus stood there in the dark as the night-time temperature plunged.

There were more people like him. Despite the darkening of the night, Marcus felt as if there might be some hope for his future.

He may be a freak, but he'd be part of a family of freaks.

Marcus entered his grandma's house. He felt exhausted, but his mind wouldn't stop thinking.

"Is that you, Marcus?" she called, peering around the door.

A warmth spread within his chest, an internal hug. Someone was waiting at home just for him. He remembered how his mother's eyes had always seemed vacant. When she was home, she seemed to be waiting for something else. Maybe the return of his invisible father.

He walked into the kitchen, where Grandma Maisey was doing the dishes.

"How was it?" she asked excitedly.

"It was . . . good," he said, eyeing his dinner plate covered with a microwave dish.

She smiled. "Yes, that's yours."

"Thanks, Gran," he said, hunger suddenly invading his stomach.

"Any nice kids?"

"Yeah." The image of the stunning girl with the red lipstick popped into his mind. Captivating and beautiful. He swallowed and distracted himself by going to get a drink.

"They do some good work there," his grandma said. "Honestly, we need more of that. Good influences, hard workers. More investment could transform those kids' lives. Do you know they have helped kids get into Oxford and Cambridge?"

"It looks depressing." Marcus chuckled to himself.

"Eh?"

"Old carpets, peeling paint. If it looked better, people would actually want to go there, you know?"

"You've been there five minutes and you already want to change it." She laughed, and her dark brown eyes sparkled. "Make the suggestion."

Marcus nodded and took out his steaming plate of brown stew chicken, rice, and peas. The familiar aromas of onions, garlic, and curry powder made his mouth water.

Leonard's conversation lingered in his mind. Maybe Bame Centre did help some kids academically, but Leonard and Amala seemed to have different plans for him. Was the centre actually about finding kids who had powers?

"Well, I'm glad you're getting stuck in, Marcus. Put the past behind you. You'll be starting a new school next week, gods willing. New friends, new start. You'll finally be able to live a normal life."

"Yeah right," Marcus said, shovelling rice and peas dripping

CHAPTER 5

with brown sauce into his mouth. "That ship sailed long ago."

Chapter 6

It was Friday afternoon, and Marcus hadn't gotten back to Leonard.

He also hadn't heard back from Crazy B.

Two separate paths lay in front of him: topple Crazy B by forming his own crew, or leave the rift behind and join a group of kids with powers. It seemed like a no-brainer. Who wouldn't want to be with other kids with powers?

But maybe it wasn't that simple. Maybe those kids would be more powerful than him. Maybe he wouldn't like them. Leonard had merely said there were others like him and that he could introduce him.

But deep down, he knew the truth: he couldn't let Crazy B get away with usurping his position. The thought was intolerable. He needed to bring him down. With a crew or alone.

A crew would give him clout and power. But if he couldn't get his own crew, maybe Dacus's gang would be the key.

Sure, it would be nice to know others like him, and no doubt it would be useful to know what they could do. Were they a threat to him? Could they do more—walk through walls, change their appearance?

CHAPTER 6

The buzz of his phone shocked him into the present. It was Tyler.

"Yo," Marcus answered.

"Bruv, you alone?"

He sat up straight. "Yeah, why?"

"I heard some rumblings about Carnell."

Marcus swallowed, and a coldness washed over his body.

"Talk of payback," Tyler said quietly.

Marcus rubbed his face. "Who told you that?"

"I heard Crazy B's boys talking. That's why you've been told to stay back. They want to see if you can dodge him."

Unbelievable, Marcus thought. Rage boiled inside him. Crazy B could've offered protection or had someone keep him in the loop, but he hadn't. Instead, the Carnell incident had turned out to be the best thing that could've happened for Crazy B: an opportunity to push Marcus out.

Well, Marcus would show Crazy B once and for all who he was messing with.

"You there, bro?" Tyler asked.

"I'm here. Thanks for letting me know. Keep listening, yeah?"

"What are you going to do?"

"I'll fill you in later."

He rung off and texted Leonard. He wanted to meet.

* * *

"Just going over to the centre, Grandma," Marcus said, coming down the stairs.

"You not going to have dinner?" she asked, surprised.

"Sorry, I forgot it was on tonight."

"Well, all right. Come straight back, ya hear?"

"I will," he said, giving her a quick kiss on her forehead. He felt bad leaving her at the last minute.

The unexpectedly cold night air made him catch his breath. The neighbouring shadowy houses started to look intimidating as the night descended, and unease snaked around his stomach. He needed to find out who these neighbours were—find out who knew who and what gangs were around. He'd start making some notes in the daylight.

He arrived at the centre in the inky darkness and pushed open the door, stepping into the dull yellow light of the entrance. This time a skinny, solemn bald man looked at him with the saddest eyes he'd ever seen.

"I'm here to see Leonard?"

"Name," the sombre man intoned.

"Marcus."

The man flicked through his notes. His smooth skin and nondescript features made it impossible for Marcus to tell his age; he could've been anything from seventeen to thirty.

The man stood up achingly slowly, went over to the door, and punched in the code to let him in. Marcus wondered what had happened to him to make him so sluggish.

They walked through the now open door, and the tall, sad figure led him to the large classroom where he'd met Sean. A few other teens were gathered inside, seated at tables. At the front, Amala was leaning back against her desk, with Leonard standing next to her.

Leonard's eyes widened, and a smile spread across his face.

CHAPTER 6

"Marcus, good to see you."

Marcus nodded and sat at one of the tables slightly farther away from the other three kids. His eyes fell on the beautiful girl from a few days before. She winked at him, catching him off guard and making his face burn. He looked away.

Against the wall slouched a well-built, tanned guy with a crew cut and piercing blue eyes; the kid's jaw clenched. The second boy had chocolate skin and was shorter with a round face.

"Well, I think this is everybody," Leonard said, looking back at Amala, who nodded in affirmation.

"What a moment this is." Leonard put his hands together and pursed his lips. He looked off into the distance for a second, as if recalling a long-lost memory. "Can I just say what an honour it is to have you all here? When Amala and I started this group, it was just to help talented kids, or kids with promise. But we noticed—"

"I noticed," Amala interjected with a cheeky smile.

"*Amala* noticed"—Leonard grinned back—"there was something different about some of these pupils. They weren't just smart but gifted with the most extraordinary abilities. We thought it was just one kid. Then we found two. As of today, we now have four, all discovered in the last few months." He started to walk around. "Your powers are gifts from the Orisha. You are channelling the abilities of gods."

Gods? Marcus shook his head. He couldn't have heard him properly. Or Leonard was having a laugh at their expense.

"You're kidding," exclaimed the round-faced boy. "Us? Coming from gods? How does that make sense?"

"We are children of Africa, Neil." Amala stepped forward. "We have spread far and wide, but we are all still connected to the Orisha."

"It's not really safe to talk about here," Leonard interjected. "We're working on a safe house, a place we can discuss this all freely, where we can teach you what we know and you can explore what you can do."

"It will be separate from what we offer here," Amala added. "This new group will be just for you, a place where you can learn more about who you are, where you're from, and what this might mean."

"How come you both know what we are?" the beautiful girl said.

"I have many years of study and experience," Amala said, her smile spreading instant warmth throughout the room. "I have encountered this before."

Silence settled over the group.

"There are more like us?" Marcus asked. "Are you one of us?"

Amala turned to him, and her kind eyes instantly relaxed him. "I am unfortunately not one of the Ebun. There are very few. You are a rarity."

"Don't worry, you won't be expected to come here to teach and assist once we have a safe place to meet," Leonard said, eyes sparkling. "There are more important things to figure out first before we do that. We will find other mentors to replace you."

"So, what are we?" said the blue-eyed boy, his fists clenched. "You saying we're freaks?"

"Far from it, Cassius." Amala rested her hand on his shoulder, and he instantly softened. "You are the descendants of all-powerful beings. Why you have these gifts and what you're supposed to do with them is another question. We'll

CHAPTER 6

figure this out together."

"We have a secluded place in mind where we can meet in secret," Leonard said. "No one can know about this. It is critically important you are protected. What you guys are experiencing hasn't been seen for centuries."

"I've got a question. Who's that guy?" Neil said, nodding towards Marcus.

Marcus stiffened.

"Oh, of course," Leonard said. "This is Marcus. It's his first week. He's new to the area, so I'm hoping you'll all make him feel welcome. Marcus, this young lady is Charlene, this is Neil, and this is Cassius."

They all nodded at him in acknowledgement.

"You all go to school round here?" Marcus asked.

"Not far," Charlene said coyly.

"Cassius and I are local," Neil answered. "We go to Hightops."

Marcus nodded. Now he understood why Leonard wanted him to go there. He'd be with the other gifted kids.

"These are exciting times." Leonard rubbed his hands together. "Hang tight. I'll let you know as soon as we have a place. In the meantime, keep coming here, okay? Let's keep in touch. You got anything to add, Amala?"

"No." She smiled, looking at Charlene, who returned her smile but cut away quickly.

"All right, well, it's getting late. You guys go straight home, okay?"

"Charlene, I'll see you tomorrow?" Amala touched the beautiful girl's arm, who nodded in reply as they all left the room.

Outside, Marcus watched Cassius put his arm around

Charlene's shoulders and immediately walk off. To his surprise, a stab of jealousy struck him. They knew each other.

He forced his eyes away, scolding himself for thinking about her that way. He'd suffered enough heartache: his cousins, his aunt . . . even his mum. Charlene had simply seen he was in trouble and tried to help him out. Nothing more, nothing less. At the most, she could be a helpful ally.

Neil walked off quickly, impatiently asking the sombre receptionist to open the door so he could leave.

Despite the disappointment with Charlene, Marcus couldn't wait to see what they could do. This group could be just what he needed.

***

That Monday afternoon, dressed in an uncomfortable green blazer with blue trimming and tie, Marcus walked home from his new school: Forest Park. Grandma Maisey had been disappointed but hadn't given up on Hightops.

He'd spent the day watching rather than talking: who looked shifty, who was eager to be liked, who were troublemakers. He'd been paired with two boys who'd begrudgingly shown him around. They at least told him who was popular and who he should steer clear from.

As he walked down the road back home, he saw Cassius with a group of other boys huddled in a corner. Their uniforms were different from Marcus's; they had red jumpers with yellow-striped ties. Laughter and plumes of smoke emanated

CHAPTER 6

from their spot.

Three girls walked past. Cassius called to one of the girls, and she came over. But it was strange. She moved stiffly, her eyes and head unwavering and still, as if she was in a trance. Marcus watched, fascinated. Her friends were calling after her, but she seemed deaf to their voices.

Cassius started to talk to the girl, then pulled her in close. He leaned in and kissed her hard, his hands all over her body.

Just as Marcus began to stride forward, one of the girl's friends grabbed her and pulled her away. The girl seemed to wake up from her daze, looking around at her surroundings as if trying to reacquaint herself with where she was. Cassius threw his head back, laughing.

Mind control.

Marcus's stomach clenched, and his fists balled up.

This guy was dangerous.

With that power, Cassius could do anything. From what Marcus had just seen, he was already taking advantage. Treating girls like that wouldn't be tolerated; he'd have to root that out. Just thinking about how Cassius could manipulate people made him uneasy.

Marcus stepped into the road. He was still staring back at Cassius and his boys when tyres suddenly screeched in front of him. He looked up to see two hooded figures swerve on their bikes to avoid him.

His heart thumped inside his chest as he watched the figures glare back at him and ride off. They were all in black with hoodies. As they disappeared round the corner, only their eyes could be seen, their faces covered with scarves. There was no way to recognise them.

Whose boys were they? Were they after him?

Marcus hurried home. He felt exposed and scared. He had no form of protection on him, and he was by himself.

Opening the front door, he called out to his grandma and was surprisingly disappointed when no answer came. He ran upstairs, took out a small knife from his suitcase, and headed outside. Grandma Maisey's old dying tree farther down the garden would make the perfect target.

For half an hour, he practised throwing the knife. It took a few tries to get it in the tree's trunk; occasionally he'd get it stuck in the fence behind. Alternating each arm, he tried to use his mental abilities to move the knife to the target. He was getting faster each time. The practise eased his tense muscles, and his aching arms distracted him from the thought of being followed. Maybe he could take care of himself now.

Still, he wanted to make contact with the Eastern European gang, gain an upper hand over Crazy B. He needed money and protection. The two cyclists from earlier bothered him. They had ridden in front of him on purpose, and the way they'd glared at him had seemed intentional. Marcus needed someone to have his back.

Back in his bedroom, he whizzed through that night's homework, then spent the rest of the evening flicking and twisting his knife around the room, practising his accuracy and control.

He'd made up his mind. He was going to see Dacus.

Chapter 7

Marcus stood outside Dacus's warehouse, his palms sweaty, his breathing shallow. He took a deep breath and dialled the number.

"Hello?" a thickly accented voice responded.

Marcus swallowed hard. "Is this Dacus?"

"Yes, who is this?"

"This is Marcus."

"Marcus who? How did you get my number?" His agitation was palpable.

"I want to help you."

"Stop wasting my time. What do you want?" Dacus growled.

"A partnership."

"Why would I want to do that? I don't even know who you are."

"I'm willing to change that."

Marcus stepped out from behind the corner and walked towards the warehouse door. Dacus spun, his phone still to his ear, to see Marcus slowly put his arms up in surrender.

"How did you know where to find me?" Dacus began to walk over to him, his craggy face etched with anger.

"I have a contact."

"Who?"

"I'll tell you, but first I need your protection."

Dacus stopped almost an inch from his face. "You are a kid. You have no business here."

"I'm valuable."

"Then why do you need protection? Only snitches need that."

"Or threats to power," Marcus countered.

"Who are you threatening?"

Marcus paused. He had two enemies right now, Carnell and Crazy B. He had to pick one. Two would be seen as too much of a liability. "I shot someone in self-defence. Now they're after me."

"I'm not getting involved in street violence."

"I just need some protection for a while. I have a lot of connections with the local gangs—"

"Then why aren't they protecting you?"

"It's complicated."

Dacus backed off, smiling now. Marcus was losing him. Would he have to reveal his abilities to convince him? That was too risky. Maybe there was another way.

"Get out of here and stop wasting my time," Dacus said. "See him out, boys."

Three of his guards came walking towards Marcus.

"Palladium," Marcus said loudly, his voice echoing around the warehouse.

Dacus paused. "What?"

"I can get you four catalytic converters tonight."

"Four?" Dacus scoffed. "I could send my men to do that."

The guards closed in.

"Ten. I could get you ten." Marcus stepped back, his hands

CHAPTER 7

heating up.

"Ten by yourself? You're working with someone—"

"If I can get you ten by myself, by the end of tonight, will you cover me?"

Dacus folded his arms and walked closer. "That's very valuable stuff you're trying to give me for free. Are you saying you want nothing from me apart from protection?"

"Not for tonight's things."

Dacus's eyes narrowed. He stroked his chin, his gaze sweeping up and down. Marcus clenched his hot fists.

"You get me those ten tonight," Dacus finally said, "by yourself, and you have a deal for a week."

"I need a month."

"I can't spare anybody longer than a week."

"How about if I get you palladium weekly. Will you extend it?"

"If you get me that palladium, then we'll talk."

Marcus nodded, quickly turning on his heel.

"And Marcus!" Dacus called after him.

Marcus spun around.

"I don't want to hear from you again if you don't bring those things tonight."

"No worries," Marcus replied with a smile. Inside, he wondered how on earth he was going to pull this off.

He'd clocked all the CCTV cameras he could find and disabled them. Next, he'd tackled the streetlights by making the bulbs blow. The last thing had been to crawl under the electric cars of a car dealership and pull out all the converters he could. It had taken him hours to locate ten, and he was exhausted.

It was four in the morning, and he had to deliver the stash before he could climb back through his bedroom window, which he needed to do before his grandma woke up at seven.

Finally, he dragged himself back to Dacus's hide out, dropping the heavy bags filled with the stolen goods.

Dacus's eyes bulged. "Let's talk tomorrow."

The following week, Marcus made his way to a park not far from where he lived: Jade Gardens. It wasn't well known to him; it was neutral territory for most of the gangs. This was where Leonard had asked him and the other gifted kids to meet.

Marcus had managed to get Dacus to watch out for him for the week, but he'd asked to be left alone on this day. The last thing he wanted was to lead Dacus to people who had superhuman abilities.

Leonard was sitting at a bench, and he smiled broadly when he saw Marcus approach. No one else had arrived yet. They exchanged a hand gesture, and Marcus sat down next to him.

"How was school?" Leonard asked.

Marcus shrugged. "All right."

"It'll get better." Leonard patted him on the back. "You look like you need some sleep though."

Marcus knew he had bags under his eyes. Twice now he'd gone to collect whatever bits of precious metal Dacus had asked for. He'd had to survive on three hours of sleep those nights.

He changed the subject. "How long you been looking for kids with powers?"

"I guess about ten years," Leonard answered, "but that was

CHAPTER 7

never intentional. It just happened, you know? Gifted and troubled kids just seemed to come my way. I had no idea some of them had these abilities. Something happens in their lives and . . . the magic just reveals itself."

"What do you mean something happens?"

"Like a big event, something that changes everything."

Marcus turned away. He didn't want to relive that night when his power fully manifested. Instead, he shifted topics. "You grew up around here?"

"No," Leonard replied. "I grew up in Essex, but life is a funny thing, and I ended up here."

"Got any family? Or are you alone like me?"

Leonard gave him a sidewards glance. "We're never alone, Marcus. You have your grandma, and us now. Ah, here we are. The others are coming."

Charlene and Cassius walked towards them, side by side. Marcus clenched his jaw. Charlene clearly didn't know who she was messing with. Cassius could be manipulating her right now, for all they knew. Neil trailed behind, a sullen look on his face and his hands pushed down into his pockets.

A wide smile was plastered across Cassius's freckled face. He leaned in close to Charlene's ear, whispering, and she smiled coyly in return. Resentment boiled in Marcus's chest, and his hands burned as he recalled the girl who had been hypnotised. There was no way Charlene knew about what Cassius had done that day.

"Hi, guys." Leonard smiled, shaking their hands as he stood up. "Let me take you to the new venue. Stay close. It's in the middle of the park."

The middle of the park? Wouldn't that be in obvious view of everyone? How would that keep them protected?

Marcus dropped back so he could watch the others, but Neil refused to walk in front of him. *He knows I'm trying to watch him*, Marcus thought, impressed. He tried a different tactic and attempted to walk beside him. "You all right?" he asked.

"Yeah, you?" Neil replied after a brief pause.

"Not bad. Had my first day at school today."

"Which one?"

"Forest."

Neil whistled. "Good luck."

"That bad, huh?"

"Depends on if you can handle it."

"Nothing I can't handle. What's the point in having gifts if we can't use them to defend ourselves?" Marcus grinned.

"Depends on your gift."

"True. You know anyone at Forest? Want to give me some pointers?"

Neil thought for a moment as they walked farther into the park, approaching a lake. "I know a couple of people. I could make some introductions if you want."

"Thanks."

The group followed Leonard into the thickest parts of the park. Dense white fog seemed to seep from the trees, damp and clinging. Marcus felt cold, as if the fog was trying to burrow into his skin.

"What is this stuff?" he asked Neil.

"Don't know . . . I've never felt fog like this," Neil replied as he wiped his coat sleeve.

Suddenly Leonard stopped. He lifted a small stone in the air and began moving his hand in a circle. A round neon-blue portal appeared, glittering and shooting sparks. Right in the

CHAPTER 7

middle was a black keyhole.

Marcus stepped back, unsure of what was before him. He glanced at Neil, whose mouth was gaping open.

Leonard turned to his astonished companions and held up a huge bronze key for them to see. "You're going to like this."

He smiled as he slipped the key into the lock. After he withdrew it, cracks began to spread out from the keyhole, each one faintly backlit by a strange blue radiance. The fog lifted slightly to reveal a small opening, and Leonard stepped through.

Marcus held his breath and cautiously stepped through after him.

There was no fog on the other side, but the density of the trees prevented any daylight from illuminating their surroundings. Ahead, Marcus could make out a large dark building made of glass. The glass front door was so thickly coated in dirt he couldn't make out what was inside. The whole scene was eerie.

Leonard took out another key, unlocked the glass door, and walked in, beckoning the others to follow him. Marcus advanced first, shoving the gnawing fear in his stomach away.

Inside was deathly quiet. Even the birds couldn't be heard. Dangling lanterns were the only things that pierced the thick darkness in which they all stood.

"How are they doing that?" Charlene stared, wide-eyed.

"Magic." Leonard smiled excitedly. "Isn't it great?"

Marcus looked closely and realised the lanterns weren't attached to anything—suspended in mid-air.

"We'll get better lighting," Leonard said, taking a torch out of his pocket. "Once we've cleaned up, you'll see how magnificent this place is. Follow me."

As they walked farther into the building, they stayed close to one another. Marcus could see just how vast it was. It had the potential to be stunning. The windows were dull and dirty, the metal frames were bent or broken, and a draft blew in from the corner of the room. The smell of something sweet, like liquorice, filled his nostrils. Yet this mysterious building was majestic. The arched windows, despite the clogged dirt, were remarkable. There were pillars surrounding them that, though dirty and stained, hinted at an old world of secrets and stories. Marcus wanted more of this supernatural realm.

"Amazing," Charlene whispered. "How did Amala find this place?"

"We're in a hidden dimension, concealed from the outside world. Luckily, Amala knows the park attendant. We created the mist in order to keep this place hidden. The only way anyone will get inside is if they have a key."

"This is madness, bruv." Marcus spun round, unable to comprehend what he'd just heard.

Leonard grinned back. "I think it's time we told you who you really are."

Amala appeared from the shadows, luminescent in her brightly coloured clothes, her face full of pride. She beamed. "Welcome to your haven."

"I was just about to tell them who they really are," Leonard said, pulling up two intricately designed metal chairs for them to sit in. Marcus felt a rush of excitement; so much metal in one place was a dream for him.

"Then I'm right on time."

Amala and Leonard sat on the rusty white metal chairs,

CHAPTER 7

while the four kids took a seat on an old metal bench just opposite.

"We're not exactly who we said we were," Leonard said.

"Or rather, we just omitted some details," Amala corrected. "You see, Leonard and I study the ancient faiths of Africa. We have spent some time travelling around the country and in Nigeria, becoming acquainted with the religion concerning the Orisha. During our last visit, we were told there had been a disagreement among the Orisha and consequences might be felt here."

"Hang on." Neil held up his hand. "What are Orisha?"

"Let me explain." Leonard cleared his throat. "The Orisha are spirit gods of Nigeria and other neighbouring villages, much like Zeus and Poseidon are gods of the Greeks, and Odin and Thor are gods of the Norse people. Powerful beings that no longer dwell on the earth. Each is a guardian over specific elements— water, fire, earth, and metal." Leonard's eyes locked on Marcus for just a moment before he continued. "They are guides for us when petitioned and generally bring no harm."

"Isn't this ancient weird stuff?" Cassius interrupted. "What's it got to do with us here and now? In London? This ain't Nigeria."

"But you are part of the diaspora," Amala answered. "The Orisha have influence wherever the diaspora can be found, as well as in Nigeria."

"You mean there are others like us across the world?" Charlene asked excitedly.

"Yes, but very, very few. There are usually only three or so born every twenty years around the world. The fact that we have now found four in the space of a year in the same location is intriguing."

"What happened in Nigeria?" Marcus asked. The idea of some "disagreement" troubled him. The last thing he needed was more problems.

"We met with some leaders of the Orisha religion called Elders," Amala replied. "They said one of the spirit gods was causing trouble here on the earth. This god has always been mischievous, but now she is becoming something sinister. She's overstepped her boundaries and wants more than she was promised. She has interfered with humans. I was involved in a case here many years ago that we believe she had something to do with: the disappearance of another gifted child. Another Ebun."

"What's an Ebun?" Charlene said.

"It means 'gifted.' That's what you all are. Gifted with extraordinary abilities from the Orisha."

"Hang on. Someone disappeared?" Neil said, his face creased with panic.

"I think we need to slow down," Leonard interrupted. "Let's start from the beginning: The Orisha are descendants of the great god Olorun, the sky father, creator of the universe. He has many children, made of pure energy, who have the ability to create and destroy. As we said, they all reign over different parts of this world: gods of hurricanes and volcanoes, wars, and defence. Others are gods of the waters and family, motherhood, and peace. There are no limits to what these spirits can influence. You have been endowed with these abilities from them, and we need to figure out why."

"Which brings us to the girl who disappeared," Amala continued. "Twenty years ago, there were three kids your age who all developed abilities. The most talented one, who lived here in London, started to display unusual behaviour, and despite all attempts to help her and guide her, she disappeared one day. Whatever happened to her must never happen again. This time we need to look out for each other and to have a place sheltered from the world. The Elders of the Orisha religion warned us to keep our eyes open for any more unusual activity. They are most interested in what's developing here."

"What about that other Orisha?" Neil asked. "The one who was causing issues?"

"That we are still trying to piece together." Amala became serious. "Strange things would happen during worship ceremonies. Accidents, illnesses, demon possession—both here and in Nigeria."

"That's messed up," Neil said, barely above a whisper.

Coldness rippled through Marcus's body. He turned and saw what he thought was a shadow next to a lantern. The lantern flickered as if a breeze was interrupting its flame. He squinted, trying to make out the shape of what he was seeing.

With a sudden movement, the shadow dashed into the impenetrable darkness. Marcus stepped back, closer to the others. His eyes darted between the lantern and Amala. Was he seeing things? He opened his mouth to say something but quickly closed it. If no one else mentioned it, maybe it was just his overactive imagination after everything he was hearing and seeing.

"Why don't they stop her? Lock her away in some part of the universe?" Cassius said.

"It doesn't work like that, Cassius," Amala answered. "All of these beings are incredibly powerful, and we don't know what alliances already exist. You can't simply imprison them.

Bargains have to be made, alliances, sometimes war . . ."

"What's her name?" Charlene asked.

Amala paused. "Names have power. We shall not utter her name just yet."

The four teenagers stood stock-still. The house felt cold and exposed.

"Why are we involved in this?" Marcus asked.

"You have been endowed with these powers from the Orisha. We will be able to determine which ones gave you your gifts based on the powers you have. Hopefully this will help us see what should be done."

"What are we supposed to do with these powers? Fight?" Neil asked. "Are we heading for war?"

Marcus stiffened, a knot crystallising in his stomach. What was he getting into?

"We're not jumping to conclusions," Leonard remarked. "We're telling you what you need to know now. We need to discover more about your abilities and help you fulfil whatever part you have to play in this."

"Have you ever seen one? An Orisha?" Charlene swallowed.

"No." Leonard shrugged. "There would have to be a grave reason for them to appear to a mortal. But sometimes their presence is felt in worship ceremonies."

Marcus wasn't sure he understood what he was hearing. This was far beyond anything he had considered. Connected to spirits from Africa—*him*, who was constantly fighting to fit in and be protected? He was expected to get involved in a battle with powerful beings?

"So, you want us to learn how to fight?" he asked. "How are we supposed to fight a god?"

"Not so fast." Leonard smiled. "First you guys need to study history and the origins of your powers and the Orisha. Each ability corresponds to an element of an Orisha's power—your abilities will be synchronised with a specific god."

"But when is this war coming?" Neil asked.

"Let's not worry about that yet. There seems to be no imminent threat," Amala said. "The most important thing is for us to clean up."

"I reckon we can do this in two weeks if we work hard," Leonard said. "It'll give you guys time to say goodbye to the kids at the centre."

Charlene gazed up at the glass ceiling. "Will the Orisha come and speak to us? Will they let us know what to do?"

"I think they will, in time, but you have to understand, they don't get involved with humans on a face-to-face basis," Amala said.

"Are we even human, or are we gods?" Cassius asked, confusion etched in his face.

"Definitely human." Amala smiled, unconvincingly. "But enhanced."

Cold uncertainty coursed through Marcus's veins. If this was true, then he really was a freak, an anomaly, which would explain so much. Why things went wrong. Why his father left, then his mum . . . and everyone else.

"Don't worry about a thing." Leonard put his arm around Neil's stiff shoulders. "In a couple of weeks, we're going to have books, teachers, and most importantly, a place you can practise your magic. Let's start cleaning!"

Chapter 8

Marcus walked out of the glass house a different person. The windows had thick black dirt, weeds and roots grew in every corner, there was broken glass and missing windows, and gnarled and twisted metal dangled everywhere. But despite the muck and grime, this place was theirs. He couldn't wait to get stuck in.

Their place of safety, once cleaned and mended, would be truly impressive, better than anything he could have dreamed of himself. A thrill of anticipation pulsed through his body at this new turn of events.

He took his phone out on instinct to text his cousins, then stopped. How could he possibly explain to them what was happening to him? These powers, these people? His throat ached as he put the phone back into his pocket. Now was not the time. He would have to think carefully about what to say.

He watched as Amala locked the hidden building behind the wall of fog and magic. Zigzags of light surrounded the lock on the portal before it faded; only a slight outline remained, invisible unless it was pointed out.

Amala caught him staring at the mysterious scene and smiled in amusement. "Marcus, how are you?"

CHAPTER 8

"Yeah . . . okay," he said with a shake of his head, forcing himself into the present.

"How are you finding life with your grandma?"

"Good actually. It's . . . peaceful."

"She is such a good woman. You take care of her now. She's been a friend of mine for a long time."

"She's been my grandma for just as long." He smiled back, his eyebrow arching up.

She laughed, a twinkle in her eye. "That might be true." After a pause, she said, "What we are building here will change everything. Do you feel that?"

He nodded. Every sense in his body seemed to flicker. His vision sharpened around the hazy trees; his ears could hear the tinkle of the nearby lake and the cracks of sticks beneath their feet. He felt the gentle breeze on his face and the heaviness of his clothing. It was as if his whole body was being activated.

"With this new generation of Ebun, I think my purpose is becoming much clearer," Amala said.

"Have you been waiting for us?"

"I'm not sure if it was for you exactly, but I was waiting for the chance to bring the past to life. To help the youth understand there are layers to this reality, not just what you see with your eyes. Have you ever had that sense? That there was more going on than what you could see?"

"Maybe," Marcus said. For him it was more about discovering people's intentions and using that to his advantage. Anything to survive on the streets. He hadn't thought much beyond that.

"There is so much to teach you all. So much for you to see and understand," she said, her head tilted towards the sun.

Her colourful patterned dress billowed behind her, practically coming to life. She looked almost whimsical as she walked through the park.

The others walked ahead, deep in their own conversations.

"Do you have powers?" Marcus asked.

"Not like you, but I have my own set of skills."

When the group emerged from the dark trees into the early evening sun, they blinked for a while, readjusting to the light, and then started to walk towards the park exit. Marcus was lost in thought. What was he supposed to do with this knowledge? How was he supposed to look after and defend himself in this new system?

From the corner of his eye, he saw Cassius laughing with Charlene.

Cassius made him uneasy. The guy was well-built, attractive, and—with his ability—dangerous to others. Marcus's intuition told him this was a snake and to steer clear, and he always followed those instincts. Yet as Cassius cosied up to Charlene, Marcus felt as though he needed to protect her. He wasn't sure what her powers were. Did she know what he could do? Could she deflect him? Did she have the same power?

Marcus recalled the first time he saw her and how he'd felt, but he brushed those memories aside. She was clearly involved with Cassius, though he had no idea why.

When they got to the exit, Leonard and Amala told the four they would be in touch to get started on the improvements. A huddled group of boys were standing across the road, staring at Cassius, and Leonard and Amala hesitated at the sight of them.

"They're with me," Cassius said with a smirk and started to

cross the road. "Laters."

Leonard and Amala exchanged glances before they said goodbye to the others and started up the road.

"Want me to walk you home, Charlene?" Neil asked, his eyes following Cassius.

"No thanks," she said, her head tilted to the sky. "I think I'll have a quick word with Marcus if that's okay?"

Looking stunned, Neil mumbled a goodbye and walked off in the opposite direction. Marcus tried to suppress the grin that was pulling at his lips.

Charlene turned towards him. "So, what did you think?"

"Of what?" he said.

"Our new place," she clarified.

"It's got potential." Marcus cocked his head to the side. The wind blew gently, and as he caught her fruity scent again, butterflies tingled in his stomach.

"My thoughts exactly. We'll get to shape this place however we want, guiding the others who join later."

Marcus's interest was piqued; she wanted an alliance. The question was, did she mean to ally with just him or Neil and Cassius too?

"You think there are others?" he asked, knowing there must be from Amala's previous comments.

"I know there are."

"Really? Do you know who they are?" He turned his body towards her, careful not to get too close, despite the magnet pull in his chest.

"One of the younger kids we mentor, and Natalie, the girl with the long brown hair?"

"So why were we the only ones they showed?"

"It's obvious. We're the ones they want to be the leaders."

Marcus felt a surge of adrenaline. Him becoming head leader might not be so difficult after all. "How do they know I'll be any good?"

Her ruby-red lips parted into an inviting smile. "You walk with your head up, shoulders back, and spine straight. A quiet confidence. The perfect combination."

None of this was new to Marcus. He'd had to carry himself with confidence in order to get things done. Yet hearing this from Charlene made him swell with pleasure. He broke eye contact and tried to compose himself. "How about you? What are your leadership qualities?"

"They're a little different." She started to walk ahead of him, and he moved quickly to catch up with her. Her beautiful scarlet lips smiled as she watched him follow her. "My gifts aren't the type you can see. Rather, they're ones that can be felt."

He knew it. His body stiffened slightly. She had some kind of magic that made people fall for her. "So . . . you can manipulate people?"

She laughed, her head tilting back. "I wish, but I can heighten feelings that are already there."

Marcus forced a smile, but a sense of unease had settled within him. How could he trust someone who might try to influence him? She could be a great ally, not just with this new group but with his plans for the Eastern European gangs. Somehow, he needed this girl onside—but maybe at arm's distance, just until he knew if he could trust her.

Despite his worries, she made him feel good, and he wanted to spend more time with her.

"Are we going to your house?" Marcus asked, suddenly realising he was walking farther from his own home.

CHAPTER 8

"*I'm* heading to my house," she said, her right eyebrow arching.

"Okay." He nodded. "Good talking to you, Charlene."

"Likewise." She winked.

Marcus held his breath, his heart beating harder in his chest as he slowed his pace and started heading toward Grandma Maisey's.

Charlene sashayed away from him as he turned to take one last glance. He'd never met anyone like her—eloquent, stunningly beautiful, and apparently just as ambitious as him. Despite himself, he had fallen under her spell. And he no longer cared.

Chapter 9

The group spent the next couple of weeks scraping, repairing, and scrubbing everything in the glass house they could lay their eyes on. Marcus had never cleaned so much in his life. When no one was looking, he would fix and straighten any bits of metal he could find. He would not reveal what he could do without seeing the others' powers first.

By the end of the two weeks, the glass house gleamed like a palace. Light streamed through every window, tinted green by the surrounding foliage. Amala had decorated the halls with paintings of African gods, rituals, animals, and ancient maps.

"I have books for all of you to explore," she said at the end of that day, handing out books to each of them. "Please familiarise yourself with Nigerian mythology."

"What about your books? Why can't we just read those?" Marcus asked with a smile as he eyed her freshly painted office; it was teaming with books.

"You need to walk before you can run, Marcus."

Amala beckoned them to follow her. They went to the back of the glass house to a slightly smaller room. Unending

CHAPTER 9

windows let in the sun's twilight rays, which landed on a small altar straight ahead of them.

"This is a very special room," Amala said, a smile spreading across her face, "one you need permission to enter. Welcome to the altar of the Orisha."

Seven large paintings hung on the wall, each depicting either a man or a woman against a different coloured background. In front of each portrait, on a red table, sat a large candle that matched the colour of its respective painting. Next to the candles were beads of various hues, a bell, and a bowl of water. Below each painting was a name.

Amala quietly closed the door behind them before moving forward. "Since you all exhibit many of their qualities, I thought it was time to introduce you to the spirits whose abilities you represent."

She pointed to the first painting. "Orula, the Orisha of wisdom and intelligence, the supreme oracle," she said with relish before moving on to the next one. "Ogun."

Marcus straightened up as he studied the picture of a bald man with amber eyes, a machete attached to his belt. As he stared, his hands flew up to his necklace.

"He embodies the spirit of war and iron," Amala continued, "a warrior of the people."

Marcus barely paid attention to the other Orisha, apart from Obatala, the creator of humans. Instead, his eyes remained fixed on Ogun's face. The man looked angry, uncompromising. His eyes seemed to pierce Marcus—daring him, challenging him to power.

"Who's this?" Charlene asked Amala, moving closer as if to touch a painting.

"Not too close!" Amala darted forward. "These paintings

are precious. A high price in more ways than one was paid for them. Eleggua or Eshu. He is . . . a complicated Orisha, known for his mischief and causing trouble for innocents. Yet he is a trusted messenger of all the Orisha, and whenever we request their help, he must be petitioned first. He carries messages and sacrifices to them."

"Why?" Marcus said. "He sounds like a troublemaker."

"Oh, he is, but to the right people and in the right circumstances, he is very trustworthy. He once saved the life of the high god. He teaches there are two sides to every story."

"I read he is the god of change," Charlene said, eyes still fixed on the painting.

"To his followers, he is the voice of choice. Of all the Orisha, he is the most complex and unpredictable."

Charlene stepped back with the others. Amala's eyes lingered on her.

"Are we supposed to worship them?" Cassius asked. He slouched back on the far wall, but his eyes watched everyone intently despite his relaxed stance. "What have we got to do with them?"

"This is your heritage, Cassius. Somehow you are all connected to these figures you see here. Don't think of it so much as worship. Think of them as guides. Directors."

"Don't people worship them?" Charlene enquired.

"Yes, but that isn't a commitment I would expect you to make. It is a very serious lifetime commitment, involving sacrifices, offerings. It isn't for everyone."

"Who do you worship?" Charlene asked.

"My Orisha parent is Obba Nani. She is one of the lesser-known Orisha."

"Why her?" Charlene's face screwed up, which surprised

CHAPTER 9

Marcus.

"Sometimes you choose your guide. Other times you are chosen by them."

"I would've thought you would have gone for . . . a more powerful Orisha."

"As I said, it's not always through choice. Sometimes you just find each other."

Marcus could tell Charlene wasn't impressed as she continued to look at the images. He may have underestimated her. She was clearly interested in power.

The evening came quickly, and everyone got ready to return home. A warmth burned in Marcus's chest that he'd only ever felt with his grandma. He felt as if he belonged here. He'd started a whole new life. Maybe he wasn't meant to just scrape by. Maybe he could live as one of the Orisha, a god on Earth.

"You all going straight home?" he called ahead to the other three.

"Why, you got any ideas?" asked Neil. He had loosened up around Marcus over the last few weeks, and he seemed to talk a lot more freely now.

"What do you want to do?" Charlene asked.

"Explore the park a bit. Get to know each other."

"I'm game," Neil said. "What about you, Cassius?"

"All right," Cassius said without much hesitation.

"Let's go," Charlene purred.

They sat on a bench next to the lake and were soon divulging stories from their schools.

"His arms were moving around like this." Neil flailed his

fists, recreating an event from school that day, his face creased with laughter. "He looked like such an idiot. I could tell without even using my powers that guy was going to get his lights punched out."

Marcus wiped his eyes. His stomach ached from laughing so hard, but the opportunity to gain information pierced through his mind. "What's your power?"

Neil calmed down quickly and looked at Marcus for a moment before answering. "I can see into the future."

"No, bruv!" Marcus jerked back. "Serious?"

"Yeah," Neil said with a crooked smile.

"You've got to show me." He turned to Charlene and Cassius. "Have you seen what he can do?"

They shook their heads, their eyes fixed on Neil.

Neil glanced around quickly. "All right, make sure no one else is watching me, yeah?"

They all looked around to make sure. No one else was visible.

Neil stood very still, almost like a statue, his eyes wide open but unseeing. Suddenly his pupils disappeared.

All three leapt back, Cassius covering his mouth with his fist.

Neil's eyes glowed brightly for a few seconds. Then the light faded and his pupils returned.

"That's madness," Cassius said, holding his head.

"I can't believe this, man," Marcus said. "What did you see?"

"Nothing. Nothing of interest, anyway. Just people walking by."

"That is so cool"—Marcus shook his head—"but really freaky to look at!"

"Yeah, I know. That's why people can't see me when I do

that."

"I bet you can predict all sorts of things."

"Only when I'm concentrating. I don't have spider senses, you know!"

They all laughed, a nervous excitement passing between them.

"It's your turn now, Charlene," Neil said suddenly. "I've always wondered what you could do."

"Well, you can't really see mine. It's more of a feeling."

"What, you mean you can make people feel things?" Neil asked.

"Yeah."

"All right then, who are you going to try it on?"

"None of you!"

"Come on, try it on me," Neil demanded.

"Suit yourself." She shrugged, then rolled back her shoulders and gazed directly into Neil's eyes. Her look was one of pure possession.

In an instant, Neil seemed to lose his normal composure. His shoulders slumped forward slightly, and he stared openly at her.

"Neil, my shoulders are sore. Would you mind giving them a rub for me?" she said, massaging her shoulder in mock pain.

Neil walked straight over, his eyes not quite focused, and began to rub her shoulders.

"Thank you so much. Could you hold my handbag for me?"

"Sure," he responded in a distant voice, taking her leopard-print bag and putting it on his own shoulder. Cassius and Marcus cracked up at the sight of stocky Neil with a dainty leopard-print bag.

"Don't laugh," Charlene said innocently. "I think it suits

him."

"You going to give him a break?" Marcus said.

"No, I think I'll let him hold it a while longer. My muscles ache." Marcus could've sworn she winked at him.

"What do you do, Cassius?" Marcus asked.

"You don't want to know what I can do."

"What do you mean?" He wasn't going to be scared off.

"What he means is, it's similar to mine," Charlene said. "He can also manipulate people."

"You mean you two have the same power?"

"Almost," Cassius answered. "Hers is more feeling- based. Mine is more, like, mind control. I can make people do things by putting thoughts in their heads."

"Huh." Marcus was speechless. Something like fear pricked at his stomach. He wished he had a cigarette to take the edge off his tense muscles.

"Do you want to see it?" Cassius asked.

Marcus knew exactly what this was: a trap to see if he could be easily manipulated. If he backed out, he would look weak.

"Don't make him do it," Charlene said to Cassius, poking him in the ribs, but he wondered if secretly she wanted to see the outcome.

"Yeah, I'll see it," Marcus said, standing up.

"Okay," said Cassius. But he hadn't moved his lips. The voice had come from inside Marcus's mind.

Cassius looked directly at him, his eyes hard and his face tense.

"Let's go for a swim," the voice said.

Marcus didn't move.

"I want to swim. It looks really inviting. And I can show them how fast I am."

CHAPTER 9

Before Marcus knew it, he was walking towards the lake. He made himself stop just before he stepped in.

"I'll show them how fast I am. I'm faster than Cassius and Neil. Might even impress Charlene."

Marcus stepped into the water with both feet. He began to fight hard now, forcing himself to stop where he was.

"I just need to get farther in the water so I can pick up speed."

"No!" Marcus shouted back in his mind. His head was aching.

"Just a little bit farther in."

Marcus was holding his breath, straining now, when suddenly the voice stopped. He felt as if his whole body had been released from some vise. He spun around to see Charlene arguing with Cassius.

"What are you doing, you idiot?" Charlene said. "Are you trying to hurt him?"

"He's fine. He should've been swimming by now anyway. He's clearly got some resistance going on."

"You're being a jerk. He's one of us."

Marcus was already out of the water, and he began to advance on Cassius. His body felt weak and depleted. "What was that about?"

"Nothing," Cassius said, his lips creeping into a smirk.

"You trying to make me look like a fool?" Marcus's hands were aflame now.

"Nah, man. You said you wanted to see what I could do."

Marcus wanted to take him out right there—put his fist through the guy's head—but Cassius was a whole other level of dangerous. He'd need to use another tactic to deal with him, or at least keep out of his way. Marcus breathed heavily, dripping in swampy water. He didn't take his eyes off the other boy.

"Are you okay? Did you step on anything?" Charlene asked.

"I'm all right."

"Yo, why are your feet wet?" asked Neil, suddenly breaking out of his own trance. "And whose is this handbag?"

"It's mine," Charlene said, taking it from him. "Marcus, do you want to get out of here?"

"Wait up," Neil said. "We haven't seen what he can do."

Marcus was in no mood to show them anything. His trainers were brown with dirt, and his soggy feet slapped the ground.

"All right," he said, eyeing the metal chain around Cassius's neck. He lifted his hand and pulled as hard as he could with his mind. Cassius's neck jerked forward, and then the chain popped off and landed in Marcus's hand.

Everyone stared at him.

"That's incredible!" Charlene said.

"Yeah, that's pretty cool," Neil confirmed.

For a moment, Cassius's face flashed hatred. Marcus offered the chain back to him, and he took it with a forced smile.

Marcus was playing with fire now.

* * *

The following night, Marcus got a text from Charlene.

Charlene: *Neil and I are hanging out tonight. Want to come?*

Marcus had homework to do, but he wasn't about to pass this up.

CHAPTER 9

Marcus: *Cool. Where we meeting?*
Charlene: *Off Franken Road, by the post office. Around 6*
Marcus: *Laters.*

Marcus sped through his homework for the next half hour, then went downstairs to get himself a snack.

"Marcus, I've told you not to eat before dinner," his grandmother chided.

"I'm going out in a bit, Grandma."

"Oh, you've made some friends?"

"Yeah, actually, Leonard introduced us."

"That's great." She smiled brightly. "Spend time with kids who will keep you out of trouble. You've had enough of that for a lifetime."

"Yes, Grandma." He wolfed down the banana sandwich he'd just made.

"What time will you be back?"

"Not too late."

"What time, Marcus? Remember your curfew."

"No later than ten." He smiled.

"Good," she said, nodding her head towards him.

* * *

"Wha gwan?" Neil said as Marcus approached them outside the post office. He briefly gripped the other boy's hand in greeting, and they bumped chests.

"Where's Cassius?" Marcus asked Charlene, who was watching him closely.

"I didn't invite him."

"Yeah, I heard what he tried to do to you," Neil said. "That's messed up, man."

"Is he always like that?" Marcus asked.

Charlene frowned. "He's . . . temperamental."

"Yeah, people don't mess with him at school," Neil agreed.

"What was he trying to do?"

"He's trying to test you," Charlene said. "He sees you as a threat."

"So he thought he'd try and drown me?" Marcus scoffed.

"He wanted to scare you. But I think you stopped him. You should have been much farther into the water, but I could see you resisting him. I haven't seen anybody be able to do that."

"So he's done that kind of thing before?"

"Not try to put someone in the water, no," she said, agitated.

"What things then?"

"Just, you know, when you see a passer-by, you try and get them to do things."

"Like what?"

"Like . . ." She glanced around, as if looking for inspiration. "There was this one time he got someone he didn't like to climb a tree and start acting like a monkey in front of his friends."

All three burst out laughing.

"Nooo, that's bad, man!" Neil said, his head rolling from side to side.

"It was hilarious." She smiled. "Another time he started a fight between two boys from his class at school."

"From a couple of months ago? Was that him? Man, that was brutal. That kid got his nose broke."

Marcus looked at Charlene; there was no smile on her face

now. He wondered if Cassius had ever tried his power on her.

A movement just past Neil's shoulder caught Marcus's attention. It was those two cyclists again, just sitting there, watching him. He thought about crunching their bikes, but without knowing who they were, he wanted to be cautious.

"Let's keep moving," he said.

Neil cocked his head. "Where to?"

"I don't know. Know anywhere with a lot of metal?"

Neil and Charlene exchanged looks.

"How about down by Edmonton Place?" Neil suggested. "Not a lot of people go there."

Charlene nodded.

Neil led the way as he chatted about school and his career plans.

"You need to get a job that involves predicting the future," Charlene said.

"Like what? The weather forecast?" He scoffed.

"No, dummy! Like investment. Like banking or something."

"Oh, right. I'm not sure how I would do that."

"Well, that's why we're part of this group," Marcus said. "We need to hone our gifts. Find ways for them to work to our advantage. If we've got an edge, we should use it. Think about it. The three of us could be unstoppable. With your knowledge of the future, Charlene's charms, and my strength, who would mess with us?"

"Strength? I didn't see you do anything strong!" Charlene laughed out loud. "You pulled off a dainty necklace!"

"All right, all right! I'll show you what I can do."

As they turned down to Edmonton Place, a small enclosure of dull grey 1960s complex flats, Marcus saw metal railings and night poles. This would do, but one day he would need a scrapyard.

"Show us what you can do," Neil said, leaning against the wall.

Marcus walked over to the railings, and after a big tug, the bottom part pulled up from the ground, uprooting the concrete on the floor.

"Wow." Neil's mouth dropped open.

Charlene's eyes were wide with surprise. "You know, I think you're the first of us who can control a natural element."

"What do you mean?" Marcus said, trying to push the railings back into the ground.

"Cassius and I can only control other people to a certain extent. Neil can look into the future. But you have control over an actual element."

"What I want to know is why we have these abilities," interrupted Neil. "I mean, it's all good, but what's the meaning behind it? All this talk of war and things is making me think twice. I don't want to be involved in that stuff. That's why I joined Leonard's group in the first place."

"We don't have a choice, Neil. Whether we like it or not, we have these abilities. We've got to use them," Charlene said, sitting on the ground.

"What do the Orisha want us for anyway? If they're gods, why do they need our help?"

"Because whatever fight is coming, it's going to be here." Charlene turned to Marcus. "It's the only thing that makes sense."

"Give the mortals the tools to do their bidding. But why are they even fighting?" Marcus said, getting out a smoke. He offered the rest around, and everyone took one.

"That I'm still trying to piece together," Charlene said. "I

CHAPTER 9

think we need to wait for Leonard and Amala to tell us what they know first."

"Why are we fighting for them?" Neil said, exhaling. "It makes no sense if it has nothing to do with us."

"Maybe it does," Charlene said. "Maybe they want to take over the world or something. Or one of them does."

Marcus listened to them both, stunned. This was a conversation he'd never imagined hearing. He wasn't sure he even believed any of what they were saying. And yet here he was, able to move and manipulate metal with his bare hands. Charlene was able to make people fall in love with her, and Neil could see the future. What a strange group of people they were.

"I'm going to research fighting gods," Neil said, flicking out his phone.

"Neil, we already know gods fight. Look at Loki and his brother Thor. Even the movies cover that. Then there are the Greek gods. Zeus and his brothers killed their own dad."

Marcus's eyebrows shot up. This was madness.

"So apparently Obatala and his son had a falling out," Charlene went on. "He now has to be of service to the world in penance."

"Let's not worry about that just yet," Marcus said. "Before we have to get serious and do the research, let's just relax, man, and have a bit of fun."

Marcus wasn't in the mood to get serious. He had enough on his mind with worrying about the hooded figures on the bikes. He didn't know who they were with, and he'd need to keep his eyes open. The heavy prospect of war with gods could wait; he needed some time alone to digest that.

The three of them spent the next couple of hours laughing

and joking, walking around the streets. Just before Marcus had to go home, Neil scared the life out of a stumbling drunk by flashing on his luminescent eyes. By the time they went their separate ways, the bond Marcus felt with these two was the strongest he'd ever felt with anybody. They were oddballs too. He could at least always belong with them.

Chapter 10

"Welcome, everybody, to the Gathering!" Leonard said warmly.

Marcus stood in the middle of the great hall. Every inch had been scrubbed and shone. Lanterns floated around the room, green foliage decorated every area, the floorboards were polished, and the benches were soft with ruby velvet cushions.

"I can't believe you guys actually finished this so quickly," Charlene mused. "It's like a palace."

"We had a lot of sleepless nights, and a lot of help," Amala said proudly.

"How did you make the lanterns float?" Cassius asked.

"Ahh, some friends helped me with that," Amala replied. "I'm not entirely sure how they did it, but I trust them that it's nothing nefarious."

This place feels truly enchanted now, Marcus thought. He never wanted to leave.

"Come with me," Leonard said. "The library is ready too."

They followed him through an ornate white door into a much darker room. The foliage outside practically covered all the windows, keeping the interior hidden from intruders and blocking all natural light from penetrating into the area.

"We need this place to be more secluded, just in case," Leonard said.

The room was almost as big as the whole downstairs of Grandma Maisey's house. There were all kinds of books, from the floor to the ceiling.

"Nearly every book you can think of about Yoruban culture and gods. There are also books here about neighbouring gods within Africa. We have a few on European, Asian, and North American gods too, in case you want to study further."

Marcus usually only read when he had to, but this seemed to be a place of treasure. Maybe somewhere in here lay the key to who he really was. Maybe his identity could be found in these books.

"Before I let you guys loose," Leonard said, "we have two new recruits joining us. Natalie and Sean."

Marcus spun round. "Sean? But he's . . . white."

Leonard chuckled. "Believe it or not, white people can have Black ancestors too."

Marcus shook his head. "What can he do? He's so young."

Leonard nodded. "He is, but he's safer with us than not. I'm not sure why his abilities have manifested so early. Regardless, we need to look out for him."

Marcus nodded. Sounded as if Sean had just as rough a background as he did. Luckily, Marcus had always been able to take care of himself and hadn't had to deal with abuse. Maybe those were the demons Sean faced.

"We are going to need the four of you to be leaders," Leonard said, "to shepherd the younger ones, which is why we brought you here first. Spend a week getting used to this place. You'll need to be able to share some knowledge of where the Orisha

CHAPTER 10

come from, so borrow a couple of books. Charlene, I believe you'll be able to point the others in the right direction."

She nodded.

"Come, let me show you the training room."

Marcus liked the sound of that. Leonard led them to some stairs.

"This place has a basement too?" Neil exclaimed.

"We had to have one put in. In record timing."

"But how? That's so fast . . ."

"We have our ways, Neil. Don't worry, all will be revealed in time. For now, just relax and enjoy what you have."

As they descended the stairs, the area got darker and a little colder. Leonard flicked on the lights, illuminating the whole of the room. It was massive.

"This is steel-supported and completely soundproof," Leonard said. "This basement can withstand a lot, but don't abuse it! We want it to last for others who need it."

He glanced at Marcus when he said that. Marcus had no intention of destroying anything. On purpose.

"Okay, I'm going to let you guys go and explore now. Enjoy yourselves and have fun . . . Cassius, could I chat with you for a moment?" Leonard ended in a clipped tone.

They all headed upstairs except Cassius, who watched the others go before Leonard shut the door. Once they got into the main room, they sat down on the benches.

"You reckon he's in trouble?" Neil asked Charlene quietly.

"Probably."

"What's he done?" Marcus asked.

"Look, I don't know. He doesn't tell me everything."

"He hangs out with a bad crowd at school," Neil said. "He brings it on himself."

Charlene sighed. "Well, I've told him about it, so there's nothing else I can do."

"He doesn't listen. I've told him too," Neil added.

"Then if you don't hear, you must feel," Marcus said. "We don't need to worry about him if he won't look after himself. We need to decide what we're going to do. Now, we could all learn all the things, bit by bit, or we could each decide to specialise in something. Leonard said you already knew about some history, Charlene. What do you know exactly?"

"Not that much. I know some of the origin story, that's all."

"Good. Why don't you focus on that? Neil, what about you?"

"I don't know."

"Pick a subject."

"Umm . . . how about looking into the predictions of the future?"

"Fine, and I'll look at the structure of the Orisha: how they keep order, who is on top, what their purpose was while they were down here."

"Sounds good," Neil said.

They all went into the library, picked out some books, and went back into the hall.

Amala came over to them as they sat down. "What have you guys got there?"

They all showed her their books: *Gods of the World*, *West African Beliefs*, and *Orisha and the Cosmos*.

"I'm glad you're all taking this seriously. You've even decided on who will read up on which subject. Smart idea."

They heard someone quickly coming up the stairs. Everyone turned round to see Cassius storming out of the long hall, rubbing his face.

CHAPTER 10

Leonard came up not long after. His face was beaded with sweat, but he had a steely look in his eyes.

Amala stood up immediately. "Do we need to go after him?"

"No, let him cool off," Leonard responded, trying not to breathe hard.

Amala walked over to him and, in a hushed voice, said, "Do we need to talk?"

"Not now," he said, still glaring at the door.

To Marcus, it was obvious what must have happened. "Did he do something to you?"

Just as the words escaped his mouth, the front door slammed shut, announcing Cassius's exit.

"Don't worry about it," Leonard said before walking off. Amala hesitated for just a moment, then went after him.

"Yo, you need to talk some sense into your boy." Neil turned to Charlene. "Turning on Leonard. That's not cool."

"I keep telling you, he doesn't listen to me like that." There was an edge to her voice that Marcus had never heard before.

"Look, no pressure," Marcus said. "But he's dangerous. Look at what he almost did to me the other day. Do you know what's going on with him?"

Charlene remained quiet.

"Charlene, I'm not trying to put this all on you. But if you know something that might help us understand why he's acting this way, maybe we can do something to help."

"You can't help," she said quietly, looking away from them all. "It's . . . it's these powers. He has these dreams . . . We both do."

Marcus stiffened. "What kind of dreams?"

She inhaled deeply. "I don't know how to explain it. It's like we're in a trance. My body is asleep, but my mind is awake.

There's always a woman there. She tells us to do stuff, tells us she'll enhance our powers if we do what she says. And she has with him. He wasn't this powerful even two or three months ago. If he'd tried what he did to you only three months ago, you would've heard his voice, but you wouldn't have felt so strongly compelled to actually do what his voice was telling you.

"I tried telling Amala about his dreams before. I mentioned I was having them. But she thought it was just a result of his trauma that he telepathically passed on to me."

"Trauma from what?"

"He's in foster care. That's all you need to know."

Neil and Marcus looked at each other.

"What happens in these dreams, Charlene?" Marcus asked.

"I'm always offered gifts. But I always refuse them because she never tells me what they are. She's tall, gaunt, like the walking dead. But her voice . . . just pierces through everything. She's like a living nightmare."

"What . . . is she . . . like an evil spirit?" Neil asked, his eyes wide.

"I . . . I think she is. I've been searching on the internet, trying to figure out who she is and where she's come from. She doesn't fit the description of an Orisha . . . but I don't know. Maybe Cassius and I are just cursed."

Marcus put his hand on her shoulder, and a thrill like electricity shot through him at the touch. He pulled away quickly and cleared his throat, trying to release his tension. "Look, I don't want you to worry about this. We're going to figure out what's going on, all right?"

Charlene looked at him sceptically. "And what can you do? Protect me from my dreams?"

CHAPTER 10

"Charlene, look at what we can do." He leaned in closer to her. "Look at what we have been gifted with! If anybody can figure this out, we can! With or without Amala or Leonard. They can't really stop us from trying to figure this out, can they?"

Charlene looked at him from the corner of her eye, biting her bottom lip.

"He's right, Charlene," Neil chimed in. "Maybe we can even help Cassius."

After a long sigh, she glanced at Neil, but her gaze eventually rested on Marcus.

"Don't worry," Marcus said, gently touching her, then withdrawing quickly. "We're not going to fail you."

That night Marcus read through his book. Tales of wonders, deception, and redemption, from the formation of humans by the hands of Obatala to the sad ending of Yemoja and her disappearance from the cosmos. Stories of the origins of the Orisha and how they were all connected.

Ogun's chapter detailed stories of heroism and drunkenness, power and abuse. A man of many contradictions. After an existence of tyranny, he turned his life around to become a protector of the weak and vulnerable, the god of iron and sacrifice. Illustrations showed a muscular bald man with a swirling tattoo on his forehead. A green robe was draped over his left shoulder, and he stood in a warrior stance with a huge lavish dagger in his left hand, his eyes blazing amber.

As Marcus lay in bed, he wondered what Ogun's role would be in the cosmic fight they were facing. He was a warrior, so whose side was he on? What could gods possibly be fighting over? These were the questions he needed answering in their next meeting.

What troubled Marcus the most was Charlene. They had left the Gathering in relative silence; she'd been reluctant to come out of her shell after their conversation. Whatever that being was who appeared to her and Cassius obviously terrified her. She'd been nervous even bringing it up.

He rolled over and grabbed his phone to text her.

Marcus: *You awake?*

Charlene replied immediately.

Charlene: *Yeah.*

Marcus: *Just want you to know I'm here for you. Yeah?*

Charlene: *Thank you, Marcus.*

Marcus: *See you tomorrow after school?*

Charlene: *Okay.*

He wanted to call her, hear her voice and tell her she'd be safe with him, but he decided against it. Too intense. She'd only think he was weird for wanting to help, despite the danger he sensed.

One thing was for sure. Cassius was in trouble. Maybe he should speak to him tomorrow too. What had he said and done to Leonard? Did Leonard know about the woman in their nightmares? It was time Charlene told everyone the truth.

As he drifted off to sleep, he wondered if this woman could also enter his dreams, and he begged the night not to let her enter.

Chapter 11

The next afternoon, Marcus dashed home after school to change into his normal clothes. He left as quickly as he could, with a quick goodbye to Grandma Maisey. That morning he'd realised he didn't have any money left, and he wasn't about to ask his grandma for some. Maybe he could find some small object to steal and sell to Dwayne.

He checked his phone. There were no messages yet. He had a couple of hours before he had to meet Charlene.

He made his way into a store that sold some electrical items and slid as many as he could into his pocket. As he walked past the alarm barrier, he bent it back while no one was looking and pulled it back up. No alarm went off. He hurried away before the security cameras could get a good shot of him.

When he reached the familiar brick-lined path, he recognised the three hooded figures at the end of the narrow passageway. Cherry walked forward and looked at his stash.

"You must be mad showing your face around here," she remarked.

Marcus pushed his shoulders back slightly as she walked back to her boss, who surveyed what he had. Two gaming headsets. Dwayne nodded, and she walked back over.

"Where did your brethren go?" she said as she handed him a wad of cash.

"I don't know," he said, avoiding her gaze by counting the money.

"You better watch your back returning here. I heard people are looking for you."

"Yeah? Well, they better watch their back." Marcus grinned as he stuck the two hundred pounds into every pocket he had.

As Marcus made his way back to his new area, he saw two people on bikes zigzagging across the road. They briefly looked at him, their eyes peering over the scarves that masked the rest of their faces. He watched them begin to cycle away, and his body tensed.

Those were the same riders from a few days ago.

He looked away for just a moment at his phone and heard them quietly pedalling towards him from another angle. They were so close he almost didn't have time to do anything. Reflexively, he moved his left hand out to the side, concentrating on knocking the bike over. The bike flipped, and the rider flew off and landed on his side, a knife falling from his grip.

Ice ran through Marcus's veins. He immediately turned to the other cyclist, holding out his arm and scrunching up his hand. The front wheel collapsed in on itself, and the rider buckled and fell onto the concrete.

Marcus looked back at the first attacker, who was on his feet, silently hunched over, a sliver of the knife now visible beneath his jacket. Marcus twisted his wrist round, and the knife crumpled up just as the attacker brought it out to stab him.

The guy glanced down at the blade, giving Marcus the split

CHAPTER 11

second he needed to land a heavy punch on the attacker's covered face. He hit him twice, and the man fell to the floor.

The second cyclist was already careening towards him. Marcus flicked his left hand this time, causing the knife to shoot out of his attacker's grasp. Stunned, the masked person turned and ran as fast as he could down the road.

When Marcus turned round, the other attacker had started scrambling for his bike. Marcus strode quickly towards him and pulled the bike apart into three pieces. The attacker staggered away, leaving only the crumpled bikes behind.

Marcus yanked off the bike chain and put it in his pocket, thinking it could be useful if the cyclists returned. Adrenaline was still racing through his body as he walked.

Those must have been Carnell's boys. They had spotted him and been ordered to sort him out.

He needed protection, and he needed it now. The streets seemed colder than ever. Without a crew he was actively part of, he was too vulnerable.

As Marcus quickened his steps, he wondered how those cyclists had found him. Had Dwayne had anything to do with this? He was on his territory, after all.

He needed to gather a group of core people to protect him. His gut told him he could trust Neil. Maybe Charlene, but he would need more assurances from her. There might be a couple of kids from school he could start to influence.

Marcus began to run now. He was beginning to panic; he didn't know where Carnell and his gang could be hiding. He prayed they didn't know where Grandma Maisey lived.

He would need eyes at the back of his head. He needed Neil onside as protection.

By the time he got to where he was due to meet Charlene,

he'd decided to get himself a bike and always carry a knife. Any small metal object would help in his defence, but he had to make sure he practised. He had to be quicker.

A thought suddenly punched him in the stomach. What if one of Carnell's boys also had powers? How on earth would he protect himself then? Or anybody else?

By the time Charlene arrived, he was sweating and in need of something or someone to calm him down.

"You all right?" Charlene said as she approached him.

"Yeah, fine." He stood up a little straighter, looking over her shoulder.

"You don't look fine."

"Just had a run-in with some people from my old place."

"Are you okay?" She leaned in and held his arms, her brows furrowed in concern.

"Yeah," he said. His fears began to dissipate at her touch, replaced by a burgeoning excitement. "Good thing I have these extra skills. I'd have been a goner without them. They rode up on me with bikes and had knives."

"You need to watch out. The next time it could be acid."

Marcus nodded; the thought made him feel sick. "Know anyone who has deflection powers?"

She smiled, and as he looked into her eyes, the feelings that started to stir in his chest terrified him. Feelings were messy and always caused hurt, and he was always the one who got injured.

"Not right now," she said, her voice as smooth and sweet as honey. "But at this rate, we're bound to find someone who can help us."

Marcus was desperate to change the subject.

"Want to go and get something to eat?" she asked, rubbing

CHAPTER 11

his back now.

"I'm not hungry." He gulped. "But I could do with a drink."

"Let's go." Her ruby-red lips smiled.

As they went to the nearest coffee shop, Marcus's eyes darted around. He carefully watched every new person they came across, his hand wrapped tight around the metal piece of bike in his pocket.

He got a drink for Charlene and himself, along with a baguette, and they slowly made their way towards the park for the Gathering.

"You okay?" he asked, munching on his baguette. "Have any bad dreams last night?"

"Actually, it wasn't so bad."

"Yeah?"

"I'm trying to learn how to control it, how to actively repel her. I'm researching objects and candles, something to ward off evil spirits."

"You found anything?"

"A couple of things, but it's where to find them. Then you have to say some magic words or something over them."

"Why don't you try asking Amala?"

"I've already tried, remember?"

"Yeah, but if this gets worse, you're going to want someone's help who knows what they're doing. We're only just discovering these things now. Amala will know exactly what to do and how serious it is . . ."

"I'll figure it out myself," Charlene said defiantly.

Marcus knew this wasn't a good idea, but if she didn't want any help, there was nothing he could do. He decided to broach his other idea to her. "Look, I'm thinking about getting a group of us together. You know, having each other's backs?"

"What do you mean? That's what the Gathering's for."

"Yeah, but Leonard and Amala will let anybody in, won't they? This will be more exclusive. The ones we know and trust."

"You mean everyone except Cassius?" she said, giving him a knowing look.

"There's that." Marcus nodded. "But, I mean, we'll look out for each other mainly outside of the Gathering."

"You want protection from this gang that's after you?"

Marcus looked away for a moment, trying to see how he could spin this story, before looking back at her. "Yeah, I do. But I won't be the only one who needs help in the future. I mean, look at us now. You're confiding in me. You didn't have anyone to do that with before. We can have each other's backs. We don't need to worry about controlling ourselves because others will be watching. We can cover for each other if anything out of the ordinary happens. We can say, 'We didn't see anything. Nothing happened.'"

Charlene looked at him, considering his offer. "It's a good idea, but I'll need to think about it."

"I have a lot more of those." Marcus smiled. "You'll see."

Charlene rolled her eyes, a coy smile playing on her lips. "I can't wait."

Marcus's heart fluttered at her reaction, and he couldn't help the grin that spread across his face.

Chapter 12

The following week passed in a haze. Marcus showed Sean and Natalie around; they marvelled at the incredible new world they had entered.

The Gathering became his haven. He found himself practising his skills every evening in the training room. He could easily move objects now without touching them; pots and pans would hover around the room, carefully guided by his hands. He couldn't wait to move bigger things next—cars and metal chairs. He needed a way to protect himself outside of these walls.

Coming straight after school, he avoided being followed by anyone, although Dacus's man would smoke at the corner of his road and give him a cursory nod. It seemed Carnell and his boys still didn't know which school he went to or where he lived. Marcus didn't know how long that would last, but luckily he had an extra pair of eyes.

Neil had been practising too. Wearing shades, he'd sit with Marcus in the park and try to predict what would happen in the next few minutes, then the next ten. By the end of the week, he could predict up to fifteen minutes.

"Man, this is dope!" he exclaimed. "I can't believe this is

what I'm doing!"

"You're killing it," Marcus said, and a spark of hope flickered within him. "You realise no one can mess around with you now. You're practically invincible."

"Nah, it's only when I'm concentrating I can do that."

"If you practise long enough, it will be like second nature. Nothing will surprise you."

Neil nodded as that sunk in.

"How's Cassius doing?" Marcus asked.

"What do you care?" A smile lingered on Neil's face.

"I don't exactly. But he is one of us. Just want to make sure he's not a loose cannon."

"He was off for a few days last week, after that thing with Leonard, but he's back at school now."

"Yeah, he hasn't been back to the Gathering, has he?"

"He seems preoccupied, you know . . . like he's not really there."

"Then where is he?" Marcus asked, more to himself than anyone else.

"Ask Charlene."

"Nah, I don't want to bother her with that. I'm sure she's got her own things to sort out."

"Sounds like the same thing if you ask me."

"She'll sort it out. We'll be right there to support her."

Neil smiled, and for the first time in a long time, Marcus felt a glimmer of safety. Maybe things wouldn't come crashing down on him as they had all the other times—if he built things up carefully.

***

CHAPTER 12

"Everyone is running late." Amala sighed, checking her phone.

Only Marcus sat in the large main room, early as usual. He was scrolling his phone for places to find more catalytic converters, but he slipped the device into his pocket as Amala approached.

"We need to be prepared for the worst." She sat heavily on the sofa opposite him, clad in a tribal martial arts outfit and clothbound hands.

"Why? What's going to happen?"

"The best offence is a good defence." She smiled. "But a bad defence is offensive."

Marcus nodded. That was a motto he could get behind.

"Did you know Obba Nani taught Ogun how to fight?" she asked, curiously.

"No." Marcus sat up straight. "Why would she need to teach a warrior how to fight?"

"He wasn't born a warrior, Marcus. He chose to become one, to pay for his . . . indiscretions."

"What did he do?"

"Maybe that's something you need to find out yourself. Learning to control your powers in self-defence will prove useful in the future."

Marcus just wanted her to get straight to the point. "So, you want us to practise fighting?"

Amala paused, casting her gaze to the floor before she answered. Marcus could see the familiar flickering shadows out of the corner of his eye. His limbs stiffened.

"We don't yet know how this situation will unfold, Marcus." Amala looked pensively at her fingers. "It's best to cover all our bases so we're ready for anything. Certainly, the material world will be affected by whatever is coming." She stood up straight and flexed her arms. "Let's go practise. You'll have a head start on the others."

"Amala," Marcus said.

"Yes?"

Marcus felt silly even asking the question, but those black shapes made him uncomfortable. His voice hushed involuntarily. "Is it me, or does it look like there are shadows moving by themselves in the corner?"

Amala's eyes flicked to the corner of the room. "Ahh . . . you have the sight." She smiled, her voice equally quiet. "You are seeing a hint of the unseen world, the spiritual realm."

Marcus swallowed, nervous now. "You mean they're spirits? Like dead people?"

"I prefer to think of them as beings without bodies."

He didn't think that sounded any better. "Are they . . . good?"

"Most of them, but try not to look at them as good or bad. They are as good or bad as either one of us."

"But what are they doing here?"

"They are everywhere, but in some places the material world and the spiritual world meld together easily. You are connected to the gods, after all."

"Could they help us?"

Amala began to move towards the stairs. "It's best not to seek their help. You never truly know what their intentions are."

The front door swung open, startling Marcus and Amala.

"Sorry I'm late," Charlene said, breathing hard and striding towards them.

"Charlene." Amala sighed with relief, quickly straightening up. "Perfect timing. We were just about to practise some self-defence."

Charlene's smile fell. "Oh, great."

"Don't say that," Amala said as she began to turn away. "You might learn something new!"

"Apparently her Orisha taught the warrior god how to battle." Marcus winked.

"She did," Amala said over her shoulder. "She also taught Oshun, Charlene."

"Oshun?" Marcus asked.

"You really should know who the Super Seven are by now," Charlene quipped. "She's the goddess of—"

"Seduction. I know who she is." Marcus arched his eyebrow at her. Of course Charlene would align herself with that Orisha.

Charlene's eyes widened in surprise.

"Why would she need to fight with those powers?" Marcus dared to look Charlene in the eye, his heart beginning to race. She looked away quickly.

"Being a one-trick pony would be kind of dull, don't you think?" A smile played on her lips.

"I'm not complaining." Marcus grinned as they descended into the gym room. "It'll just make this practise very easy for me."

"We'll see about that." Charlene tilted her head away. Marcus noted her steps mirrored his own.

His palms started to sweat; he hoped he wouldn't embarrass himself.

Amala turned to face them in the middle of the training room. "I'm going to ask you both to fight. I want to see what springs naturally to you both."

Charlene glanced at her. "Can we use our powers?"

"Of course. Use whatever you can to gain the upper hand."

"This'll be too easy." Charlene smiled wide, her perfect teeth framed by her ruby-red lips. "Let's see how resilient you are."

"Is that a challenge?" Marcus grinned back, excitement igniting within his chest. "You just worry about protecting that beautiful face."

"You think I'm beautiful?" she said, tilting her head to the side. Her dark brown eyes seemed to bathe him in warmth.

Marcus tried to shake the feeling off, scanning the room for metal. He was reaching out for a bar across the room, wanting to draw it towards him, when he felt his legs being swept out from under him. His feet flew up as he crashed onto his side. A strange thrill raced through his body as he looked up to see Charlene towering over him, her smile triumphant. She was an equal. A beauty, no doubt, but something so much more.

He quickly jumped up. "That was sneaky."

"I'm not just a pretty face," she said, observing her perfectly polished nails before winking at him.

He quickly found the metal rod and pulled it towards him with heated hands.

They squared off, Marcus manoeuvring the metal pole without the help of his ability, swiping and jabbing at Charlene's legs to try to knock her off balance.

"Use your powers, Marcus!" Amala called.

He knew he was distracted. Beating Charlene was the last thing he wanted. Sparring with her? He could do that all day.

Another wave of warmth came over him when his eyes connected with hers. His thoughts and actions became slow, and a strange magnetism that was hard to resist pulled him towards her.

"You don't have to fight me, Marcus," she purred. "Just let

CHAPTER 12

me win."

"You'd like that, wouldn't you?" he replied with a smile. Instead of sounding resilient, he seemed desperate to please.

A ringtone broke the trance he was in, and they both looked at Amala. She was fumbling in her pocket.

"Sorry," she said, observing her screen. "I need to take this. You two carry on."

Amala swiftly left the room.

Without a moment's hesitation, Marcus swept his feet underneath Charlene's own. She flipped over, her eyes wide with surprise. Fear swept through him at her shocked expression, and he immediately bent down to help her up.

"You okay?" he said, his heart hammering.

"Yeah," Charlene responded, taking his hand.

The shock of her touch ignited every sense in his body, blood rushed to every part of his anatomy, and he let go of her hand the moment she had risen.

"Thanks," said Charlene, barely meeting his gaze.

"Yeah . . . umm . . . shall we keep sparring?" Marcus didn't know whether to stay or go.

"You know, I think I'm going to use the bathroom." She twirled a strand of her short curly hair.

"Okay," he replied, relief washing over him.

Smiling sheepishly, Charlene disappeared from view.

Sean stood in the training room of the Gathering in his bare feet, looking nervous.

"Come on, show me what you can do," Marcus said, leaning up against the wall with his arms folded.

"No one's ever seen me do this before." Sean rubbed his

buzzcut head.

Neil looked at him sceptically. "That's not true. I heard Amala has seen you." "Well . . . no one else apart from her."

Marcus smiled. "Look, I won't tell anyone if it's embarrassing. You can trust me, bro, and neither will he." He cocked his head towards Neil, who rolled his eyes.

Sean's gaze darted around the room, and then he walked towards the wall and gingerly began to climb. With no ladder or rope. As if he had natural suction on his fingers and toes.

"No way, man. You've got to be kidding me. You're Spider-Man!" Marcus exclaimed.

Sean grinned widely. "Yeah, I like that. Better than being a freak."

"You're in good company, bro."

Sean began to scurry around the wall like a spider. Marcus couldn't believe what he was seeing, this small kid defying gravity.

"How did you discover what you could do?" he asked.

Sean jumped down, and his stance recoiled slightly. "Hiding from my dad."

Marcus nodded, trying to calm the anger swelling in his chest, and walked over to him. "Don't worry, little man," he said, putting his arm around Sean's shoulders. "We'll look out for you. If he starts bothering you again, you let me know, yeah?"

Sean looked up at him, wide-eyed. "What do you mean?"

"I mean if he's causing you problems, we can look out for you. Pay him a visit, you know?"

"What will you do?" Sean's gaze fell to the floor. He nervously picked at his right elbow.

"I'm not making plans to hurt your dad, Sean. But look

CHAPTER 12

at what we can do. We should use these powers we have to defend ourselves and each other, right? We've got to look after each other."

Sean nodded. "I'd like that," he said and straightened up slightly.

"Anyway, it's time to see who Leonard wants us to meet. Let's go."

They headed up the stairs. Everyone was at the Gathering that night, waiting to see the guests Leonard had brought in.

"Hi, guys," Leonard said as Marcus, Neil, and Sean entered the room.

The sight of Cassius sitting in the corner put Marcus on edge, and he immediately went to stand next to Charlene. For some reason, he felt as though she needed his protection.

When they all sat down in their chairs, Charlene inched closer to him, and Marcus felt his body relax. A calmness seemed to emanate from her, and he welcomed it.

"I want you all to meet two special people: Abeo and Ezra." Leonard stepped back, his arm sweeping out towards two older men sitting just behind him. "I've known these men for a long time, and you're going to find them fascinating. Abeo, would you like to introduce yourself first?"

Abeo nodded and stood up. An older man around seventy years old, he wore a red cap on his bald head, a blue-and-white-checked shirt that came down to his knees, and jeans. He had deep smile wrinkles around his mouth, and his rich dark skin seemed to glow. Nodding at Leonard, he turned to everyone else in the group

"Hello, my dear friends. It is an honour to be in your presence this evening." His voice was warm and inviting. "I am astounded by what I have heard about you all and look forward to getting to know you. I have other duties to attend to, but I know you are in good hands with Amala."

He stood up a little straighter. "I am what you would call a priest of the Orisha, a worshiper and petitioner to them. In particular, I venerate Olorun, the creator and ruler of the heavens. The father of all Orisha. Of all the gods, he is the least accessible but, I find, the most rewarding once you are able to do the work.

"Each of you has a specific gift. It will serve you all well to get to know the Orisha that your powers emulate. Only then might we be able to ascertain what your role will be moving forward."

Ezra rose from his chair. He looked as if he was from another time. An older, smaller man, he had short salt-and-pepper hair and wore a green-checked jacket, with a red handkerchief poking out of one of the breast pockets. He walked forward, peering at everyone over his glasses.

"An interesting bunch." Ezra paused, looking at each teen individually, his hands behind his back.

Marcus rolled his eyes; this guy clearly thought he was better than everyone else. He sank lower in his chair, shoving his hands into his pockets.

"I look forward to getting to know you all more closely." Ezra cleared his throat before continuing, "My name is Ezra. I am a professor of the Yoruban religion. I have made it my life's work to uncover the mysteries of the gods and to understand their relationship to us. I went to Oxford and Cambridge to earn my degrees and PhDs. I have spent five years in Nigeria, travelled the world, and taught in every setting you can imagine. I keep in close contact with the Elders, who specialise in the teaching and worship of the Orisha. One of them, my dear friend Abeo, is here with us today.

"I will be your teacher. I will teach you the theoretical and historical context of the past and what you now find yourself in. Whereas Amala, with the help of Abeo, will be your spiritual guide, I will be more of a practical help."

He sat down rather abruptly, as if that was all he had to say on the matter, his head tilting up as if he smelled something unpleasant. Marcus couldn't believe Ezra's arrogant air. He hoped they wouldn't have to work with him much.

Leonard moved forward to stand next to the guests. "I think it's time to show you what these kids can do, my old friend," he said, putting his arm around Abeo.

They all descended the stairs to the training room. One by one, each member of the group showed Abeo what they could do—all except Cassius and Charlene.

"Charlene, would you like to go next?" Amala asked. "Is there anyone in particular you would like to be your volunteer?"

"If it's all right, I would like to be the volunteer," Abeo interjected. "I would like to assess her strengths."

A coy smile flickered across Charlene's face as she sashayed towards Abeo. Marcus could tell she enjoyed this; she couldn't wait to watch Abeo fall under her spell. A pang of jealousy shot through him. It felt cold without her warmth at his side.

Abeo's expression suddenly changed from calm to uncertain; his relaxed posture stiffened. His eyes became sharp, unwavering, as he focused in on Charlene.

"Hi, Abeo," she said, walking over to him. "How are you?"

"I am very well, thank you." He smiled back, his eyes never leaving her.

She crossed her arms and stopped about a metre away.

"How old are you?"

"I'm seventy-two years young," Abeo said. He sounded like a small boy eagerly waiting for sweets.

"If I asked you to run away with me, where would we go?"

"Back to my home in Nigeria, a nice quiet village."

"Why would you take me there?"

"I could show you all the wonders of the world, the layers beneath the world, how the wheels and mechanics of this world work." He was leaning forward slightly. Marcus wondered if he was about to tip over.

The others all tried to stifle their laughs. Marcus couldn't help but smile too at this old man fawning over Charlene, but something deep inside him began to stir. Maybe he had underestimated her. If she could do this to an old man, one of the Elders, what could she do to *him*, who'd only learned about these powers a few weeks ago?

He tried to shake off the feeling. She liked him, and she wasn't like Cassius. He'd make sure to keep it that way.

"Do you want to kiss me?" Charlene purred.

"I think that's enough!" Amala quickly interrupted. A flash of anger crossed her face as she shot a look at Charlene.

Anger flickered inside Marcus too. Humiliating an old man was not necessary to prove her powers. Maybe he should be more careful around her . . .

Charlene stepped away, and Abeo's eyes relaxed as he came back to himself. He looked around for a moment, as if trying to put some puzzle together, and his eyes fell on Charlene again. Marcus thought he saw him shiver. Amala still looked annoyed.

"Very interesting," he said. "And now you, dear sir."

Abeo turned to Cassius, who sat away from everybody

else in the corner, his face obscured in shadows. Marcus watched uneasily as Cassius walked forward into the middle of the room. The boy had dark circles under his eyes, and the corner of his mouth was turned down. What would he do to a vulnerable old man?

"Would you like to show me what you can do?" Abeo said, his hands interlocked behind his back. His smile crinkled his eyes.

"You asked for it," Cassius said, and without a moment's notice, Abeo's mouth flew open, his eyes going so wide the whites could be seen all around his irises. His gaze darted around in terror; his stance changed as if he were about to run away.

Leonard and Amala looked at each other before dashing to his side. Cassius turned away from all three and sat back down. Abeo's eyes returned to normal and his mouth closed, although he was still breathing heavily.

Charlene glared at Cassius. "What did you do that for?"

"What? He wanted to know what I could do."

"He's an old man. You didn't have to scare him like that," Charlene said, edging closer to him.

"He shouldn't have asked then, should he?"

Marcus looked at Cassius more carefully. When he'd first met him, the guy had acted as if everything was a joke. Now he looked distressed, disturbed.

"I'm all right, I'm all right," Abeo insisted as he flapped Amala away. Leonard glared at Cassius.

Abeo straightened his clothes and walked towards the slouching Cassius. "You have been through a lot in your life," he said gently. "You can find some peace here. Come and see me after this is all done."

Cassius flinched, as if the words were physically painful. Charlene stared at Cassius, her hands fidgeting nervously by her side. Marcus was confused by this. She was no longer scornful but looked worried.

Abeo turned back to Leonard and Amala with a wide but weary smile. "Come. Let us all go back upstairs and enjoy some food."

Ezra stood at the back of the room, his eyes locked on Cassius. Not a word had passed his lips, and he hadn't moved one inch during the whole display.

After a bellyful of food, it was time to return home.

"I've got to go. It's getting late." Marcus was starting to worry about running into the hooded cyclists. It was harder to discern what was going on late at night; he hated not being able to see clearly and looking out of control.

"It ain't that late, bruv," Neil remarked.

Marcus glanced at his watch. It was nine thirty. "Yeah, but I promised I'd be home early. It's on the other side of town."

"Yeah, I mean, you are living with an old woman." Neil shrugged. "I guess you're turning into one."

They all cracked up, and Marcus smiled despite himself.

"Where do you live?" asked Sean. "Anywhere near here?"

"You got wax in your ears?" said Neil, rubbing Sean's head. "He said on the other side of town. You looking for someone to walk you home?"

Sean looked at the floor sheepishly.

"It's okay, Sean." Marcus put his arm around him. "I can walk you some of the way if you want."

"I'll take him," said Natalie. "He's not far from me."

CHAPTER 12

Marcus nodded. "I'll see you later in the week, yeah?"

They all got up except Charlene.

"You coming?" Marcus said, turning to her.

"I'm going to wait for Cassius." She was avoiding his gaze, her legs crossed neatly as she fidgeted with her short curly hair.

"You sure?" Marcus asked, surprised, his voice lowering.

"I'm just checking he's okay." She inspected her perfectly red nails.

"He's not safe," Marcus said, his brow furrowed. Why would she want to be left alone with a guy like that? "I can wait for you."

"No, I need to speak to him alone."

"Charlene, you shouldn't be alone—"

"I can look after myself." She shot him a glance through slitted eyes. "I need to know what's happening to him." She turned away, continuing to coil her hair around her fingers, and bounced her crossed leg. She was nervous.

Marcus swallowed hard and straightened. She was acting strange tonight—first embarrassing an old man, now insisting she stay and talk to someone she knew was unstable. What was going on between her and Cassius?

"I'll call you later?" He wanted to offer her some comfort. He wanted her by his side. Cassius wasn't going to get to her; he couldn't allow that to happen.

She smiled, nodding slightly. "Okay."

He forced himself away and headed to the exit with the others. Why was she trying to protect Cassius? What hold did he have over her? Had they met up earlier?

"She's mad if she thinks she can fix him," Neil said.

Marcus turned to him, surprised.

"What happened to him?" Natalie said. "He's so weird now."

"We don't know." Neil shrugged.

"Then what makes you think she can't help him?" Natalie asked.

"He's a loose cannon, and he's dangerous. He's always been like that."

"But he'd never take it out on an old man like he did today. Something's changed."

"Maybe," Neil conceded.

"Well, we better figure it out," Marcus said. "He's going to cause havoc with a power like that. He'll take us all down with him."

Chapter 13

Neil and Marcus talked the entire way back to their side of London.

"The thing is, bruv, if he gets worse, what will happen to Charlene?" Neil said. "She's dead set on protecting him, but she seems to be getting more insecure too."

"What do you mean?" Marcus asked.

"I walked home with her the other day. I was asking her what she thought Cassius's problem was. She dodged the question, saying it was probably his past issues coming up. Then she asked me if I could look into certain people's future. I said I didn't know. She got me to try and look into her future, so I did. I told her for the next couple of hours she'd be fine."

"What did she say about that?"

"Nothing, but she was fidgety, you know what I mean? Like she was scared something was going to happen."

"I'll talk to her," Marcus said, although he had no idea how. "Is there something between them two?"

"I don't think so. They've always been tight ever since they joined. I always thought they bonded because their powers were so similar."

"It's just weird, you know? She's determined to figure this

whole mess out by herself."

Neil rubbed his chin. "What if she caused this?"

"What do you mean?" Marcus glanced at him, tension tightening his throat.

"I mean, what if she did a mind trick on him or something, and this is what happened?"

"She told us they both have nightmares and a woman is making him do this."

"I know. But what if she caused the woman to appear? What if she somehow manifested this thing—demon or spirit or whatever—and now it won't leave them alone?"

Dread rose in Marcus's stomach. Hadn't Charlene mentioned that she'd researched these things? He'd just assumed she meant after the dreams started happening, but what if she'd started before . . . and this was the result?

Marcus tried to dismiss the thought. "I don't think she'd do that."

"Why?"

"I just don't think she would."

"Bruv, you've only been here five minutes. What would you know?"

"All right. I'll talk to her. See what she says."

"Make sure she tells you the truth. We can't have any funny business going on. He's messed up as it is. Between you and me, I heard he's gone back into care. The family couldn't handle the mood swings anymore."

Marcus nodded. If Charlene got too close to Cassius, he would have to cut her out of his plans. There was no telling what Cassius would do to her, and she clearly didn't want to be told any different. The thought made him mad. "We need to talk to Leonard and Amala. Whatever path he's on,

CHAPTER 13

he needs to be stopped. We'll protect her."

"I'm not sure she wants your protection, bro." Neil shrugged.

Later that night, Marcus couldn't sleep. He kept debating whether to call Charlene that night or the following day.

It bothered him she wanted to spend any time with Cassius, who was clearly a spiteful bully. Charlene was smart and wanted to be a leader, taking interest in the most powerful Orisha and being visibly unimpressed by anything not matching her ambitions. So why so much attention on that deadbeat? There had to be something else going on. The clue must be in their nightmares.

He picked up his phone and, despite it being nearly midnight, pulled up her number.

"Hey, you okay?" he asked, nervously playing with a coin in his hands.

"Yeah, I'm okay." She sounded wide awake—unable to sleep, Marcus guessed.

"Did you get a chance to speak to him?"

"Yes."

"And . . . how was he?"

"Better."

Marcus paused. Did she not want to speak to him? These short answers seemed dismissive, and yet she had still answered the phone.

He pressed on. "Did he speak to Abeo?"

"Yes." Her tone sounded bored. He clearly wasn't getting anywhere with her.

"What did he say?"

"I'm not sure."

Marcus's patience was wearing thin. He forced a smile on his face—he didn't want her to hear his irritation—and pushed for more information. "Did you sort him out? He can't go around frightening old people."

A chuckle burst through his phone. "Something like that," she said, trying to stifle her laugh. "Don't worry, it's handled. I told him to relax, leave things to me, and stop getting into trouble."

Leave things to me? What did she mean by that?

"You said you were going to sort him out then?" Marcus asked to keep the conversation going.

"Yeah, he's just worrying about things too much, you know? It makes him lash out."

"What's he worried about? Those nightmares?"

There was a brief silence.

"Yeah." Her voice was unusually high. "But you know, his powers are changing and there's stuff at home—"

"His powers are changing?" Marcus scolded himself for interjecting so soon. "Sorry, you go ahead."

"We're teenagers, right?" she said cautiously. "It makes sense since we're all still growing."

"I guess so." Marcus nodded to himself, although he didn't buy a word of it. "Well, I just wanted to check you were all right. You know, after what he did, I was just worried he would try something on you."

"Thank you, Marcus."

The words were like silk in his ears, and a warmth began to build in his chest.

"I know what Cassius can do," Charlene went on. "I can take care of myself, but I appreciate your concern."

CHAPTER 13

"Cool... I'll catch up with you later, yeah?" He didn't want the call to end, but he knew he wasn't going to get any further. He needed to think through what he'd just heard.

"Sure... and, Marcus... thanks for calling." Her voice suddenly sounded strained.

"Are you sure you're okay?"

"Yeah... I am."

"Okay, laters."

Marcus cut off the call and flopped onto his back, staring up at his dark ceiling. His fingers continued to twist and flip the metal coin.

Why was Charlene, a well-spoken, impeccably dressed beauty, spending her time trying to save an unlikeable bully with a troubled background? Was it just because they both had powers of the mind? It had to be deeper than that. The two were having similar dreams. Somehow, they were deeply linked.

She'd instructed Cassius to leave things to her. Did she mean she was going to look after him, or did she have her own agenda—something different from Marcus's own ambitions? Did she want to be the leader and push Marcus out? He'd been there already...

Any warm feelings he'd felt for her began to dissipate. He didn't know if he could trust her.

As if she could read his mind, Marcus's phone pinged.

Charlene: *Do you want to come to mine tomorrow?*

Marcus swallowed. He wanted to get to know her better, and he wanted to figure out what was going on. Maybe she really did have influence over Cassius. Plus, if she wanted to be a leader with him, he needed to know who he was getting into bed with.

Marcus: *Sure, where shall we meet?*
Charlene: *Meet me at the gates of my school.*

Chapter 14

Marcus exhaled deeply; the cool of the evening brushed across his face.

He waited for Charlene by her school gate, his nerves jangling in anticipation. He'd changed his school jumper so no one would know which school he went to.

A stream of teenagers flowed out of the school gate. After a few seconds, Charlene broke through the crowd, her eyes finding his. His cheeks burned as he glanced away for a moment before looking back at her.

Her luminescent skin glowed, and the curve of her lips as they smiled at him sent ripples down his spine. Despite himself, a wide smile broke across Marcus's face.

"Hi." She gently touched her hair as she approached.

Marcus felt as if a magnet were pulling her towards him. He wanted to hold her close and feel the smoothness of her skin on his face. He shoved his hands into his pockets, trying to distract himself as he stepped back slightly. "Hey."

"Ready to go?"

"Sure."

"I just need to grab something from the shops if that's okay?"

"Of course, whatever you want." Marcus's head was

spinning. Why exactly had she invited him to her house? What did she want from him? He couldn't help but hope it was something romantic.

It felt wrong to want that. He'd been hurt so many times, and of all the people he could be falling for, he'd ended up liking someone who had the ability to manipulate emotions. But this felt different. *She* was different. She was special, like him, driven by the desire to get on top and do well. Surely their meeting couldn't have been chance.

"I'm going to make you my favourite snack," Charlene said coyly as they entered the local supermarket.

"Really? Sure you're not trying to poison me?"

"Now, why would I do that?" Charlene smiled.

"That way you'd definitely beat me."

Charlene jabbed him in the ribs with her elbow. "What must you think of me?" she said, looking at him through the corner of her eye. "I'm not always a sore loser."

As they headed to the chocolate section, Marcus noticed a familiar figure with a fancy scarf round her neck.

"Marcus!" Grandma Maisey exclaimed.

Marcus wished the ground would swallow him up. "Hi, Grandma."

"Well, what are you doing here? And who is this stunning young woman?" Grandma Maisey barely concealed her surprise at seeing Charlene.

"Grandma, this is Charlene. Charlene, this is my grandma." Marcus wanted to escape.

"So nice to meet you," Charlene said. "Your scarf is beautiful. Is that silk?"

"Why, yes, it is." His grandma smiled.

Charlene leaned in closer. "It looks Italian."

CHAPTER 14

"It was a gift from a friend who went to Italy. I'm impressed you would know that."

"My mum loves silk. She has so many designs from Italy."

Marcus couldn't believe what he was hearing, amazed by Charlene's ability to charm even his grandma.

"I have another one at home, which I save for special occasions," Grandma Maisey said. "You'll have to see it sometime. I have quite the collection."

"I'd love to." Charlene beamed and glanced at Marcus, who simply nodded back.

"We don't live too far from here, down south past the main road," his grandma went on. "We're the block of houses on the second road on the left."

"That's so kind of you," Charlene replied.

"Marcus, make sure you invite this lovely girl round for dinner sometime," Grandma Maisey said as she began to make her way past. "Nice to meet you, Charlene. Have a lovely evening."

Charlene nodded. "So nice to meet you too."

Grandma Maisey squeezed Marcus's arm and walked off. That touch of assurance infused him with courage.

"Your grandma is so refined," Charlene said, impressed. "Stark contrast to you."

"How would you know?" Marcus grinned, enjoying the ribbing.

"I haven't seen anything to suggest otherwise."

"You'll have to wait and find out. I want to hear why your mum has Italian silk."

Charlene rolled her eyes as they approached the checkout. "My mum's been all over. She and my dad used to go to Italy every year when they first started dating. He'd whisk her off to Milan and buy her a scarf every time."

Marcus didn't know much about fashion, but he knew Italian clothing had to be expensive. Her parents were probably loaded. He felt nervous; his life was so far removed from that existence. "Have you ever been?" he asked.

"Apparently." She sighed, bagging their purchases. "I was far too young to remember. I cried so much they swore never to take me again."

"Mentally scarred them, huh?"

"Something like that."

She walked quickly towards the exit. Marcus hurried to keep up with her but made sure to keep his distance.

As they wandered through the streets to her house, Marcus learned all about her high-flying parents; her dad was an international surgeon, her mum a psychologist.

"They used to travel first class everywhere," Charlene said nonchalantly. "Have dinners with international dignitaries, politicians, humanitarian-aid officials."

"Powerful people then?" Marcus's eyebrows shot up.

"My parents love the spotlight. They like to be seen by people who have power. They like connections, but they never really did anything with it."

Marcus suddenly found himself in a new area of town. Each house was obviously worth over a million. The streets were clean and palatial, and there were trees everywhere. He hadn't even known places like this existed in East London.

Charlene turned into her front garden and alighted on the front steps.

"Do you think they wasted their opportunities?" he asked her.

"Definitely!" She cracked open her front door. "They

could've been heads of departments if they wanted. Campaigned for real change or influence. Instead, they were happy to ride on the coattails of others."

Marcus wasn't sure what a coattail was, but he thought he understood what she meant. "Power isn't for everybody," he said as he shut her front door.

"That's why people lose it. They don't value what they have right in front of them."

The massive hallway had dark tiled flooring, and the walls were a deep forest green with accents of framed black-and-white African art. A wide carpeted staircase was to the left of the hallway. Even the scent of the house seemed expensive—a stark contrast to his grandma's dated two-bedroom home that smelled of cheap lavender. Marcus shifted on his feet uncomfortably.

"Follow me." Charlene slipped off her shoes and made her way towards the kitchen, her figure swaying as she walked. Marcus swallowed; his heart had begun to beat harder now that he was alone with her on her territory.

The kitchen looked like a showroom. The sleek white and black décor was immaculate.

"Do your parents still travel?" Marcus asked.

"They go away every few months," Charlene said, avoiding his gaze.

"Do you go with them?"

"I used to, but I've wanted to stick around more often now. They say I need to take the next few years seriously because of my exams."

"Where have you been?"

"Mainly Africa and Asia. Zambia, South Chad and Nigeria, Hong Kong. My favourite was Dubai. Anyway, enough about me. What about you? Have you ever travelled anywhere?"

Marcus smiled, trying to hide his embarrassment. "Not yet, but I have plans for the future."

Charlene put a bottle on the counter, presented a chocolate fountain and a pile of strawberries, and started melting marshmallows in the microwave. She switched on the fountain, crumbling the just-bought chocolates into it. Marcus watched in silence. Her moves were graceful and seductive, each one ending with a flourish. He tried to avoid staring at her lithe figure as she reached up to get two wine glasses.

"Ta da!" She spread her hands out once she'd finished. Her smile made his heart melt. "It's not much, but I like it."

"It looks perfect." Marcus grinned, taking the metal stick from Charlene but avoiding touching her hands.

"So, where would you like to go?" Charlene said as she poured some wine into their glasses. Marcus had never tasted the stuff.

"Nigeria would be a good place to start. Find more Ebuns like us, learn the history."

"Are your family from there?"

"Nah . . . we're from the Caribbean."

"Which country?"

"Jamaica."

"I've always wanted to go there." She sighed, her eyes drifting to the ceiling.

"Really?"

"People know there are other dimensions to the world there." Charlene twirled a strawberry in the chocolate, then dipped it in the marshmallows. "It all goes back to Nigeria, doesn't it?"

"What do you mean?"

CHAPTER 14

"People talk about these things there. They'll tell you where to avoid, what to do if you get sick. People will always explain things if you want to understand. Here? Everyone is so closed-minded. It wasn't until I met Cassius when I moved here that I realised I wasn't alone." She paused before putting the dripping fruit into her mouth.

Marcus licked his lips and quickly averted his eyes. Her connection to Cassius now made sense, but he forced back the stab of jealousy. Charlene had chosen him to spend time with right now. "I wondered why you guys were friends. He's so different from you."

Charlene shrugged. "He saved my sanity. When you're constantly moving, it's hard to make friends. Especially when you're so . . . different."

Marcus cleared his throat. He really didn't want to talk about Cassius. "My grandma used to be superstitious like that, always talking about duppies in certain areas of town."

"Duppies?"

"Yeah, it means 'ghosts.'"

"Are they common?"

"I don't know. Those stories weren't important to me back then." Marcus took a big bite of his marshmallow-covered strawberry.

"Are you close to your grandma?" Charlene asked seriously.

Marcus opened the bottle on the counter for some liquid courage. "You could say that."

"Do you live with her?"

"Why?" he asked, more forcefully than intended.

"No reason. That's just how it sounded when she invited me over."

Marcus gulped; his throat tingled as the liquid went down.

"Yeah, I live with her. Is that a problem?" His voice was harsh, but this was the last thing he wanted to discuss.

"It's not a problem. I just wanted to get to know you better is all. I've told you all about my family."

"Yeah, well . . . there's not much to tell. Only kid, whose parents abandoned him." He couldn't mention his cousins. The thought made him ache inside. His family seemed completely broken in comparison to Charlene's.

"You mean they just left you with your grandma?"

"Well . . . with my aunt, actually."

"What happened to her?"

Marcus paused. He realised how pathetic this must sound, how it painted him as a complete reject from his own family. He couldn't stand the idea of being seen that way.

"There was . . . an incident. It was best we went our separate ways." He shifted uncomfortably on his feet, then took another swig of the drink.

"Were you hurt?" Charlene asked, her voice a little quieter this time.

"I was fine." He swallowed hard. Memories of that night began to crowd his thoughts: the menace in Carnell's face, the cry of pain from his cousin as he was struck. A cold, hollow feeling seeped through him, and he tried to control his breathing.

"Hey," Charlene said, touching his shoulder.

A charge of energy pulsed through his body, snapping him back into the present, and he turned to her. Her bright almond eyes looked up at him through long lashes. He felt himself melting under her gaze.

"We don't have to talk about it if you don't want to." A small smile lifted her cherubic cheeks. "Your grandma seems

CHAPTER 14

amazing to me. You're lucky to have her."

"I am." Marcus nodded. "It could be worse. I could have no family."

"You'd be surprised," she said, leaning into his chest; his heart hammered against his ribs and his face flushed, warmth spreading across his body. "Even being with family can be . . . lonely."

Marcus's arms encircled her, and he breathed in slowly. She smelled of cherries and honey. He held her tight, closing his eyes, feeling the warmth of her body pressed against his.

"You're not alone anymore," he said, stroking her hair.

She looked up at him, and her eyes shimmered as her gaze ran over his face. "Neither are you."

Her lids drifted closed, and her full red lips parted. Marcus leaned in, his lips pressing against hers.

A clang shocked the pair apart. Marcus's head whipped to the front door.

A tall, slender woman came bustling inside. She halted when she saw the two of them in the kitchen.

"Mum!" Charlene remained close to Marcus and subtly wiped her mouth with her fingers. "I thought you were working late tonight."

Two hawk-like eyes looked back at them. The woman's face was pointed, her hair scraped back into a tight bun—a stark contrast to her daughter's softer, tender features.

"My last two meetings were cancelled," her mum said impatiently as she took her shoes off. She looked Marcus up and down, barely concealing her disapproval.

"I'm Marcus," he said, stepping forward. "It's nice to meet you."

"Hi," Charlene's mum responded, making no move towards

him. She whipped off her coat. "Charlene, we're going out to dinner. Be ready in ten."

"Mum, I have plans with Marcus."

"Family comes first, Charlene. We have important things to discuss tonight. I'm sure your friend will understand. Have a good night."

She nodded at Marcus and stalked off, her footsteps retreating up the stairs.

"I can't believe her." Charlene's furious voice was deeper than he'd heard before, almost husky. "She's so rude. Sometimes . . . I just want her to listen . . . to really pay for how she belittles me."

Her beautiful features darkened, her eyes narrowed, and the corners of her mouth turned downwards. A coldness emanated from Charlene that made Marcus step back slightly; the change in her unsettled him.

She wasn't just annoyed. There was hate in her eyes.

"It's okay." Marcus took hold of her shoulder, and her face instantly softened, her gaze refocusing on him. "We'll catch up another time."

He headed for the door and put on his shoes.

Charlene followed him. "I'm really sorry about this. I'll make it up to you."

When he opened the door to leave, Marcus turned back to her. She looked small and alone as she hugged herself. He embraced her hard, inhaling the sweet smell of her soft skin so close to his mouth.

"You're not alone," he said, then kissed her on the forehead and stepped out into the dark.

CHAPTER 14

* * *

The next evening, Marcus made his way to the Gathering.

He'd barely concentrated at school that day. His thoughts had been on Charlene, how lonely she seemed despite having her family around her and living a life of privilege. The darkness that had crossed her face when her mum ruined her plans worried him. He'd felt cold in her presence.

Cassius had been there when she needed someone, even if he was troubled. Hopefully, she wouldn't need him soon.

Maybe Abeo would be able to heal Cassius, root out whatever issue was troubling him. Marcus could use someone with Cassius's abilities when he took his rightful spot in Q Block. He'd graft all the Ebuns he knew into the crew: Charlene, Neil, Natalie, and maybe even Sean, though he was so young. He would build his partnership with Dacus and take over from Crazy B.

His mind raced as he got closer to the meeting point. There was so much potential that he needed to scope out, and he didn't want to wait any longer. What these guys needed was a night off, to relax and not be so serious after their lessons with Amala and Leonard. As soon as they'd finished, he would convince them to hang around in the park. He had some smokes in his pocket.

That evening was spent listening to Abeo tell stories of the past: how the Orisha revealed themselves through possession of the living, and the importance of paying homage to ancestors. Marcus felt something spark within him at that last point.

"But what if you don't know your ancestors? What if they don't want anything to do with you?" he asked. He felt no connection to his family members who had gone before. The living ones didn't even care.

"Unlikely," Abeo mused. "But in that eventuality, the Orisha could more than make up for it."

"Why are the ancestors necessary if you can just go straight for the Orisha themselves?" Charlene asked, holding Abeo's gaze.

"There is a hierarchy, my child." Abeo broke eye contact and shifted in his seat. "Showing respect for the ancestors proves you respect the order of power and age-old tradition. In order to attain more power and wisdom, you must walk before you can run."

Charlene simply nodded in response.

Marcus still found this difficult to wrap his head round. Could this all be real?

He glanced around the room and studied everyone's reaction to Abeo's words. Cassius sat towards the back. He at least seemed more rested, his dark circles not quite so pronounced. Clearly Abeo or Charlene had been able to help him, but Marcus just didn't feel comfortable with him being in the room. He was too unpredictable and dangerous.

Everyone else was watching Abeo intently; even Charlene seemed engaged and interested in what Abeo was saying. Marcus tried to concentrate, but what he really wanted to do was speak to Leonard.

When Abeo had finished his presentation and the others were dismissed to do their own personal study, Marcus approached Leonard.

"Marcus, what can I do for you?"

CHAPTER 14

"I was wondering if I could have a word, in private."

Leonard looked at him for a moment before glancing around. "Let's go into Amala's room."

They slipped down the hall into Amala's study, and Leonard shut the door behind them.

"What's going on? Are you okay?" The man's eyebrows knit together.

"I'm fine. It's Cassius I'm worried about."

Leonard looked at the floor before folding his arms.

"Leonard, the kid's a loose cannon. Look at what he did to Abeo the other night, and he's still here?"

"Where else is he going to go, Marcus? He's in foster care. He needs to have a space to just be himself and be left alone."

"He's dangerous, and we're all going to pay the price!"

"Marcus, we've put some parameters in place for him. If you've noticed, he's much better today. I promise you we're keeping an eye on him."

"And what about Charlene?"

Surprise flickered across Leonard's face. "What about Charlene?"

"She said they're both seeing this demon woman in their dreams."

Leonard squinted, a worry line creasing his forehead.

"I'm just thinking, if that's the reason why he's acting this way, it might be only a matter of time before she starts acting differently too." Marcus felt good finally putting words to his fears.

Leonard rubbed his face with both hands. "Are you sure that's what she said?"

"I swear." Marcus crossed his chest with his finger.

"All right, leave it with me. I'm going to have to consult

with the others."

Marcus nodded and opened the door to leave.

"Marcus," Leonard called, "thank you for looking out for us. The Gathering will be in good hands with you here."

Marcus nodded and shut the door. He felt a pang of guilt. He wasn't doing this for the Gathering. He was doing it for himself.

An hour later, after a bellyful of Nigerian food that Abeo and Leonard had brought in, Marcus went to grab a book before he re-joined the others. They had already agreed to hang out for a while before heading home. As he was about to open the door to the library, he heard loud discussion coming from Amala's room. Glancing around, he moved closer to listen in on what was being said.

"You didn't think to mention this to me before?" Leonard said angrily.

"Leonard, you know I didn't know Cassius was having those dreams," Amala answered firmly. "We've only just discovered this. Charlene told me about her dreams months ago. I didn't connect the dots. I'm sorry. But we don't even know if they're experiencing the same thing."

"Abeo!" Leonard snapped. "What's going on?"

"My boy, I am as puzzled as you are, but it's clear to me this is a spirit of some kind," Abeo responded gravely. "In one way, that is good, because the hex I have put on him should hold for a while. The problem is, unless we know what this spirit wants or what kind it is, it may be able to break free."

"He needs to be closely observed." Ezra's voice penetrated the door. "As does Charlene. Do we know what they do in their spare time? How much time do they spend together? And crucially, do we know what they have been doing? It's entirely possible they themselves have opened a door they do not know how to shut."

"Charlene has been showing an interest in mind control and the gods and spirits connected to that," Amala replied.

"Amala, you will need to take her aside and see what you can get from her," Leonard said. "We need to stop this before it gets out of hand."

"I'm aware of that, Leonard." Amala sounded cautious. "But a balance has to be struck here. If we move incorrectly, whatever is influencing him could make things perilous for everyone. Not just us here. We need to make sure they feel safe so they can mature to follow whatever path the Orisha have laid out for them. We can't just act for the sake of it."

"Our inaction has led us here! Is there a way for us to just take his gift before it gets any worse?" Leonard asked.

"No!" said Amala and Ezra in unison.

A deafening silence followed.

"It takes a very high price to do that, Leonard." Abeo's calm voice pierced the quiet. "And the consequences are dangerously unpredictable. Let us think on this tonight, and we will convene again tomorrow. I am due on a flight back to Nigeria next week. Let us find a way forward quickly."

Recognising the end of the conversation, Marcus quickly slipped into the library and released his held breath.

They were all in uncharted territory, it seemed. Even the Elder wasn't sure what was going on. Marcus would have to watch Charlene. If things went wrong, at least she would have him. Maybe if he kept her occupied and away from Cassius, whatever bond they had would be broken and she would be safe. Whatever was happening to Cassius had the potential to get worse.

What worried Marcus the most, though, was hearing Leonard's words about removing Cassius's gift. Their powers could be stolen.

Fear crept in; he felt as though control were slipping from his fingers. He'd found a way to navigate the disappointments in his life, but this was an entirely new threat. Marcus had to clench his fists and take deep breaths to gain control of the welling anger at his own helplessness.

He wouldn't be beaten. He just needed to find a way to get a handle on this situation and protect himself.

He hunted through the rows of books and landed on *The Spirits and Ancestors of the Nigerian People*. Everyone would be wondering where he was, so he quickly scribbled the title in the borrowing ledger and placed the book in his bag. He opened the door wide and nearly bumped into Amala and Ezra, who had been talking outside of the door.

"Oh, sorry," he said, trying to avoid eye contact.

"What's your name, young man?" asked Ezra. The question sounded more like a statement from his mouth.

"Marcus."

"Marcus." He looked him over with small scrutinising eyes. "I think you have the favour of your friends. I need you to watch Charlene for us."

"Why?" Marcus asked, not liking this man's directness. He was not about to be bossed around by anyone.

"Because she will need your help, as you know. I suspect she is in far deeper than she knows."

"Deeper in what?"

"Trouble." Ezra stepped towards him, the man's ego more than making up for his lack of height. "Keep your eyes open. We will be doing all we can for Cassius, but you need to look

CHAPTER 14

out for any warning signs from her. If we are able to tackle what's going on with him, we will need to do the same for her, although maybe not as drastically. But if you notice any change of personality, you must come straight to us."

Marcus nodded.

"Marcus." Ezra looked intently at him again. "I am not being flippant when I say this. Your story has only just begun, and it will end just as quickly unless we protect it. Whatever is controlling Cassius could destroy not only us right here but everyone in this town. Everyone will be at the mercy of this being. All of your family and friends."

"I'll keep an eye out for her," Marcus responded.

"See that you do."

Amala stood by quietly, her large, troubled eyes looking up at him. He couldn't tell if she approved or disapproved of how Ezra had addressed him, but he didn't want to stick around to analyse it. He walked off quickly, joining the others in the large hall.

"Where you been, man?" Neil asked.

"I was choosing a book."

"Were you reading the whole library?" Sean asked. Everyone turned, stunned that the timid boy had made a joke.

"Shut up, man." Marcus laughed, and Sean smiled. Marcus felt a small surge of hope that Sean was beginning to come into himself and be more confident. "Anyway, how about we all hang out in the park for a bit? Blow off some steam."

"I'm up for that," Charlene said, standing up and sauntering towards him. She hooked her arm through his and flashed her perfect smile.

Marcus grinned, trying to push the doubts about her away. He'd watch her carefully and handle whatever came up. "Cool, let's go," he said.

Neil, Natalie, and Sean began to follow.

"What about me?" came a voice from far off. "You guys are always sneaking off. You never invite me."

Marcus turned and looked straight at Cassius's smirking face. "You want to come? Come," he replied, trying to break the tense atmosphere.

There was a moment when no one knew what Cassius was about to do. Neil focused on the guy for a moment, his eyes glowing.

"That's it, Neil." Cassius grinned. "You know I'm not going to do anything."

Neil nodded.

Heat rose in Marcus's throat, and his fists balled. Cassius was mocking Neil, and had Neil even seen how the guy would act? Or was Cassius manipulating him?

"It's all good." Marcus tried to steady his racing heart. "Come spend some time with us if you want."

He turned quickly towards the door, and the others followed suit. As much as he hated Cassius, making an enemy of him would be worse. He could pay him a bit of lip service for a while, at least until he had more bodies to protect him. Dacus's men would be a temporary protection until they found more Ebun kids.

They headed towards the front of the Gathering, everyone exchanging nervous glances. Marcus knew Cassius was putting them all on edge, but they needed to stop showing their fear. Maybe getting everyone to relax would help.

They walked to the other side of the park, away from the entrance. It was dusk now, and the sun was setting. Other groups of kids passed them, and Marcus tried to put some

CHAPTER 14

distance between them.

"Thanks for inviting him," Charlene said, leaning in. Marcus caught a whiff of her floral scent, and his heart skipped a beat. Her closeness was intoxicating; he couldn't deny he enjoyed it.

"He's one of us," Marcus said with a smile. She didn't need to know what he really thought. "We need to look out for each other."

Natalie and Sean walked slightly ahead of them, and Neil walked with Cassius behind.

"You should come over to mine again," Charlene said quietly.

Marcus looked at her, a smile playing on his lips. "With your mum there? I don't think so."

"She won't bother you again."

"She looked like she wanted to throw me out." Marcus arched his eyebrow at her.

"Yes, she can be like that," she said, her almond eyes locked on to his. They seemed different in the dark, almost a different colour. "It was just because she doesn't like surprise visitors."

"Okay, when's good for you?"

"How about this weekend? My parents will be out for most of the day."

Marcus tried to disguise his pleasure; he didn't want to look too eager. She would sense she could control him then.

"I think I can squeeze you in." He smiled.

They arrived at the picnic benches and sat down. The next half hour was spent chatting about schools and powers, friends and family for those who had them. Marcus watched everyone cautiously, making mental notes on each personality. Even Cassius relaxed and laughed casually.

"Yeah, my family is pretty messed up," Cassius proffered. "The last foster family I was in kicked me and my brother out because he set fire to a bus."

Neil stared. "Why did he do that?"

"He was being pressured by some kids to do it. He wouldn't stick up for himself . . . so I made him do it. To get them off his back."

Everyone sat there, stunned.

"You manipulate your brother a lot?" Marcus asked. He knew this could trigger Cassius, but he needed to know.

Cassius's eyes narrowed, but his face remained relaxed. "I did it so he could save face, so those guys would leave him alone. It was the first and last time. We don't live together anymore."

Marcus nodded. He understood the logic. As the younger brother, Cassius couldn't be seen to intervene, so he had to do something more subtly. But if he could control his brother, there was no one he wouldn't manipulate.

"Anyway, enough about me," said Cassius. "Natalie, let's see what you can do."

"I can't believe you haven't seen it," Neil said. "It's freaky, man."

"Watch this," Natalie said, taking a swig of her beer and placing it on the table. She took a deep breath and ran straight through one of the picnic tables.

"You can run through objects? That's mental!" Cassius said.

"Yeah, I know." Natalie laughed. "When my mum first saw it, I had to convince her she was dreaming."

"And she believed you?" Charlene said.

"Of course she did! Would you believe your eyes if you saw that? Without knowing what we are?"

CHAPTER 14

"We're like a bunch of freaks," Neil said, laughing as he inhaled his roll-up.

"Yeah, but we're looking out for each other, so it's all good," Marcus said.

Cassius looked directly at Marcus and took a drag. "Even me?"

"That depends," Marcus said, playing with a metal coin in his hand.

"On what?"

Marcus thought about his words carefully. "If you want to be."

"Want to be what? You're talking in riddles, man."

"Looked out for."

"What, you don't think I want to be part of this group?"

"I didn't say that."

"Or you just don't want me. Think I'm too much trouble."

"Cassius, no one is saying that," Charlene interjected.

Cassius stared at the ground and kicked at the grass before he looked back at Marcus.

"All right, I'm in." He grinned.

* * *

"You fight?" Neil looked sceptically at Amala.

Amala descended the stairs while wrapping her hands in some kind of binding, dressed in what looked like a karate uniform with African-patterned cuffs.

"Yes, Marcus and Charlene have already started having

lessons." She smiled as the other members of the Gathering followed her down into their new training room. "I've been a black belt in karate for a number of years now."

"That's incredible," Charlene enthused. "Did you seek guidance from the Orisha for this?"

"Actually, yes, I did." Amala nodded at her.

"Which one?"

"Obba Nani, the teacher of the hearth of the home and wisdom on earth. Also a teacher of the martial arts. She taught Shango how to fight."

Charlene frowned yet kept her lips shut.

"I don't remember seeing her in the hall," Marcus said.

"She's not one of the main Orisha, but she has a lot of influence with them. Much can be learned from her story."

"Why, what happened?" Charlene asked with an almost bored expression on her face. Marcus was surprised by her lack of respect.

"That is for another day," Amala said, ignoring the edge to Charlene's voice. She walked towards the middle of the training room. "Now! It is time for your first martial arts class."

She widened her stance, her fists a little farther out from her hips.

Cassius flung his head back and laughed. "You expect us to take lessons from you? We've got powers."

"You must master yourself, Cassius—in all ways, not just your powers. These are exercises in discipline. You can come first. Hit me."

Cassius's smile faltered as he looked around at all of them. "You serious?"

"Come and hit me."

CHAPTER 14

Gingerly, Cassius moved forward. Marcus held his breath, his jaw clenched. He knew what this guy could do and had to be ready to stop him.

Cassius launched his fist towards Amala, but in the blink of an eye, she had stepped to the side and had him by the scruff of his neck, bent towards the floor. Cassius gasped. She quickly let go and straightened out her clothes.

"Now, shall we get started?"

* * *

It was Saturday, and Marcus's hands were sweating like crazy, his heart racing. He was wearing his new metallic silver bomber jacket and a gold chain round his neck; he must have checked his reflection dozens of times in shop windows. Charlene was always impeccably dressed. He wanted to make sure he could keep up. Luckily, he'd done some extra jobs for Dacus and managed to earn some extra money.

Her street was a world away from his own. Tall leafy trees were everywhere, and these red brick homes dated way further back than his own greying 1960s one. These houses were enormous and stylish. If he'd had a different life, with a different family, this life could've been his.

He took a deep breath; he wasn't going to wallow in self-pity.

When he knocked on her door, it opened immediately.

"You're early." She smiled. Her skin shone so much it looked as if it had been polished. Her short skirt revealed glowing legs, and even from this distance, her smell almost made his eyes roll back.

"I like to make a good impression." He stepped in and handed her a single red rose. His heart was already pumping hard, anticipating her skin against his. He'd spent a lot of money on new clothes, so he hadn't had much left for an impressive gift. He hoped the flower would do.

They sat on the sofa, and all of Marcus's cares and concerns about Charlene melted away. The living room was beautiful: dark green walls with brown leather sofas, tall green foliage in the corners, and brightly coloured paintings of every style he could think of.

"Do your parents know I'm here?" he said as he sank back into the sofa.

"Yes, they do." She folded her bare legs close to his, her skirt only just covering the tops of her thighs.

Marcus placed his hand on her lower leg, not daring to move it up. Her skin was soft and silky smooth, and her heavenly fruity aroma made him giddy.

"I've been thinking," he said as Charlene shuffled closer, "about where our abilities come from. Could any of it have come from our parents?"

"Unlikely. My mum's as stiff as a board, and so is my dad."

"What do you mean?"

"As I said before, they don't believe in this stuff." Charlene held his hand tenderly. "They don't believe in magic and powers. They think it can all be explained away with science."

"Have they seen you do something?" Marcus leaned in closer, concerned.

"Oh no, and even if they had, they wouldn't think it came from me. You can't exactly see what I can do." She winked at him as she took a swig from a glass. "They've travelled the world. I spent my first four years in Africa, where my dad worked for doctors abroad. They encountered all these different people, and they were . . . so dismissive. I found other mythologies fascinating. Especially the gods."

"So you've known about these things for a while then?" Marcus smiled.

"I've always had a sense about these things." Charlene looked off into the distance. "And one time . . ."

"One time what?" Marcus asked, waiting for a reply.

She paused before she continued. "This man—a really tall man, dark and bald and skinny—was watching me from the shadows when I was playing in the compound one time. He came over to me, and I remember he was dressed all in red and black."

An image of one of the Orisha flickered into his mind. That sounded like Eshu.

"He told me I was special," she continued. "He told me to use the gifts I had and that I would be one of the greats in this world. That I would be of great influence."

"He told you that?" Marcus's mouth hung open.

"Yeah," she said, her eyes drifting back to him.

Marcus swallowed. "Charlene, that man sounds like the painting of Eshu in Amala's shrine."

Charlene nodded. "Exactly. I've been doing some research. Let me go and get my book."

She got up slowly, allowing her skirt to swing around her hips before she twirled round with a coy smile and disappeared from the room.

Marcus's phone buzzed as soon as she left, and he wriggled it out of his pocket.

Crazy B: *Let's talk tonight.*

Marcus gritted his teeth. He'd enjoyed not hearing from him, but this confirmed he'd have to deal with him sooner or later.

"Look at this," Charlene said, re-entering the room.

"What is it?"

"It says here that Eshu is the leader of the Aganju: evil spirits."

Marcus took the book from her and straightened up. "What are you saying? That Cassius might be possessed by him, or a spirit he controls?"

"He wouldn't be possessed by him." Charlene shook her head, barely lifting her own gaze from her book. "I doubt Cassius even knew who Eshu was before Amala showed him the shrine."

"Well . . . you don't know that," Marcus said.

"I know more than you think." She stiffened for a moment; she'd revealed something she hadn't intended.

"Okay." Marcus leaned back in his chair, the book on his lap. "Tell me what you think."

"What I mean is, why would Eshu want him? You heard what Amala said. Eshu straddles both sides. He offers people choice; he doesn't control them."

"Says here he's also the bringer of misfortune," Marcus said, pointing at a page. "If this isn't what's going on with him, I don't know what is."

Charlene sighed and closed the book. "Look, I've been reading about these things, trying to figure out what's happened to him. We've been friends for a long time. I would know if he'd been tampering with Eshu."

"Okay . . . how about any other Orisha?"

CHAPTER 14

Charlene moved closer, then looked Marcus directly in the eye. "We'd been reading about Abata and Erinle—the Orisha of having it both ways, of secrets and wealth—but I don't see how either of those could be dangerous."

Secretive and dangerous go hand in hand, Marcus thought.

"I'm the one who . . . directed him to this stuff," she said. "I see the power these Orisha have, and the fact one of them, or at least one of his followers, appeared to me must mean something."

Marcus nodded before he froze. Hadn't a tall, bald, darker-toned man appeared to Donovan, telling him to make Crazy B head boy? Was Eshu bringing misfortune to Marcus's life? His mouth suddenly went dry.

"What is it?" Charlene asked, so close now Marcus could almost feel her breath on his face. He wanted to lean in and taste her pillowy lips.

As best he could, he recounted what had happened in Q Block crew and how he had been pushed out in favour of Crazy B. How Crazy B now wanted him to do deals with Dacus.

"Curtis Ben? I know him." She rested her head on Marcus's chest.

His heart banged so hard he was sure she could feel it. He began to stroke her bare arms, enjoying every moment of being in her presence. She was full of surprises. How did this rich girl know a petty criminal from the streets?

"I'm surprised you'd know guys like that."

She chuckled gently. "I know a lot of people. I know the people he surrounds himself with. They go to my school."

Marcus's mind buzzed.

"I could come with you next time you speak to him," she

said. Her brown almond eyes looked up at him, and he felt his very insides melt. His normal caution and resistance failed to protect him from her overt charms.

"Why would you do that?"

"Why would I not help you, Marcus?" She sat up to face him, her hands pressed against the top of his legs. Marcus could barely breathe in anticipation. "If Eshu showed up in your life as well as mine, it must mean something."

"I don't know what it means," he said. He couldn't think straight. Any fear he'd had that she was manipulating him vanished. This felt real. It felt inevitable.

"We could all use an ally. I know I could," she breathed, and her gaze lowered to his lips.

"Sure you're not going to seduce him with your power?" he whispered, awaiting her soft touch.

"I prefer being in the background. You're the real leader."

She opened her mouth to close it around his lips. Marcus pulled her lower back close to him as pleasure filled his body, as she gripped his shoulders.

Finally, he felt accepted for everything he was.

"Marcus."

"Yeah?" Marcus lazily rested on Charlene's shoulder, his legs up on the sofa, her hand on his chest.

He'd spoken to Crazy B, and they had planned to meet later in the week to discuss their new "terms and conditions." Marcus had wanted to scoff at those words, but he'd restrained himself. He and Charlene had decided they would go and see him together.

He kissed her fingers, which were entwined with his.

CHAPTER 14

"I discovered something last night," she said quietly.

"What?" He smiled, his head now tilted on the back of the sofa.

"I think I've discovered another power."

"You have two powers?"

"Well, not exactly . . . more like an extension of what I can already do."

Marcus's eyebrow arched up. "Okay . . . what is it?"

"Well, instead of making people feel love or desire . . . I think I can make them . . . afraid."

Marcus's stomach unexpectedly constricted. Why did this make him nervous? "Yeah? How did you discover that?"

"I was having this fight with my mum, and she just . . . she just never listens to me, you know? Like, she literally doesn't care what I say, or even what I do. It goes through one ear and out the other. I might as well just be a ghost to her. As long as they get to live their perfect lives . . . Anyway, so I'm staring at her thinking, *I wish I could make you feel something . . . something bad, just to wipe that vacant look off your face.* Then I tried. I tried pushing out this coldness that was in me . . . and it worked."

Marcus faced her. "How do you mean?"

"Her face just changed. She went from babbling about some party she and Dad needed to be ready for to silent. She was looking around the room, like she was waiting for something to jump out at her. Like a little kid." Charlene smiled in wonderment, then looked briefly at the wall. "It was incredible, Marcus. I felt something change inside, like I've had another beat added to my song, you know?"

"Yeah." Marcus tried not to show his nerves, but he couldn't look at her.

"Do you want me to show you?"

"Really?" His head screamed no, but his heart . . . his heart wanted to trust.

"Don't worry, I'll be gentle. I just want to see if I can do it again."

Marcus swung his legs to the floor, his whole body rigid despite his efforts to relax. This would be the one and only time he'd open himself up like this.

Those dark starry eyes looked back at him. Her lips pressed together in concentration, and a slight crease formed between her eyebrows.

A chasm of fear began to widen inside Marcus's chest, terror paralysing his mind. The hairs on his neck stood up; his fingers trembled as he gripped the sofa beneath him.

The feeling quickly dissipated, leaving him deflated and drained. Despite himself, he looked around the room. He felt as if they were not alone.

"Are you okay?" Charlene searched his face. "Was that too much?"

"No." Marcus took a deep breath. "No, it was fine. That's mad what you're able to do."

He felt as if something were crawling on his skin. He wanted to get out of this house. If the fear was gone, why did he feel like this? He rubbed the back of his neck.

"Are you sure you're okay?" she asked quizzically.

"Yeah. You know, it's late. My grandma is going to come back from her club soon."

Charlene's face scrunched up, and she looked at the time. Her eyebrows rose. After a moment, she peered into his eyes. "Marcus, I'm sorry. I shouldn't have done that."

"It's okay . . . I'm sure it'll wear off."

CHAPTER 14

"It's not okay . . . and I did it to my mom too." She looked at the floor and shook her head.

Marcus reached out to touch her shoulder, but his fingers instantly recoiled. He felt as if she was contaminated.

"I'm really sorry about this." Her eyes were big and scared.

"Charlene, it's okay. I'll call you tomorrow, yeah?"

She walked to the front door. Marcus followed at a distance.

"Okay." She shrugged. "I'll see you tomorrow?"

"Definitely."

As soon as he was outside, Marcus walked quickly away without a backward glance.

Chapter 15

Marcus entered the Gathering's greenhouse quietly. He'd considered not coming. He didn't want to see Charlene and be reminded of that dark crippling fear. Every time his mind had wandered that day at school, he'd been sucked back into that place: a cold isolation that burrowed into his chest.

He'd settled on arriving late, after the meeting had already started, to avoid any conversation. At least that was late by his standards. Being early was important to him. He found it easier to gain the upper hand that way.

Today was not one of those days.

After closing the wide ornate door carefully behind him, Marcus turned to see Cassius quickly heading his way. The guy's eyes were barely focused, and they looked different. His top and jacket fit his body in odd shapes, as if something was stuffed under his shirt. His shoulder knocked into Marcus as he walked past.

"Yo!" Marcus whirled round angrily.

Cassius stumbled, his eyes still glazed over, but the stuffing under his clothing began to drop out. He scrambled to stop it, but it was too late. Several things clattered to the ground: a book, various beaded necklaces, and a curious stone. Cassius bent down to pick them up, in no particular hurry.

"Cassius, what you doing, man?"

Cassius continued to pick up the spilled items, as if Marcus hadn't said anything.

"Are you sneaking things out?" Marcus crouched down, about to pick up the gem, but the other boy snatched it from him without a glance. Instead, Marcus turned and picked up the book: *Ancient Rituals of the Sub-Saharan Communities*. He froze for a moment and looked Cassius in the eyes. They were purple. "Bruv, what is this?"

Cassius's face twitched. "Don't worry about it."

"Why are you sneaking this stuff out?" Marcus opened the book and scanned the table of contents: Birth Ceremonies, Coming of Age, Marriage, Death, Sickness, Possession, Ascension. He looked up at Cassius's eyes again. Why had they changed colour? What had he done?

Cassius tried to snatch back the book, but Marcus moved away quickly.

"Why do you need this, bruv? Are you doing some kind of ritual?" he asked. Fear trickled through his thoughts.

Cassius swiped at the book again, and Marcus dodged.

"Does anyone know about this?" he pressed.

"Just give it back." Cassius lunged quickly this time, tumbling into Marcus.

As they grappled, Marcus shoved the other boy hard into the wall, making his head thwack backwards. Without waiting for Cassius to recover, Marcus reached out toward the nearby metal railing. As soon as he felt the familiar pull in his fingers, he swiped his arm to the left, and the metal piece obliged, wrapping around Cassius's torso and locking him in place.

Marcus glanced around. No one was coming yet.

Cassius opened his eyes and tried to rub the back of his head, but his arms were locked in place. He looked around, his gaze finally landing on Marcus. His irises were blue again.

"What's this about? Get me out!" He began to strain against the metal. His items still lay strewn on the floor, but he barely gave them any heed.

Marcus watched him wordlessly.

"You just going to stand there?" Cassius growled. "Did you do this to me?"

"You were sneaking out with Amala's ceremonial things. Why?"

The other boy's eyebrows furrowed. "What are you talking about?"

"I mean this stuff on the floor." Marcus nodded.

Cassius looked down and shook his head. "That's nothing to do with me."

"You literally bumped into me, and this stuff fell out of your clothes."

Cassius's face screwed up again. "You're lying. Let me out of this before I shout for someone to come."

"And who do you think they're going to believe? Just tell me what you were doing, and I might let you go."

"I didn't do anything." A look of panic flitted across his face. As if he was afraid.

One of two things was going on here. Either Cassius was buying time until someone else got here and he could get free and take those things home, or he really had no idea why he had been carrying those things.

Marcus looked again at the book in his hands. "You really don't remember?"

CHAPTER 15

Cassius lowered his head, shaking it slowly.

Marcus had to think quickly; he could hear someone coming from behind. He knelt and placed the book back on the floor. "I can get you out of this."

"Then do it."

Marcus cocked his head to the side. "What's in it for me?"

"What do you mean?"

"I mean, I can use someone with your skills. You have a great gift, Cassius. We could be a good team. You get me?"

Cassius's brows furrowed. "No way. You're a snake."

What did he mean by that? Did he know about Charlene? Was Cassius jealous?

The footsteps were even closer now.

"Suit yourself." Marcus stood up and stepped back. This was a guy who had a death wish. He couldn't be helped. He turned to see Amala's confused face as her eyes flitted from him to Cassius. "I caught Cassius trying to sneak some of your stuff out."

Amala stared at her possessions on the floor. Her eyes widened as she knelt down to gather them up.

"I had to restrain him because he tried to attack me. Don't get too close."

Amala paused. "I can take care of myself, Marcus." She looked at Cassius. "Is this true?"

Cassius shook his head and tried to lift his arms. "I don't know what he's talking about. He put me in this metal trap!"

"But did you take my stuff?" she said through gritted teeth.

"N . . . no . . . ," Cassius stuttered. "I mean, I don't remember."

Her eyes widened as she recognised the book. Her shaking hands picked it up off the ground.

"Marcus must have something to do with this. I don't know how I got here," Cassius snarled, glaring at Marcus

He sounded desperate. No way would Amala believe him.

"Marcus, can you go and get Leonard for me?" Amala stood slowly, her eyes fixed on Cassius.

"Sure thing." Marcus nodded and walked off.

If Cassius won't join me, he's out on his own, Marcus thought. *And good riddance.*

Marcus kept his head down for the rest of that evening. He was rethinking everything.

It was now clear Cassius had no intention of being friends with him. He didn't even want to be cordial, preferring to get in trouble with Amala and Leonard than let Marcus help him get off the hook.

The thing that troubled him the most was Charlene.

He'd never allowed himself to be so vulnerable with anyone. She knew about his powers and about his plans to eventually overthrow Crazy B. But he couldn't shake what had happened last night. Could he keep someone that close who could cause such fear in him? What would stop her from turning on him? His heart felt as though it was being pulled apart.

"Yo, Marcus." Neil turned to him. "We going to the park again tonight?"

He didn't want to go, but he knew if he pulled out, it would draw attention to himself that he didn't want. Charlene would know it was about last night. He needed to save face.

"Yeah, man." Marcus forced a smile, then lowered his voice. "Got some smokes too."

He turned to Charlene and winked at her. Her cherubic

smile almost melted his defences.

Almost.

Marcus sat on the park bench, watching plumes of smoke swirl through the fading light, while Charlene huddled next to him in the chill of the evening. Sean giggled. Neil and Natalie chatted excitedly.

"They need to just take his powers, man," Natalie said slowly. "We shouldn't all have to live in fear of him."

"He's had it rough, you know," Neil countered. "So many rumours about his family. Hard to know if any of it's true."

"So? He's a liability." Natalie shrugged. "The way I see it, you're either for us as a group or you're against us. There's no in between."

Marcus liked Natalie. She got it.

"It's not that simple," Neil said. "We can't help where we come from. He's no different."

"It doesn't matter," Marcus joined in. "Natalie's right. If we have a loose cannon, he's going to hurt us eventually, as well as everyone else. Amala and Leonard need to act."

"Act on what?" a voice said from a distance.

A chill ran down Marcus's spine. He forced himself to turn very slowly. He needed to show Cassius he wasn't afraid of him, although the fear was obvious in everyone else's eyes.

"You all right now, bruv?" Marcus asked as he puffed his roll-up.

"You talking about me?" Cassius asked, slowly approaching them.

"We're worried about you," Neil said. "You were caught stealing today. What were you thinking?"

"I wasn't, all right?" Cassius touched his head, as if trying to think through a problem. "I don't . . . remember what happened."

Charlene broke away from Marcus, and his resentment towards Cassius began to flare up. His hands burned, and a knot formed in his stomach.

"Cassius," she said softly. "What do you remember?"

"I was just sitting in the Gathering with you lot . . . then I, like . . . drifted off to sleep. Next thing I knew, you were standing over me." He jabbed his finger towards Marcus.

Marcus rolled his eyes. He was past caring about him.

"Cassius, let's talk about this later. Come have a smoke with us." Charlene passed him her joint.

For the next few minutes, they all puffed away quietly.

"You know what?" Cassius mumbled. "I don't need you lot."

There was an awkward silence as everyone tried to figure out what he was going to do, but he remained still.

"Do you know those boys over there?" Cassius asked casually.

Marcus whipped around. A group of seven older teenagers were walking towards them, their postures stooped, their hands deep in their pockets.

It couldn't be Carnell's boys, could it? They wouldn't know to come to this park. Dacus's men should have been round his house today, so he couldn't have been followed. He had covered his tracks so carefully.

"Does anybody know these guys?" Marcus asked as he rose, looking at the others.

"No idea, bruv," Neil said. Everyone was now on their feet.

Marcus stepped towards the advancing group. "Wha gwan?" he asked. He'd encountered other gangs and crews before;

the key was to not be hostile even if they were.

The tall blond guy swung for him.

"Freak!" he yelled as Marcus ducked.

"Easy, easy." Marcus stepped back, both hands up.

"Freaks. We don't want your kind here." He lunged for Natalie, who quickly dodged and ran towards Sean.

"Let's get out of here," she said quickly.

They turned around, only to find another group of kids had suddenly approached and stood at the ready. The six of them were completely outnumbered by about twenty people.

"Look, we don't want trouble." Marcus tried to keep his cool. "We're just here smoking our joints. We can smooth this over. Who's in charge?"

His mind raced clumsily through the fog of weed in his system. He only had his bag with a couple of metal pieces. How was he supposed to defend everyone else? Sean, Natalie, and Charlene might need help, but Neil and Cassius should be okay.

Cassius. Marcus spun around and saw Cassius still sitting on the picnic table, carefully watching him through slitted eyes.

"Is this you?" Marcus asked him.

Cassius grinned back silently.

Suddenly, Neil, Natalie, and Sean all looked at him, the same angry look in their eyes.

"You can't stop me, Marcus," he said quietly. "You think you can come in and lay claim to my friends?" His eyes lingered on Charlene, who looked between the two. She was fighting whatever Cassius was doing to her.

"Things are going to change around here, and you are going to listen to me," Cassius went on. He stood up and began to walk slowly towards Marcus. "Ever since you got here, you've thought you're a big man. Worming your way into everyone's good books. Well, that ends now, and just so you don't forget . . ."

A dark cloud descended on Marcus's thoughts. They became jumbled and unclear; he could barely register what was occurring. He saw Cassius pull his fist back, but he couldn't move. He was paralysed on the spot—awaiting the crack of the punch.

But the collision never came. The mind fog lifted, and Marcus could see Cassius struggling. A huge man who towered above them held Cassius's arm and punched him in the head with his free hand.

Cassius dropped to the floor.

The man then turned his gaze to Marcus. He had to be the biggest man Marcus had ever seen. His skin was the colour of copper; his bald head shone under the sky. A feather necklace and beads hung around his neck, and a belt that looked like copper coiled around his waist, a dagger dangling from it.

Everyone looked around as if snapped from their trance. The strangers who had approached them began to walk away. The Gathering, however, stood open-mouthed, gaping at this giant.

"What is this . . . hmm?" the giant man's voice boomed. "This is who is entrusted with taking care of this rising generation?"

"I'm sorry," Marcus said, trying not to be rude. "Who are you?"

"Who am I?" The man smiled as if Marcus had been making a joke. "The question is, who are you? You are an imbecile. Eshu has really made a mess of this." The giant shook his

CHAPTER 15

head. "What are you doing allowing this boy to get high? Can't you see he is a danger to himself and others? You treat these powers as some sort of game?"

Marcus remembered where he had seen this man before. He'd seen him in Amala's shrine.

Ogun.

"You are supposed to be a guardian," the man continued, "to keep the others safe. Instead, you give the one who is infected things that will make his condition worse."

"You're Ogun," Marcus managed to get out.

"Congratulations," Ogun mocked. "You are not that bright, I see. I should have known better than to listen to Eshu. I should have come and seen you myself."

"Wh . . . why?"

"Eshu doesn't take anything seriously." He pointed to Cassius. "You better get him back."

"What condition does he have?" Marcus stammered.

"He has Ogbanje."

"What is that?"

"Go and tell your Elders that is what I said. I shouldn't even be here rescuing you. You should be able to do that yourselves. Now go and tell them Ogun sent you. And keep away from that poison. You will rot your brains! I should know . . ."

He turned and went quickly into the woods, where there was a flash of blue light.

Charlene dashed to Marcus's side. "I can't believe it," she said quietly.

"What?" Marcus said, still dazed.

"That was Ogun, the warrior god."

All five of them stood over the slumped body of Cassius.

"Is he dead?" Sean asked, shaking.

No one moved. Marcus wasn't about to check. For all he cared, Cassius could stay there and rot.

Sighing loudly, Charlene bent down and checked his pulse and lungs. "He's alive," she said, standing up.

"So, Ogun, huh?" Neil looked around the park. "Are we expecting any more gods to pop out of the woodwork?"

"Why did he call you an imbecile?" Natalie asked Marcus. "None of us know what is going on."

Marcus wasn't sure. Was it possible Ogun knew that Marcus had eavesdropped on the leaders' conversation? He was a god, after all . . .

"He was harsh, man," Neil said. "None of us could've known Cassius would act like that."

"It's common sense," Marcus said plainly. "We knew he was vulnerable. We should've said no."

"Do you really think he would've accepted that?" Natalie interjected. "He's a loose cannon! Honestly, I don't want anything to do with him. I don't want to be near him."

Everyone looked away. Marcus knew it was true. No one wanted to take responsibility for this—or for Cassius.

He pulled out his phone.

"What are you doing?" Charlene asked as he began to dial.

"I'm calling Leonard."

She tried to grab his phone, but he moved away quickly.

"You can't call them, Marcus," she said.

Marcus stared at her. "Are you blind? Did you not see what just happened?"

"Do you know what they'll do to him?" she shot back. "He could be put in a mental institution, or worse, they'll take his powers."

"Charlene, wake up." Heat rose in Marcus's chest. "He's not stable. He was ready to take me out, permanently. He controlled all of you. None of you could help me. I was alone. No one to defend me."

He took a deep, shaky breath and stepped away from her. "Look, I don't want to do this any more than you do," he lied, punching in Leonard's number. "But they need to be told."

Charlene stepped towards him, but this time Natalie blocked her. Leonard's phone rang.

"Hello?" Leonard answered.

Suddenly Natalie stepped away and walked next to Charlene, her gaze distant. Charlene's eyes seemed different again, almost lighter in the surrounding darkness.

"Leonard? Something's happened with Cassius." Marcus's eyes flitted around the group.

"What? Where are you?"

Sean walked towards Charlene. Cold gripped Marcus by the throat.

"He turned on us. He tried to attack me."

Neil was the next to move to Charlene, but his steps seemed stunted, as if he was grappling with his actions.

"Charlene, stop it! What are you doing?" Marcus shouted, then hurriedly spoke into the phone. "We're on the other side of the park by the benches. It's Charlene too! Ogun said it's Ogbanje!" he managed to say before turning off the call.

He knew he couldn't outrun this. Charlene had him. She had them all.

"Charlene . . . don't do this . . ."

"Marcus, you leave me no choice . . ."

Chapter 16

Marcus startled awake.

He spun around, trying to see through the darkness, until he recognised the vague dark shapes. He was in his room. Switching on the lamp, he rubbed his eyes and checked his phone. One thirty in the morning.

Marcus had no recollection of how he got home. He couldn't even remember what day it was. The last thing he remembered was talking to Charlene . . .

He looked at his phone again, and relief spread over him; it had only been a few hours since then.

He knew she'd influenced him, but why did he have no memory of it? She wasn't supposed to have that ability. Her powers were centred around feelings, not mind control or memory loss.

Fear twisted his insides. Ignoring the time, he called Neil.

"Hello?" his friend answered groggily.

"Neil, fam. What happened?"

"Huh?"

"What happened tonight? I don't remember anything."

"Bro, it's one in the morning."

"Neil, listen to me. How did you get home? Do you have

any memory of it?"

Neil was silent. "No . . . no, I don't."

Marcus muttered a cuss word under his breath. "Okay, do we have any idea where Charlene is? Can you think of anything?"

"Wouldn't she be at home? It's past midnight."

"Maybe. Laters."

"Be careful."

Marcus rang off.

Next he dialled Leonard's number. The man didn't pick up.

Marcus was beginning to sweat. Who could he ask for help now? He lay back on his bed, his mind wide awake and racing. What had he done? Ogun, that huge man, had blamed him. Why? Why was he the one being blamed? Was he even officially the leader?

The only thing he could think to do was grab the book he'd borrowed from the library out of his bag. He turned the plain cream book round in his hands. Could anything in it possibly help? He flipped straight to the Index and found the word *Ogbanje*. Turning to the indicated page, he saw the subtitle "Possession."

If this was an evil spirit they were dealing with, they would need the help of Abeo and Ezra to sort it out.

Marcus's phone rang, startling him. It was Leonard.

"Marcus, are you all right? Where are you?"

"I think so. I'm back home."

"How did you escape?"

"I . . . I don't know."

"So you didn't overpower her? Did you run?"

"I don't know. I can't remember anything. Neither can Neil."

"Neil?"

"Yeah, I just called him. He's at home too."

Leonard sighed deeply. "Okay, well, we found Cassius. He was alone at the benches when we got there. We assumed you guys had run off or tried to overpower Charlene."

"No. I think she put us under some sort of . . ." Marcus dropped his voice. "Influence."

"This is bad," Leonard said quietly. "This is really bad. Look, I'll call you in the morning, yeah? We'll sort this out. Don't worry. Thanks for telling us about Ogbanje. How did you know?"

"Umm . . . Ogun told me . . ."

"*Who?*"

"This big guy came . . . said he was Ogun. He's the one who knocked Cassius out."

"Oh boy . . . ," Leonard croaked.

The next day, they all sat in complete silence in Amala's office. Everyone except Charlene and Cassius.

"You were sitting in the park . . . doing drugs?" Leonard said slowly, his anger palpable.

Neil had just finished telling him what had happened the night before, and Leonard was nearly bursting a blood vessel in his temple.

"We didn't know Cassius would act like that," Neil protested. "We were all fine."

"You knew how unstable he was. You undid all the hard work we did to get him under control!"

"He is stabilised now," Abeo said calmly, entering the room behind Leonard. "I find it most interesting, Marcus, that you say Ogun came and spoke to you. Is this true?"

Marcus nodded.

"That is . . . unusual. Normally when deities want to communicate with humans, they go through official sources, their priests, or at the very least their worshipers."

"I'm just telling you what happened," Marcus replied. "I'm not saying it was or wasn't him. That's what he said."

"We all saw him," Natalie piped up. "He was a giant. Not just tall but big. I've never seen anything like it. Then he disappeared in this bright blue flash in the woods."

"Hmm," Abeo replied.

Leonard paced around the room.

"Sit down, Leonard." Amala beckoned toward a chair. "You're making everybody nervous."

Leonard sat down next to her. "And you mentioned Eshu was involved . . . how?"

"Ogun said he should have known better than to listen to Eshu," Marcus answered. "He should have come and seen me himself."

"Have you seen Eshu?"

Marcus shook his head. He had no concrete evidence his old crew leader had even seen him.

"Let's say Ogun really did appear to you, Marcus." Amala stood up. "If there is precedence for this, it makes sense. Marcus mimics some of his powers. Do we have any evidence of Ogun having done this before?"

"Not as far as I am aware," Abeo said. "How about you, Ezra? Any record of this having happened in the past?"

Ezra shook his head. "At least not on the African continent. I can double-check my sources, maybe even try some contacts in the diaspora, but this all seems highly dubious."

"So what was it then? A ghost that saved me?" Marcus said incredulously.

"Leave it with us," Amala said. "We'll have to do some digging to find out what's happening. You can all go and spend some time relaxing in the main room if you want."

They all got up, but Marcus practically stormed away. Neil ran to catch up.

"You all right?" he asked.

"Those guys don't know what they're doing," Marcus responded, fuming. "They're sitting there, all comfortable, and they can't even see what's going on in front of them."

"What do you mean?"

"This is a takeover, bruv! And somehow Charlene and Cassius are doing it. And the adults are busy in there debating about whether or not we actually saw what we saw. We know we did!"

Natalie and Sean came over then.

"They didn't believe us," Natalie said, shaking her head.

"I don't understand," Sean added. "Why wouldn't they believe us? We wouldn't lie."

"Because it's never happened before, that's why," Marcus said, "and because of that they're wondering if we were under the influence of something else. Maybe deceived. We were smoking, after all."

"It's possible," Neil said. "Look at all the crazy things that've been happening, especially with Cassius. Now Charlene's run off. They probably don't know who to trust."

"What's going to happen if they don't trust us?" Marcus asked them. "What's going to stop them trying to control us if they don't think we're telling the truth, or if they think we're turning against them? Look, I'm grateful for everything they've done for us so far, but we've got to start looking out for ourselves."

Charlene was slipping through the cracks, messing with their memories. Disappearing. Marcus's hands were unusually clammy, his throat tight at the thought of her. He swallowed hard.

"So you're saying we shouldn't trust them?" Neil asked, his eyebrows furrowed.

"I'm saying we need to put our needs first."

Chapter 17

Marcus headed home angry. That display of authority from Leonard had made him sick to his stomach. No one was going to speak like that to him.

Natalie, Neil, and Sean were all going to his house once they'd picked up the books they had chosen to study. Marcus sat down on his bed and flicked open his own book. Scanning the pages, he found something on extracting bad spirits. He went straight to "Hexes" to see what Abeo had done; he needed to recreate it. It seemed these gems could be used to bend energy, or magic, to the will of whoever used them, to control an outcome. With no abilities of his own, this would be one of the most powerful tools Abeo could use.

Banging at the front door shocked Marcus, and he dropped his book onto the floor. Fear gripped his stomach as he slowly and noisily made his way down the stairs. The banging continued. His mouth became dry, and his heart thumped in his chest as he looked through the spyhole in the door.

Neil, Natalie, and Sean stood waiting for him.

Relief washed over Marcus, and he opened the door. "Come in," he said, letting them pass by as he quickly scanned his road. No one seemed to be there. "Did anybody follow you?"

"No," Natalie replied.

"Neil, do a scan just to make sure."

Neil became completely still, his shoulders sloping down and his eyes glowing white. A moment later, the darkness of his pupils came back and refocused. "Nothing's going to happen in the next twenty minutes."

"Good," Marcus said. "Let's get to work. I want you all to research as much as you can about your powers. We need to figure out a way to find Charlene and keep her away from Cassius."

"Why?" Neil asked.

"I dunno, exactly." Marcus rubbed his head. "They're connected somehow. She keeps trying to protect him. Remember how you said they were involved in something together before all this weird stuff happened? She knows more than she's letting on."

"Maybe we should actually talk to Cassius about it," Natalie said, picking up one of the old photos that were on Grandma Maisey's mantelpiece.

"Put that down," Marcus said sharply. She'd picked up the one of his mum.

She shrugged and gently returned it.

"Leonard and Amala have already done that," Marcus said, turning his attention back to Neil and Sean.

"What did they say?" Natalie walked over with folded arms.

Good question, Marcus thought. The adults hadn't mentioned anything to them. They were being kept in the dark. "They never told me."

"They're keeping too much from us," Natalie said. "We just need to get to the source. Does anyone know where Charlene lives?"

"I do," Marcus said.

"Okay, do we know where Cassius is?"

"I think he's actually staying at the Gathering," Neil replied. "Amala knows people in social services, so I'm sure she's pulled some strings."

"When does Abeo leave?" Marcus asked.

"Tomorrow," Natalie said. "I think he's going to be meeting with us all individually this evening to say goodbye and give us advice."

"All right, we all go to the Gathering tonight. I'll try and see Cassius somehow. The adults are not to know. They'll stop us."

"What if Cassius attacks you? Who's going to help you?"

"No one will be able to help me . . ." Marcus trailed off but then had a thought. "Maybe you can . . . but let's get to work, fam. We need to know about evil spirits, what our powers can do, and which gods might want to help us."

All four walked back to the Gathering, a nervous, chilling energy surrounding them.

"Do you think she'll be there?" Sean asked.

"I don't know, but don't worry about it, all right?" Marcus said. "We're all here together."

"But she managed to overpower us before."

"True, but as far as we can tell, nothing bad has happened to us. Maybe she just wanted to get us all away from the scene so she could escape."

"But she left Cassius there for Leonard to find him. Why would she get us out of the way only to leave him behind

CHAPTER 17

anyway?"

Marcus didn't know; that was a detail he hadn't considered. Her powers clearly made them blind and forgetful. How was she able to acquire and harness that much power? The only explanation was that the evil spirit fed her abilities somehow.

"I just can't believe she's turned on us," Natalie said. "I know she probably couldn't help it if she's possessed, but . . . it still hurts."

Marcus's whole body tensed. He didn't want the others to see how much it felt like a dagger in his heart.

Neil put his hand on Natalie's shoulder. "We're going to sort this out. Marcus will speak to Cassius, see what he knows. It's our job just to keep everybody occupied until he's done."

"It won't take long," Marcus said, trying to reassure everyone. What he really wanted to do was punch Cassius's lights out—after all, he was to blame for putting them all in danger—but that would only make everything worse. "I'll just ask how Cassius is doing, then I'll know if it's safe."

As they approached the trees and fog descended, Sean walked closer between them. "This part always gives me the creeps."

"It's supposed to." Neil smiled, with a wink. "Keeps the wimps away."

Sean straightened up at that.

Finding the special opening, with its swirling blue magic, Marcus took out his key, opened the way up for everyone, and carefully closed it behind them. Then they entered the Gathering house. Even after everything that had been going on, this place still felt like home. Somewhere he wanted to be and belong.

Walking along the candlelit corridor, Marcus wondered if

the magic that held up those candle cages was the same that held Cassius and Charlene hostage.

"Okay, let's figure out where Leonard and the others are," he said, "and remember to hold their attention until I'm back. I'll be with you to start off with, and then I'll leave."

"We'll try the training room and library," Neil said, breaking off with Natalie.

"You all right, little man? Think you can do this?" Marcus asked Sean as they headed towards Amala's office.

Sean nodded his head. His face and body looked smaller than ever.

Marcus knocked on the door.

"Come in," said Amala.

Marcus and Sean walked in to find all four adults standing there.

"Marcus, Sean, hello." Amala smiled.

The tense atmosphere made Marcus uncomfortable; he knew they'd walked in on something important. He opened his mouth to speak, but Sean beat him to it.

"I'm sorry to disturb you all," Sean said. "But I was wondering if someone could explain to me the cosmological connection to Yoruban religion."

Everybody stared at him, including Marcus.

"Well, erm . . . ," Marcus said, beginning to back away. He was about to tell them they would come back later.

"Fascinating question, young man!" said Abeo. "What an insightful boy you must be. Did anyone put you up to this?" His eyes flicked to Marcus, who held his gaze.

"No, Mr. Abeo. I took the book out a couple of days ago, and no one could explain it to me. I think I asked Leonard about it."

Leonard looked around, slightly bashful. "He did actually," he said quietly. "How about you ask Abeo about it in a few minutes?"

Sean nodded.

"How is Cassius?" Marcus decided to push the moment. He'd planned on getting Amala alone to ask her what was going on, but maybe it was better to ask now with all of them in the same room.

"He's doing much better," Leonard said sombrely. "We think he'll be okay. But it'll take some time for the ritual to work fully."

"We can talk about this later," Ezra interrupted. "I'm afraid, Marcus, we don't have much time with Abeo's departure. Please excuse us."

Marcus's throat constricted. Restraining himself from a rude outburst, he nodded, turned, and left with Sean.

They walked a little way down the hall, where they bumped into Natalie and Neil.

"We can't find anyone," Natalie said.

"That's 'cause they're all in Amala's office. It's perfect."

"How?" asked Neil.

"They'll be easier to control if they're all in one place. You just have to stall them until I'm done talking to Cassius."

"I don't know if they'll talk for very long," Sean said. "They did say they'll be just a few minutes."

"I reckon they'll be longer. They were right in the middle of it when we interrupted. Anyway, I won't need long."

"Is he stable?" Neil asked.

"They seem to think so. That's all we can go on." He took a deep breath. "Wish me luck, and all of you text me when they leave the room, all right?"

All three of them nodded nervously.

"Good. I'll be back in a bit. Stay calm." Marcus tried to steady his racing heart as he walked towards the spare room.

He knocked on the door, trying to control his breathing.

"Come in," came a tired voice from inside.

Marcus clenched his jaw as he pushed the door open.

Cassius was lying on a red sofa. When he turned and saw Marcus entering, he immediately sat up.

"Wow, chill, it's okay," Marcus said, lifting both hands before he shut the door behind him. "I just want to talk."

Cassius leaned away from him, that familiar shadow back under his red-rimmed eyes.

Marcus sat down on a table near the door, keeping his distance. He couldn't hear any voices, so Cassius seemed to be giving him a chance.

"What are you doing here?" Cassius asked.

"I'm here to see how you are."

Cassius snorted. "Why?"

"'Cause we don't know what's going on with you." Marcus leaned against the wall, trying to relax his posture. "They're not telling us anything. How are you doing?"

"Better," Cassius replied, reclining on the sofa and avoiding Marcus's eyes.

"You remember anything?"

The other boy cast him a sidewards glance. "Not everything."

"We don't have to get into it. We just need to know how you are."

"You mean you *want* to know. The others would have told you if they thought you should know."

Marcus paused for a moment. "We don't have to be enemies,

CHAPTER 17

Cassius. We can work together, you know."

"Why would I want that?"

"We've got something pretty good going on here." Marcus gestured at the whole room. "We're special, man. We don't need to fight."

"Look, I'm going to be honest." Cassius leaned forward. "I don't like you."

Marcus stiffened, waiting for the invasion of his mind. He quickly scanned the room for any metal implements, calling on the burn in his hands.

"But I don't want to hurt you," Cassius said, looking away. "I just have this need to control everything . . . and when you come around? I want to control you the most."

Marcus put his hand in his pocket, where he kept a coin and some keys, and swallowed hard. Was this Cassius talking, or was he being controlled? "Why me? Is it that thing inside you?"

Cassius smirked. "You think you're better than everybody else. But this is beyond that . . ." He paused.

Marcus decided not to interrupt, although he wanted to punch the guy's lights out. He gripped the keys in his pocket until the metal dug into his flesh.

"Leonard and those guys think it's some kind of evil spirit," Cassius went on. "I've been having dreams and stuff that make it seem like it's controlling me."

"Do you know how it got in your head?"

Cassius froze. "I don't really remember. It was a few weeks ago."

He knows, thought Marcus. "Does Charlene know about this?"

"Yeah, she knows. She has those dreams too."

"No one can find her, you know. Any idea where she's gone?"

"No." Cassius closed his eyes. "If they don't find her, this thing is going to get worse."

"What did this spirit even want?"

"Look, I think you've asked enough questions." Cassius looked straight at him.

Marcus held his gaze. "Just one more."

"All right."

"Did she do this to you?"

"Who?"

"Charlene." Marcus stiffened as her name escaped his lips.

Cassius's face turned dark. "You need to leave."

"I just want to know why you're protecting her." Marcus could hear a small whisper; he wasn't sure if someone was outside or if this was Cassius.

"You don't want to know. You need to leave."

Marcus stood up quickly, again showing his hands in an attempt to be nonthreatening. "I'm going. Get well soon, yeah?"

"Like you care," Cassius said bitterly as Marcus closed the door.

Marcus breathed out heavily and started to make his way back to where he'd left the others. Luckily, he heard Leonard's voice before he reached them.

"Hi, Sean. Where is Marcus?"

Marcus whipped out his phone and emerged from around the corner. "I'm just here. I was on my phone."

"Oh," said Leonard, surprised at his sudden appearance.

CHAPTER 17

"Okay, good. We wanted to speak to you all. Where are the other two?"

"They went down to the training room, I think," Sean said.

"Okay, I want to meet you all in the main room in ten minutes, all right? Go get the others."

Leonard turned back to Amala's study while Marcus and Sean quickly headed down to the training room.

"What happened?" asked Neil when he saw Marcus enter.

"I told you to stay by Sean. What you doing down here?" Marcus tried not to explode.

"He had it handled," Neil said.

"You think he could have stopped all four of them upstairs from finding me? Think, bro, think!"

"Sorry, it's my fault," Natalie said. "I wanted to show Neil something."

"What?" Marcus said impatiently.

Natalie walked towards the wall and then passed through it.

"She could already do that," Marcus said, unimpressed.

Then she popped just her head and her arm out, picked up an object, set it back down, and disappeared in the wall. Her whole body re-emerged a second later.

"What am I looking at?" Marcus asked, not understanding.

"I learned how to control my body composition better. My whole body can be malleable, but I can make my hand and head solid."

"Okay," said Marcus, nodding. "Not bad. Look, we need to go back upstairs. They're going to be waiting for us. But I wanted to tell you what Cassius said."

"I'm surprised you came out alive," Natalie muttered.

"He is a bit better, but listen. Charlene is involved in this somehow. He wouldn't tell me how, but she definitely is. He doesn't know where she is." The thought that she was involved filled Marcus with dread, but he pushed those feelings down as far as he could and tried to concentrate.

"Should we go round her house though?" Neil asked, surprised. "Especially if she's got that thing inside her?"

"Depends on what Leonard and the others are going to tell us now," Marcus concluded.

"Well, the good thing is she isn't as powerful as Cassius. She can't make us do things we don't want to," Natalie said.

"I don't know," Neil said. "Hers is just different. You can't think clearly when you're under her spell. You just feel like you want to make her happy, do whatever she says."

"It's like you're in a fog," Marcus added, not wanting to tell them about the fear she had projected onto him a few nights earlier. "I'd say she's equally dangerous. Being near her is like someone's pulling you towards them. Hard to explain."

Natalie looked at the floor. "That's exactly how I felt when I tried to stop her from getting to you, like I was being seduced."

"So now we all know how it feels when we're being influenced by her." Marcus nodded. "When she tried it on me the first time, I fell for it completely. The second time I knew what was happening, and I was able to resist. Little good that did."

"Look, the good thing is, nothing bad happened to us," Neil chimed in. "Somehow she just led us all home."

They headed upstairs to the main room and sat down, trying to relax.

"Once all this is done, I better be second-in-command," Natalie joked.

"You? No way." Neil giggled. "That spot is mine."

CHAPTER 17

"Who's number one?" Sean asked.

"It's big boy here." Neil gestured towards Marcus. "Remember what that giant man told us."

Marcus looked at Neil, who nodded in acknowledgement. A calm swept over him.

Neil trusted him to lead.

He could finally prove himself. Keep himself and his new friends safe.

Save Charlene.

"Could that really have been Ogun?" Natalie asked. "I mean, have we found a way to verify it?"

"We're not exactly going to find photographs of him, are we?" Neil scoffed.

"We don't need to," Marcus interjected. "He looked exactly like the painting in Amala's shrine."

"Even if those guys don't believe us," Neil said, "that was some crazy stuff right there."

Amala, Leonard, Abeo, and Ezra walked into the room.

"Thank you for being so patient with us," Amala said. "These are untested times, and we needed to discuss together how to best move forward."

"We have discovered two more people, gifted like yourselves," Leonard said. "But we have decided to hold off inviting them into this group until things settle down with some of us. It is best they remain unknown to you all."

"Why can't we know who they are?" Marcus piped up. "We could look out for them. There's nothing wrong with us."

"I don't want them wrapped up in this. When they join, they will join with a clean slate. With all these kinks worked out."

"So what are we going to do with Cassius and Charlene?"

Natalie asked. "I mean, we don't even know where Charlene is."

"She is at home with her family," Amala said. "I know them, and I checked in on them. They said she's just taking some time for herself right now. They seemed unconcerned."

"They're probably under her control," Marcus said, more to himself than anyone else.

"Yes, I suspect they are. At least some of the time. But unfortunately, there's nothing we can do."

"What do you mean?" Marcus said. "She could be doing whatever she wants in that house, making all kinds of plans that are against us and the community!"

"We have to lure her out before we can help Charlene," Amala answered.

"Who's 'her'?" Neil asked. "Are we not talking about Charlene?"

"We suspect it's a female spirit," Amala said. "We need to offer her something she wants."

"What's that?"

"Power. She can do a lot with Charlene, but ultimately Cassius is the one with the true power."

"So we're going to give her Cassius?" Marcus asked in disbelief.

"Yes."

"What will happen to him?" Sean cried.

"Nothing. It will only be a ploy to draw her out. Then we can put something in place that will trap her."

Marcus didn't like the idea of using Cassius as bait because of his powers, but at this point, what choice did they have?

They sat in silence.

"I feel like Cassius is being offered as some sort of sacrifice,"

CHAPTER 17

Natalie said quietly.

"I have extended my stay," said Abeo. "I have dealt with possession before. Admittedly, not with Ebuns such as yourselves, but I don't anticipate it to be much different."

"Ebun? What's that?" Sean asked.

"Why, that's what you are, dear boy. Ebun means 'gift.'"

Chapter 18

Marcus headed home, with Neil walking alongside him.

"I'm just glad he didn't attack you, bruv." Neil sighed. "I checked to make sure nothing bad was going to happen."

"Thanks," Marcus said. "I appreciate it."

"But the fact they're going to use him as bait . . . man, that seems cold."

"Don't think about it too much. We need to get rid of that thing in them, whatever it is. That's what's most important."

They reached the corner where Neil would turn around to make his own way back home.

"Think we're going to be able to save Charlene?"

"I don't know." Marcus shrugged. "It looks like we're only just hanging on to Cassius, although losing him wouldn't be a huge loss."

"That's harsh, bruv."

"No, it's not. The guy is trouble. I could tell even before he started acting weird—"

Neil's body suddenly went stiff, as if he were stuck in time, his eyes glowing.

CHAPTER 18

"Neil?" Marcus's whole body froze. For a moment he didn't know what to do. His eyes darted around. Was Neil sensing danger? Was someone controlling him?

"Neil, Neil!" Marcus shook his shoulders, and Neil's eyes quickly normalised. He focused on Marcus for just a moment before tyres screeched to a halt in the middle of the road.

"Get down!" Neil shouted as he dived at Marcus, pushing him behind a nearby wall.

Car doors opened and slammed. Marcus's heart was in his throat.

"They've got guns," Neil whispered, his breath rattling out of his body.

Marcus nodded and closed his eyes momentarily, trying to feel the metal behind the wall that protected them. He'd heard three car doors and sensed three guns.

As the adrenaline coursed through his body, he took a deep breath and stood up as quickly as he could.

In a split second, he'd clocked the assailants. The one at the front already had a gun aimed directly at him. Marcus pointed at it, feeling the magnetism of the gun, and flung his left arm far to the side. The gun flew out of the attacker's hand.

The second assailant's firearm went off, luckily missing Marcus, no doubt because the man had been distracted by what had just happened. Marcus formed his hand into a fist and punched straight up, and the gun struck the second man in the face. Marcus kept pumping his fist up, and the gun kept pummelling his attacker.

The third man hesitated. Marcus used that time to fling the guy's gun onto a nearby roof.

The first attacker was scrambling after his gun. Marcus

drew it towards him, the man trailing after it as fast as he could. As soon as the weapon leapt into his grasp, Marcus pointed it directly at the guy's face. With his other hand, he kept punching the second attacker. The third was in the car, about to drive off.

Marcus shot the first attacker in the foot, and the man crumpled to the floor. Dropping the gun by Neil, he used both hands to swipe to the right. The car crashed into a metal pole.

"Let's go!" Marcus called to Neil. "Give me that gun."

Neil scrambled up, thrusting the gun into Marcus's hand as they ran off into the night.

Panting heavily, they arrived back in the park.

"Why are we back here?" Neil asked.

Honestly, Marcus didn't know. He just knew he couldn't lead those people to his grandma's house. That was completely off-limits. Plus, at least here they could disappear into the foggy woods. The followers would either get lost or be unable to pass through the door because of the magic lock. "Look, we lost them. That's the most important thing."

"Did you shoot that guy?"

"Had no choice," Marcus said, feeling sick as the events flooded his memory. He'd shot two people in two months. What was happening to him?

"How did you stop them all?" Neil stared at him, wide-eyed.

Marcus turned away. "I just took their guns off them."

"Then what was that crash sound?"

"I stopped the car too."

Neil checked over his shoulder. "Who were they?"

CHAPTER 18

"Just some people I used to know. Anyway, why didn't you spot them before?" Anger rose in Marcus's chest. "They could have taken us out."

"I did spot them."

"That was too close, man."

"I don't have premonitions like that. We were lucky that I got it in time."

"You need to practise to feel it sooner."

"Look, man, I saved your life." Neil straightened up, his hands clenched and his teeth grinding.

"Yeah, I know . . . sorry, man." Marcus rubbed his head hard. Every part of his body ached with tension. He felt as if he was about to snap.

"Who are those people, Marcus?" Neil slowly sat down on a bench. "I have a right to know. They could be after me next. Or I'll be collateral damage."

"My aunt's ex-boyfriend. We had an . . . altercation. I had to leave my home and school and come here."

"What did you do?"

"I shot him."

Neil flinched, his eyes widening.

"No, it wasn't like that," Marcus responded, suddenly realising he must look like a cold-blooded killer. "It was in self-defence."

"Look, I'm not getting involved in gang stuff. I've worked too hard to keep away from that stuff, man."

"He was beating my cousin, and he pulled the gun on me!"

Neil stood there awkwardly. Marcus didn't know if he was going to stay or run.

"Look, don't worry about it," Marcus said. "I was defending my family. My cousin messed up, and this guy was beating him bad. Threw my aunt across the room. Nearly knocked out my other cousin. He pulled the gun on me. What was I supposed to do? You've seen my power. He was going to shoot either me or someone else."

"So you did it first."

"Not on purpose . . . It all happened so fast." Marcus shook his head. He couldn't talk about this right now. He tried to gather his thoughts. "I'm not going to let anything happen to you, Neil. This is what I do. I protect my own. My cousin is blood, been there for me through thick and thin. Look at what you did for me today. I'm not going to forget that."

He put his hand on Neil's shoulder. "Do you hear me? I'm not going to let anything happen to you."

Neil looked at him for a few seconds before nodding.

"Good." Marcus allowed himself to relax slightly. It was absolutely necessary that someone like Neil was on board with him. "I'm going to need you, Neil. You're my closest friend. If you just keep working on your gift, we'll be almost invincible."

"Yeah," Neil said as they bumped fists and clasped hands. "So you crashed their car? You're nuts."

Marcus smiled, a trickle of relief spreading through his insides. "Yeah, man . . . I've never done that before!"

"You're going to have to do that again just so I can see it!"

"No way! Someone will probably film it, knowing my luck, and I'll be all over the news."

Their laughter died down.

"Do you think it's safe to go home now?" Neil asked after glancing at his phone.

"Sure, but let's try going different ways, yeah? Check for the next fifteen minutes, can you?"

CHAPTER 18

Neil stiffened up, his pupils disappearing. A moment later, he came back into consciousness. "We're good for the next fifteen."

"All right. Text me when you get back so I know you're okay."

After saying their goodbyes, both boys turned and ran. Marcus was going to have to ask Dacus to step up security.

It normally took thirty minutes to walk home from the park, but Marcus ran for his life. The underground wasn't an option; there was nowhere to hide down there, even if he could get home much quicker that way. His best bet was to run and hope the extra five minutes would be uneventful.

Feet pounding the pavement, his heart hammering, he felt as if he had razors in his throat. The streetlamps flashed by, and the neighbourhood looked only vaguely familiar in the dark.

Carnell was serious. He wanted Marcus dead, not just injured. This wasn't merely a message being sent.

He swallowed hard, his mouth completely dry. In his panic, he thought about running past his grandma's house. Just running forever, never stopping. To the ends of the earth, or at least until his legs collapsed underneath him. When he came to the turn he would normally take to get home, he instead went round the back alley and climbed over her rickety old fence. He crouched, allowing his body to slow down for a moment, before he opened the back door.

His grandma gasped. She stood there in the kitchen, fright written all over her face.

"Sorry, Grandma!" he said, reaching out to her. The last

thing he needed was for her to have a heart attack because of him.

"Goodness me! Why are you using the back door? You scared me half to death!"

"Oh . . . sorry. I couldn't find my front door keys this morning, so I took the back door ones instead."

Her hand was still on her chest as she looked away from him.

"Do you need to sit down?" he asked, trying to show some kindness.

"No, I'm fine. You better find those keys!"

"I will. Do you need some help with the cooking?"

"No, I'm all right."

Marcus hurried upstairs to shower off the night's events. Sooner or later, he was going to have to deal with Carnell. He couldn't spend his whole life running from him. He had hoped he could use his new band of friends to help in some way, but that was now out of the question. It was too dangerous.

Cassius would have been invaluable. He would have been able to conquer Carnell's whole gang. No one would have messed around with Marcus again after that. But there was no chance that would ever happen. Cassius just didn't like him, and there was nothing to be done about that. They could have been an invincible force if the guy weren't so bad.

As the hot water washed away most of the day's memories, Marcus was left with thoughts of Charlene. She could have been his right-hand woman. She was stunning and smart. No one could resist her charms—not even him. Last night sitting on that bench, he'd still felt proud to have her by his side, despite the fear she had inflicted on him the night before.

An ache formed deep within him. He'd wanted her to be

CHAPTER 18

on his side. She had captured his attention from the get-go. After that first meeting, he'd thought they had a connection. He had wanted to see where their flirting could go.

He could never trust her now, even if he was able to rescue her from this demon possession.

He stepped out of the shower, unable to shake her from his mind. If there was something he could do to help her, get her back to herself, maybe she would come round. Maybe after some time, they could be that team he had envisioned. Maybe more than that. His throat tightened at that thought. He missed her fruity smell; he missed her soft touch.

Quickly dressing, he reached for his phone and saw the message from Neil saying he got home safe. He replied that he had too. Then he scrolled to Charlene's name and pressed Call.

It rang right through.

In some ways he was grateful. He didn't even know what he would have said to her if she'd picked up. He just longed to hear her voice.

"Marcus! Come, it's time for dinner," his grandma called, her voice ringing up the stairs.

He came down and ate in relative silence, while she chatted away happily. Marcus felt as if every inch of him was on high alert, hoping and praying that no one had followed him home to disrupt his tranquil dinner with his grandma.

Marcus could barely bring himself to leave the house that night to see Dacus, but he needed to give Dacus more of what he wanted in order to get more protection. He hid a metal bar inside his jacket and walked in the shadows as best he could. He felt heavy; fear threatened to take over his mind. He gripped the bar, which helped give him some peace.

As he drew closer to the warehouse, he could hear shouts. He froze for a moment before proceeding carefully, creeping up to peer through the peephole. Shadows flitted through his limited vision. He didn't know what the voices were saying, but there was no doubt those men were panicked.

After a deep breath, he forced open the front door, clenching the metal handle.

Three of the men were arguing with one another, while Dacus was in the corner, shouting down a phone. When he caught Marcus watching, he turned off the phone and marched towards him.

"You . . . you know anything about this?" He tipped his head towards the back of the room.

"About what?" Marcus glanced quickly over Dacus's shoulder. Spray paint covered the back of a corkboard littered with papers. Drawers were strewn all over the floor.

"You sent them here?"

"What? No, man."

"Took everything back, did you?"

"Take what back?"

"Everything you brought me in the last two weeks. It's all gone."

Marcus's blood ran cold. "Who took it?"

"That's what I want to know." Dacus's eyes bored into him.

Marcus tried to think quickly. Who knew he came here? Crazy B? Was it possible Cassius had found him here?

"I'll find out. I'll get it back." Marcus tried to hold his ground, but Dacus continued advancing towards him.

"This doesn't happen to me. People don't mess with me. I

come back and find two of my men tied up and my things taken. You . . . I don't know. You come here and offer me big volumes of expensive metal. Next thing I know, I am robbed."

Dacus's fist flew forward at such speed Marcus barely ducked in time. A blade, nestled in between Dacus's fingers, had passed inches from his face.

The man swung again, but this time Marcus was ready. His hands burned as he focused on the blade and flicked his arm across the room. The blade flew out of Dacus's hand and soared through the air, burying itself in a poster on the wall.

Dacus watched it; his face only lost focus for a second. "You promised those things to me."

"I don't know who took it," Marcus said as loudly as he could, calling on all the courage he could muster. "But I can find out."

"No one steals from me." Dacus launched himself at Marcus, who, in that same moment, spied a chain around the man's neck.

Marcus pulled his hand into a fist and tightened the chain. Dacus's hands flew up to his throat, trying to stop the chain from embedding itself into his skin.

Walking backwards, Marcus kept one eye on the other three men as they looked on in horror. One broke forward to help Dacus, who bared his teeth and desperately clawed at the chain digging into his flesh.

"I'll find out who took it," Marcus said before he turned and ran. He finally released his tight fist, leaving Dacus gasping for air.

Marcus spent most of the next day in bed.

He used the excuse of having a headache, but in reality, he was crumbling inside. Every muscle ached, every memory hurt, and he felt cold.

He was supposed to meet Crazy B that evening, but with Carnell trying to pop him off and Dacus turning on him, Marcus was fast running out of options. How was he supposed to be safe on the streets now? Would seeing Crazy B be too dangerous?

His resolve began to return. There was no way he would miss the chance to speak to Crazy B. To not show up would be cowardice. Marcus couldn't live with that.

He swallowed back the sadness that Charlene wasn't with him. Together, they could've conquered his old crew in a matter of days.

Marcus racked up to their old meeting area twenty minutes early and sat on the cold grey stone wall, his hood firmly over his face. He'd gone to a charity shop and bought a faded red hoodie to change up his look; he didn't want to be instantly recognisable. With extra time on his hands, he began to plan.

Putting Crazy B at ease was paramount. Marcus would paint himself as a liability because of his history with Carnell, and he'd suggest that Crazy B should strike a deal with Dacus on his own. He didn't need to know Marcus was already being hunted, or that he'd already been working with Dacus and things had gone bad.

Marcus rubbed his head. Another puzzle that needed solving.

If he got a chance, he'd speak to Jermaine—see if he could get a better description of who'd changed Donovan's mind

CHAPTER 18

for the leadership.

Marcus saw a large group heading towards him and sniggered to himself. Typical of Crazy B to show off his supposed influence. Marcus would offer to be his informant for now, nothing more or less. He had to reduce his exposure, at least until he had things handled back at the Gathering.

As the group got close, Marcus slowly stood up and held his head steady, looking straight at them.

Charlene was arm in arm with Crazy B.

Marcus's heart nearly stopped beating. Blood drained out of his face. It was all he could do to remain standing.

She had formed an alliance with Crazy B.

He dared to look at her. He wanted to look into the eyes of his betrayer.

Her irises were that strange colour again, a hazy purple.

He swallowed hard and tried to hold himself together. She was not herself.

"Marcus." Crazy B held out his fist.

Marcus stared at it for a couple of seconds before he returned the greeting. He kept his mouth shut, shame and anger firing through him. His hands were aflame.

"Sorry it's been a while, bruv," Crazy B said, lighting a cigarette. "You know how busy it can get. You're so . . . in demand."

Marcus wanted to tie him up with the nearby lamppost, but instead he simply nodded.

"I'm going to need you to see the Eastern guys tonight. We've got some things to shift in two days."

"I can't do that, bruv," Marcus said, his voice steady.

"What do you mean?"

"I've got a target on my back. Someone tried to take me out

last night."

Crazy B stiffened. "Who did that?"

"I don't know. Do you?" Marcus wanted to make him uncomfortable.

"Nah, man." Crazy B rubbed his head. "I can't have my first big deal get messy." He turned to Charlene and whispered to her.

"I see you've made a new friend," Marcus said, looking straight at Charlene.

"Yes," she purred back. A smile played on her lips, and her voice was deeper than normal, just like the time she'd shown her real feelings towards her mum. "Curtis is . . . magnetising."

Marcus felt as if he were being torn up inside. He was done here. "B, I know you're a busy man. Let me do some informant work for you. We can touch base, wait until things calm down."

"I don't need any more informants. I need you to do this deal. No one else can shift it that quick."

"Bro, I can't do it. Let me call around, and I'll find someone for you."

Crazy B shook his head as he inhaled his cigarette. "You know, I guess you're not as good as I thought you were. Donovan was wrong about you. He made it seem like you could move mountains. I don't need you, bruv. You go home and stay safe with your grandma."

Instinctively, Marcus reached inside his hoodie for the bar, but he stopped himself and tried to control his anger. Four of Crazy B's boys also had their hands in their pockets and hoodies. All with weapons—most likely metal-based. He could take all of them out.

CHAPTER 18

He clenched his jaw. He knew he couldn't do that here. He'd have to sort Crazy B out another time.

Instead, he put his hands up. "Suit yourself."

"Come on, boys," Crazy B said. "Remember this day."

Marcus used all his strength to stay rooted to the ground and not take him out. He couldn't risk upsetting someone else.

Charlene was the last to turn away.

"I'll be in touch," she mouthed as she left with Crazy B.

As soon as they were out of sight, Marcus slumped against the wall, trying but failing to stop his uncontrollable sobs.

The next day, Marcus had made up his mind. They would see Charlene today, without the adults, and try to extract information from this being within her. Maybe it would drop some clues as to why it wanted Charlene. Then he'd know how to free her.

He stood outside of school with a boy from his last-period Spanish class, waiting for a second kid he had asked to hang out.

"How long is Dev going to be?" Marcus asked.

"He'll be here in a bit," Luke said.

Dev and Luke were the two he'd felt he could trust. They were like him; they kept themselves to themselves. They weren't interested in showing off.

He texted Neil to tell him where they were going to meet, and a second later, Dev walked over.

"All right, so here's what we're going to do," Marcus said. "I'll meet you over by the grocery store in an hour, yeah? Don't tell anyone where you're going. You get me?"

They both nodded.

"All right, in a bit."

They all bumped fists and left in their separate directions.

He texted Natalie next but paused at Sean. The kid was two years younger than the rest of them. He couldn't involve him, especially because Marcus didn't know how things were going to go down.

On his way home, he watched the streets as carefully as he could. Without Neil with him, there was no telling what might happen.

Once he was safe in his room, he got dressed and put a few metal items in his pocket. He really needed a crowbar of some sort. Or even a gun, though that was more unpredictable. His grandma would never forgive him if she found a gun in her house.

He walked back down the street, his hood up, looking everyone he passed in the eye. Not far ahead, he could see Dev and Luke where he'd asked to meet them.

"Who else we meeting then?" asked Dev when Marcus approached.

"Some really good guys. They'll have my back and yours. I literally just need you two to keep watch. I'll be in the house trying to sort out some business. Anything that happens out of the ordinary, just text me, yeah?"

"Why do you need us to wait outside though?" asked Luke. "Won't you need most of the manpower in the house?"

"I might have people following me," Marcus said, averting his gaze. "I just need some eyes on the street to make sure I can do what needs to be done."

Just then, Neil and Natalie approached.

"What's up, fam?" Marcus said, greeting them both. "This

is Dev and Luke. They'll be helping us out."

Natalie's face dropped. "You're joking."

"Look, we know what we're doing," Luke said. He had a lazy drawl to his London accent.

"Bruv, come here," Neil said, beckoning Marcus to the side. "You can't involve them boys. They don't know what they're getting into."

"It's fine. They'll be outside—make sure no one follows us. She won't even know they're there."

"This makes no sense." Neil shook his head.

"Neil, there's only three of us. I'm not involving Sean. They are going to stand just outside her gates so she won't know they're there. If I've got people trying to hit me, I've got to know."

"Wait, what?" Natalie said, looking at him. "Someone made a hit on you? Why?"

"Don't worry about it, man."

"I'm not going anywhere with you until you tell me why someone tried to get you."

"It's just my past. Look, we've got to stay focused, get to Charlene. You brought the hex, right?"

Natalie looked at him uncertainly. "Yeah."

"Did Amala see you take it?"

"I can walk through walls, remember?"

"Good. We'll return it as soon as we get back to the Gathering tonight. Whoever holds it needs to focus on deflecting her powers."

"Let's keep this small, Marcus. We don't want to get anyone else involved."

"What if I get jumped again, huh? Then what will happen to us? Do you think the giant man is going to come and help us again? He's going to let us fall. He warned us to do more, and that's what we're doing."

Natalie and Neil looked at each other.

"All right, bruv." Neil nodded. "Let's go"

"Good," Marcus said with as much authority as he could fake. "Trust me, we're going to help her. If not, we'll at least get more information."

He walked back over to Dev and Luke.

"Everything all right?" Dev asked.

"Yeah, everything's fine. Let's go."

They all headed down the road, Marcus using his phone's GPS to guide them to Charlene's home. Finally, they approached her large Victorian house and well-kept front garden, with a big bush that had been trimmed neatly.

"Right, you two, stay out here," Marcus said to Dev and Luke. "There were a couple of boys riding around on their bikes. One time it was a car, a big black one. Stay a bit out of sight so they won't know you're still here."

They both nodded. Dev crossed the road, while Luke walked a little farther down to a post box and waited there.

Marcus took a deep breath and ascended the steps to Charlene's house. He pushed the bell. All three peered through the living room window to see if anybody was coming.

"Marcus," Natalie said, nudging him.

He followed her gaze to the window upstairs. Charlene was looking down on them, but she disappeared into the darkness behind her.

"Think she's going to try and take our minds?" Natalie asked.

"Yep," Marcus said. "Stay close, Natalie. Don't step away

CHAPTER 18

from us, for no reason. The moment the hex gets too far away from us, that's it. She's got that person's mind."

The door opened, and Charlene's mum stood in front of them. "Hello," she said in a dreamy voice.

Marcus paused for a moment. She sounded the complete opposite of how she'd been in their last encounter. She sounded drained and seemed to look straight through them. "Um . . . hi. We're looking for Charlene. Is she in?"

"Yes, she's here. Would you like to come in?"

For a brief moment, Marcus wanted to say no. He felt underpowered, but he was here now, and there was no going back. He wanted to show some ounce of trust. "Yes, thanks."

The dreamy lady stepped back as all three went through the door, which shut behind them. The whole house felt cold and empty.

"She's just upstairs," the lady said, pointing to the blue-carpeted staircase. "She will be down in a moment."

Then she just stood there, motionless.

"So . . . are you Charlene's sister?" Neil asked, trying to make conversation.

A noise that sounded like a cough—or a laugh, Marcus wasn't sure—came out of her mouth. "I'm her mother," she said, placing a dainty hand on her chest. "Please, come into the living room."

Marcus preferred her mean streak. This woman was washed out.

They went into the living room and took a seat on the sofa, all of them perched on the edge.

"We have visitors?" a deep voice said from farther in the room. A tall man sat up slowly at the table, looking at them. All three jumped when they saw him.

"Yes, my love. They are here for Charlene. I will go get them some water to drink."

Charlene's mum drifted out of the room, and the man sluggishly went back to his work.

"Have you seen their eyes?" Natalie asked quietly.

"Yeah," said Neil. "They're tinted purple!"

"Look, we know what's going on," Marcus hissed. "Let's just keep our calm, yeah?"

"It's rude to whisper in a stranger's house."

There stood Charlene by the living room door, the same elfin face yet her beautiful eyes somehow distant—and purple.

"So good to see you." She smiled as she slid into one of the luxurious armchairs, her voice still deeper than usual. Her house was devoid of any feeling; even the once vibrant plants in her living room seemed to be wilting. "What can I do for you all?"

Her eyes shifted to each of them. Neil inched closer to Natalie.

"We just came to see how you are," Marcus said. "We haven't seen you in a while."

"I'm fine, just at home, as you can see."

"I tried to call you, but you didn't pick up."

"I've been busy."

"Doing what?"

"Oh, just planning to take over the world." She laughed, her mouth unnaturally wide, distorting her pretty features. "I'm just joking."

"Are you? You don't seem to be yourself lately."

"What do you care?" She looked directly at him, shifting her position to lean in closer.

"We're your friends," Natalie piped up. "Friends check on

CHAPTER 18

each other."

"Do they now? Well, then I'm going to need a lot more friends in the near future."

All three looked at one another as she moved to the armchair right next to Marcus. She must have realised her powers weren't working on them. Or was she even trying? He didn't know and didn't care to find out.

"What is it you want, Marcus? You're such a lonely person. No mother or father. Abandoned by his parents. I bet you just need someone to look after you."

It felt like a punch in the gut to hear those words. He should never have opened up to her. He balled up his fists, trying to swallow the ache that throbbed in his throat.

It isn't her. It's the monster, he told himself.

She leaned in and stroked his face. He tried not to flinch. He didn't want to show he was afraid, though he could feel the beads of sweat pricking his forehead and armpits.

"How about you, Natalie, the oldest of five?" Charlene said. "I wonder what your mum thinks about you leaving her instead of taking care of your younger siblings."

Natalie stiffened. "I do help. As long as I get all my chores done, I—"

Marcus put his hand on her arm, and she stopped talking.

Charlene grinned. "And you, Neil, I know you've always had feelings for me. You are so loyal to anyone who shows you any attention."

"What do you want, Charlene?" Marcus said before she could say any more.

"I can give you all what you need."

"What are you talking about?"

"This group is directionless, Marcus," she said softly. "It

has no purpose. You are collectibles to Leonard, Amala, and Ezra. Abeo is the only one who has any idea what is going on beneath the surface. I can give us all purpose and direction."

"Is this anything to do with the nightmares you've been having?"

Charlene smiled. "As you know, Marcus, I have a visitor—or friend, shall we say—who is offering to give us a little extra power and a little extra knowledge. She sees how important it is for us to be able to explore these gifts we have, how we could become like deities on earth. The world would be our oyster. We could have anything we wanted. Can you imagine that, Marcus?"

He looked at the other two. "This isn't you, Charlene. You're being used."

"How do you know this isn't the real me, unleashed? I can come and go as I please, as you can see. There is no one to stop me." She turned and looked at her parents, who were now both sitting at the table. "Imagine it just for a moment: Being unafraid of your abilities. All of us together working towards finding others like ourselves. Our own secret society, not controlled by people who are afraid of us. You know that, don't you? That they're afraid of us? They have no powers. Any control they have is what we choose to give them."

Marcus said nothing for a moment. He couldn't let seeds of doubt creep in now. "They brought us together for a reason," he finally said. "They told us something is coming, and we need to be prepared for it. What you're doing is distracting us."

"Is it?" Charlene sat back on the sofa. The purple in her eyes seemed to shift and swirl. "There *is* a war coming, but we need to be on the right side of it. One thing is for sure: this world won't be kind to us once they know we exist. *That's* what we need to prepare for. Protecting ourselves."

"But I thought we didn't want the world to know we exist," Neil piped up.

"We don't, not yet. When the time is right," Marcus cut in.

Charlene laughed again, flinging her head back. It seemed maniacal, a wildness that was the complete opposite of her usual natural elegance. "Your band of merry men wouldn't stand a chance. We have a different kind of knowledge from Leonard and the others, something that will truly give us the edge in the battle to come. You should choose the right side now, before you have no choice."

"Charlene, if you can hear me, try and break free," Marcus said to her. "We're here for you. We still want to help."

"She is happy to share her body with me. She will be rewarded handsomely for it too. Now, if you don't mind, it's time for you three to leave."

They all stood up as Charlene led the way to the door and opened it wide. The three of them shuffled out together, Marcus fighting to find the right words to say. At the bottom of the stairs, he saw Dev and Luke waiting. His eyes darted around for any sign that they'd spotted someone, but the streets appeared empty.

Then he saw their eyes.

He whipped back round to Charlene. "What are you doing? They have nothing to do with this!"

"They do, because you brought them here."

"Not for you! Let them go."

"Hmm . . . well, it seems maybe you do need our protection then, don't you? They stay here." She slammed the door.

Dev and Luke looked on as the three passed them by.

Marcus rounded the corner and rubbed his head, trying to make sense of everything.

"Now what are we going to do?" asked Neil.

"Is she just going to keep them there? Like guards?" Natalie asked, looking back at the two boys.

"We got some info. We know more than we did," Marcus said hopefully. "We know that Charlene really is possessed now and that thing is using her."

"We knew that before!" Natalie said impatiently. "I knew this wasn't a good idea. What are we going to tell Leonard and Amala?"

"Nothing yet," Marcus said, trying to sift through his thoughts. "We know that she hasn't started whatever war is going on, but she wants to be involved and on the winner's side. She wants us to be exposed to the world."

"But how does that help us now?" Neil asked.

"We have a few more pieces of the puzzle. That'll give us something to work with."

"We need to concentrate on getting Charlene back," Natalie said, the anger in her voice palpable.

"Not so fast," Marcus said. "Whoever that thing is in her has knowledge we don't. While she's in Charlene, we need to get as much info from her as possible."

"Are you saying we should leave her in there?"

"No, of course not! We need to find a way to get that thing out. I'm just saying that while we're working on that, we could also get some extra help. We need to think long term here."

"Marcus, I don't like the sound of this." Neil shook his head.

"I don't either," Marcus said grimly. "But let's face it, Neil. We don't know much about this fight with the gods, and neither do Leonard and that lot. How can we do anything if we don't get the knowledge to protect ourselves?"

"And how are we going to do that?" Natalie folded her arms and glared at Marcus. "Do you honestly think Charlene wants to see us again?"

"She will if she believes she's convinced us to join her side."

"You've lost your mind," Natalie said. "You want us to pretend to be on her side? Do you have any idea how dangerous that is? She could use our powers for anything! The amount of damage she could do with any of us . . ."

Marcus's eyes fell to the floor. She was right. They were too powerful. Metal was everywhere. Natalie's ability to walk through objects would give Charlene access to anything she wanted, and Neil's power to see into the future would propel her to change everything.

"There's one person . . . ," Neil said quietly.

Natalie stared at him. "No . . . he's too young."

"The kid needs to have a chance to prove himself," Marcus said.

"You don't have to do this." Natalie shook her head. "Marcus, don't get him involved. It's not right."

"Do you think I want this? Any of this?" Marcus said bitterly. "But how are we supposed to protect the future and everyone else unless we do this? She knows she'll never get me onside, or you two. It has to be him."

Natalie folded her arms. "Are you sure about that?"

"Come on, Natalie," Neil said.

"No, really. You're acting like a monster."

"You're out of line," Marcus said, his face beginning to burn with frustration. "I'm trying to make sure we do what's best for everyone. It's called being strategic."

"It sounds to me like you're trying to use people—both Sean

and Charlene. Were you just pretending to care for her all this time? Even Cassius never did that. They both knew what they had was just a fling."

Marcus felt his stomach drop.

"Look, I don't care what they did or didn't have," he exploded. "If any of us are going to survive this, we've got to be smart. Stop getting emotional and use your head. We're going to find out what this war is about, then we can save her!"

"Against the gods?" Natalie looked Marcus up and down. "You really think you or any of us really know how to go up against any of them? You're stupider than you look. I'm out of here."

She spun around and stalked off.

"Natalie, come back!" Neil shouted after her, but she ignored him.

"At least let us have the hex," Marcus called.

She threw it straight at his head, and he caught it an inch from his eye.

"Good luck returning that!" she shouted back.

Chapter 19

"Bro, what are we going to do now?"

Marcus stood there for a moment. Natalie had just walked away from him. No one had ever walked away from him like that, just brazenly turning their back on him. He felt himself turning to ice inside. If that was how she wanted it, then that was up to her.

"Let's go get Dev and Luke," he said.

They walked over to the two boys. As if a spell had been broken, the pair blinked and looked around wildly.

"Where am I?" asked Luke, dazed.

"Wake up, bruv," Marcus said, trying to be light-hearted. "You been asleep on the job? I asked you both to come with me, remember? Anyway, we're finished now. Let's go and get something to eat."

Neil walked up close to Marcus. "What are we going to do about Natalie?"

"If she doesn't want to be part of this, we can't force her."

"How are we going to put the hex back? How are we going to do this alone?"

"We have to, innit? We don't have a choice . . . There's always Sean. Text him and see if he's going to the Gathering today."

Neil got out his phone and started texting.

Marcus could hear Luke and Dev talking behind him.

"How long were we there for?"

"No idea, fam. I don't remember anything."

Marcus swallowed hard as they turned into the shops on the high street to get some food. He wasn't backing down, but it was clear to him there was no leadership in the Gathering. The adults were clueless, and Natalie couldn't handle tough decisions. Cassius was a liability. Charlene was the only one who could possibly have brought everyone together;, yet she had left them, and left him.

He was the only one staying true to the cause. He needed to be protected; Then in turn, he could protect everyone else. Maybe this was finally his turn to lead.

After eating and a bit of small talk, Luke and Dev went home.

"You heard back from Sean?" Marcus asked Neil.

"Yeah," said Neil. "He's not coming."

"What?" Marcus shot Neil a look. "Why?"

"He didn't say."

Marcus kissed his teeth. Next to Natalie, Sean was the best one to sneak something back. He was smaller, and his skill would enable him to hide in unusual places if needed. "Come on, let's go and see him. Do you know where he lives?"

Neil nodded.

"We're just going to ask him to put the hex back, that's all. I don't want him involved in anything else. Okay?"

"Sure," Neil replied. "But, Marcus, we need a plan."

"Don't you think I know that? I just need some time to

CHAPTER 19

think. Have you got any bright ideas?" Marcus's head began to throb.

"I think we should just tell Leonard and the other adults. They know more than we do."

"Yeah, and what have they done?" Marcus shot back.

"I don't know what they've done, because they haven't told us!"

"Exactly! We're trying to figure this all out by ourselves." Marcus began to pace, trying to think more clearly. "They're keeping us in the dark."

"Maybe we just need to lay it all out for them. Maybe they'll tell us once they know how much we've pieced together."

"Look, I don't know why they're not telling us everything." Marcus was exasperated. "Maybe it's because they realise we have more power than they do and we're the only ones who can make things happen."

"You reckon they really are afraid of us?" Neil's voice was tinted with disappointment.

"I don't know," Marcus said sombrely. Charlene's words were going around his head. He couldn't quiet them down. Were the Ebuns being constrained? None of them had been consulted about how to construct this group. They'd had no say about rules and what they could or couldn't do.

No. They had all been *told* what to do, brought together with a supposed agenda. Maybe they did need to speak to Leonard. Somehow, they needed to clear the air, but Marcus wanted to be ready when they did have that conversation.

They reached Sean's block of flats. Seeing it gave Marcus flashbacks of his own time in the block of flats with his cousins. He wondered how they were. If they remembered him at all. If they hated their new life now without him. Or if, even worse, they preferred it.

Neil went to the ground floor and knocked on an old brown door. A few moments later, a bedraggled man with pale skin and the beginnings of a beard opened it.

"Yeah?" he said, looking the boys up and down.

"Umm . . . is Sean in?" Neil asked.

"Sean!" the man yelled, not taking his eyes off Neil. "There's someone at the door for ya. Don't be long."

Sean walked heavily to the door, his head bowed. A shiny purple bruise disfigured his eye.

"What the?" Marcus gasped. "What happened to you?"

"I was being clumsy," Sean mumbled.

"He did this, didn't he?"

"It was my fault. Don't worry."

Rage enveloped Marcus and he lunged forward, but a strong arm kept him back. Neil held him tight, his eyes glowing white. He was stiff yet strong. Slowly, his pupils came back.

"Are you all right?" Marcus asked Sean, trying to regain his composure. He shrugged Neil's arm off.

Sean nodded. "It's not worth it," he mumbled. "It's not that bad."

"Do you want to come out with us? I'll buy you some dinner."

"Not allowed."

Marcus couldn't believe this. He tried to peer into the living room, where he guessed the scumbag was. He bent down close to Sean. "I'm going to sort this, yeah? Be tough, little man."

Sean nodded.

"We've got to run, but we'll catch you later, okay?" Marcus said, guilt punching him in the stomach.

"Be strong, yeah?" Neil said to Sean as they walked away.

CHAPTER 19

Once they were far from the flat, Marcus blurted out, "I should've asked him to come earlier. He wouldn't have gotten beaten."

"You don't know that," Neil said. "I bet this isn't the first time."

Marcus shook his head. Things were slipping through his fingers, and he could feel an energy rising up inside him, a fire that hadn't been there before. "Can you check ahead, make sure everything is clear?"

Neil turned towards him so no one could see.

"We're going to need you to get some sunglasses, man," Marcus muttered.

Soon, Neil's pupils came back. "We're good for the next twenty."

"Okay, let's head back."

Despite Neil's assurances, Marcus felt a sense of foreboding as they walked to the park. They tried to make small talk, but it was awkward. The Gathering had started off with six gifted people. Now one was in confinement, and three others weren't attending today. Only two were left functioning and working towards the cause.

Was it worth it? What was he saving exactly? Marcus didn't even know. He barely noticed as they entered the fog, his mind heavy as Neil unlocked the secret door. The cracks of light appeared around the lock, as if the air itself were breaking, and then the portal opened and they stepped through.

They entered the house a short while afterwards. It seemed eerily quiet.

"Let's just get this done," Marcus said quietly. "Let's find out who's here."

They headed towards the library and poked their heads in. No one. But when Marcus pulled his head from behind the door, he nearly collided with Abeo.

"Hello, boys." The old man smiled.

Marcus tried to hide the shock on his face.

"I'm sorry to have frightened you. You seem on edge."

"Nah, we're good." Marcus took a deep breath, trying to steady his nerves.

"Are you sure?"

"Yeah, you just surprised me."

"Unfortunately I have been summoned back to Nigeria early," Abeo said, "so I must leave today, but I wanted to see you all first. What time is everyone else getting here?"

Neil and Marcus looked at each other.

"It's just us," Neil replied.

Abeo slowly looked at each of them. "Has there been some falling out?"

"Maybe," Marcus conceded.

"I know it is not easy to be a teenager, especially with the talents you have. But you have to find a way to get along. Stay together at all costs. Not just the two of you, but all of you. You will be easily overcome if you are fractured."

Marcus's heart felt heavy. He had never managed to keep anything together. In fact, things were supposed to fall apart around him.

"Don't give up on yourself," Abeo said, touching his shoulder. "You have an important mission here. You are the only one who can bring everyone together."

"I didn't do that. That was Leonard and Amala."

"They will never be enough to hold everyone together. They will not even be with you for the whole of this journey."

CHAPTER 19

"Where are they going?" Neil asked, looking worried.

"You both have hard decisions to make, but whatever you do, make sure it is in the best interests of *all* of you."

"I don't know how to do what you're asking me," Marcus said. Abeo's words felt like a weight around his neck.

"I will send you help, Marcus. There will be a promise of some marvellous things in the future, to equip you for the war that is coming—a war this world hasn't seen in a long time. But this can only happen if you hold this fort. If you prepare the way."

Abeo turned to Neil. "Neil, remember who you are. Remember that even the most loyal can stumble if they are not watchful." He seemed to look off behind them, as if he'd heard a noise. "It has been a pleasure getting to know you all."

Marcus nodded. "You too. Are you going to see Cassius?"

Abeo avoided his gaze. "Cassius is stable for now and will continue to be so, if he so chooses. You all have extra abilities, and I don't know how that will interfere with the help I've given him. Ultimately, it will be up to him."

Neil and Marcus nodded.

"Goodbye, sir," they both said.

As they began to walk away, Abeo grabbed Marcus by the arm and leaned in close to his ear. "The gods are watching you, Marcus. Tread carefully."

After a final glance, Abeo let go and walked off.

Marcus hurried to catch up with Neil. What had Abeo meant by that? He swallowed and pushed down the fear creeping into his stomach.

Why were the gods watching him? What kind of help was Abeo referring to? None of this made any sense. He had always been the outcast. At the Gathering, at least, he'd thought he could be like everyone else, but even that wouldn't be the case. He would be held to a different standard. At first glance, that seemed like a good thing. He'd wanted to be a leader, but that was before every corner of the world had decided to turn on him or take him out.

The two boys approached Amala's door, looked around briefly, and then stepped inside.

"Quick, bruv, do you know where Natalie got it from?" Neil asked.

"No, I didn't ask," Marcus muttered.

No surface looked as if it had been home to this crystal. The room was completely dust free. Marcus opened Amala's desk drawers before looking over to a wardrobe in a dark corner of the room.

Something flickered at the edge of Marcus's vision, and he spun round.

Shadows seemed to swirl in the corner of the room, completely detached from anything, like inky spirits scuttling across the walls. Marcus froze, but he knew he had to put the crystal back. He tore his eyes away from the shifting shapes to find a cupboard slightly ajar. As he moved closer, he could see a row of beautiful stones inside, with an empty space ready for the one he had. He put the stone in line with the others and shut the cabinet.

With a sigh of relief, Marcus prepared to sprint out of the haunted room.

"Got what you needed, did you?" a sharp voice said from behind.

Marcus spun around to see Ezra standing in the opposite corner. "Umm . . . I found this on the floor and picked it up to put it back . . . How did you . . . ?"

CHAPTER 19

He knew Ezra hadn't been there before, so how did he get there?

"There are many doors in this house. I simply used one you didn't know was there."

Sure enough, behind Ezra was another door, dark and faded, barely visible to the naked eye.

"What were you doing with those crystals?" Ezra asked.

"Look, I'm just putting it back."

"You must think me a fool, Marcus." The man sneered. "You may be able to charm your way out of trouble with the others, but not with me."

"I swear I didn't come to take it."

"Maybe not, but you certainly had it in your possession." Ezra brushed past him to get a closer look at the exact gem Marcus had put back. "These are very powerful, Marcus! Did you go anywhere near Cassius with this?"

He thinks it was for Cassius, Marcus realised. "No."

"Don't lie to me, boy! These gems can be used in many ways, but first you have to know what you're doing. Why would you pick up a deflection crystal if not to get closer to Cassius?"

Marcus tried to think fast on his feet, but his mind was blank for a moment too long.

"Don't try to take matters into your own hands," Ezra said. "You don't know what you're dealing with."

"Do you?" Marcus asked. "Do you know what they're seeing when they close their eyes at night? Charlene told me about coming to you guys for help, and you failed her. Not me."

Ezra's eyes squinted, scanning every inch of Marcus's face. "Did you go and see her?" His face suddenly contorted. "You went to see her! You stupid boy! We were setting things up. We were going to take that crystal to add to the strengths we had already amassed. Now she will know that we are coming and what we will use. We won't be able to take her by surprise!"

Marcus's stomach sank. Had he really messed things up for them?

"Get out of my sight, you idiot! All this planning for nothing. Who knows what she's going to do now?"

Marcus stepped around him and left the room. Neil was waiting outside.

"Was Ezra in there?" Neil panicked. "Yo, how did you not see him?"

"There's a secret door. Can you believe it?" Marcus said more to himself than to Neil.

"What? Bruv, we need to get to know this place better."

"You're telling me," Marcus said as they both headed down the hall. "This opens up whole other issues. They could be spying on us, and we wouldn't even know. Sliding in and out of rooms, and we'd have no idea."

"What was he saying to you in there?"

"He said they had some plans. He reckons we've messed them up."

"Why, what were they going to do?"

"I'm not sure exactly, but we can't worry about that now. We need to see if we can figure out who this war is going to be between. We can't go back to Charlene. We need to see what Cassius knows."

"You're just going to walk in there?" Neil looked scared.

"What choice do we have? We need something!"

They approached Cassius's door.

"I just need ten minutes," Marcus said. "Do I have that?"

Neil paused for a moment, as if searching for clues in

CHAPTER 19

Marcus's eyes, and then his own eyes became pale. His pupils returned to normal after a minute. "It's a bit unclear past ten minutes, but you've got until then."

Marcus knocked on the door.

"Come in," Cassius said.

Marcus walked in with Neil right at his shoulder.

"So, Marcus, Neil?" Cassius lay back on the sofa, his legs stretched over the cushions and his hands behind his neck. "What can I do you two for?"

Marcus sat down at the opposite table. "We don't want no trouble. Just wondered if you could help us out."

Cassius grinned. "Now, why would I want to do that?"

"Because it involves Charlene."

His smile faltered. "I'm listening."

"We want to know what this war with the gods is about." Marcus leaned back in his chair. "We know that . . . thing was inside you. She said she knew about the coming war and that we could be on the winning side. What did she tell you about that?"

Cassius went silent, his hands on his lap as he looked off into the distance. "I don't recall much about that"—he rubbed his forehead—"other than Olukan's being unhappy and that another god was making the others nervous and uncomfortable. There were never any other specifics."

"So this thing that was in you, she wasn't one of them?"

"No. She said her time hadn't come yet. She had something she wanted to do here first. To get things ready."

"Ready for the war," Marcus finished. "What exactly?"

"She wanted us mobilised."

"We were doing that anyway. What's that got to do with her?"

"Because she said she was one of us."

"How? I mean, she's dead."

"I don't know. I just know she was in my head and those are the bits I made out."

Marcus thought for a moment. Why was she claiming to be one of them? Was she a teenager? Was her body trapped somewhere else and her spirit was inhabiting another? Who could he ask to help figure all this out?

He nodded slowly. "How are you doing?"

"Like you care," Cassius retorted.

"Look, for what it's worth, I don't hate you. I want you to get better, bruv. We can work out all of this together, maybe figure out what's really going on."

Cassius paused for a moment, looking at his hands. "I think we both know that's not going to happen."

"All right." Marcus stood up and headed for the door. "You don't have to be a prisoner to her, you know. You can choose to be free."

Then he and Neil walked out.

"What a waste of time." Neil heaved a sigh as they exited the Gathering.

Neil and Marcus walked through the park, heading home. Marcus felt cold, inside and out. He felt as if he had nowhere to turn. He needed to go home, lie down, and have a think.

"At least he agreed to see you and didn't kill you in the process." Neil smiled.

"Yeah, look, I'm going to take a couple of days off. This whole thing is stressing me out, man." Not one to admit he was tired, Marcus felt as if he'd been hit by a truck; every part of his body ached, and his eyes wanted to close.

"You all right?" Neil sounded concerned.

"Yeah, it's just been intense, you know?" All he wanted to do was sleep. The feeling was overwhelming.

"I know what you mean." Neil nodded.

"Could you check for me?"

Neil's eyes went white, and then he told Marcus he was good for the next twenty minutes.

"All right, keep safe, yeah?" Marcus said, bumping Neil's fist.

"I will, and keep out of danger!"

They smiled as Marcus headed off down the road.

Too tired to run, he walked as quickly as his legs would allow. He couldn't recall the last good night's sleep he'd had. His thoughts were becoming a jumbled mess of gods and spirits, betrayers and friends. He'd never wanted to see his cousins so badly. He wondered if he could give them a call and decided to talk to Grandma Maisey about organising that.

He desperately wanted things to work out. There were so many loose ends in his life; clearly, he had dropped the ball. He wanted to save Charlene, despite her callousness towards him. He needed more resources to cover his back without Dacus. He still didn't know who'd looted Dacus's hideout; he hoped it had nothing to do with him.

Maybe he could do some recruiting. If Leonard could find gifted Ebun kids, then so could he. Plus, he'd know if they were truly trustworthy, if they had what it took to really defend and protect the Gathering.

Leonard and Amala—what were they going to do with him once Ezra told them he had ruined their plans? Throw him out? Unlikely, he concluded. They hadn't thrown Cassius out yet, and look at the havoc he had caused. They were even trying to rescue Charlene.

Marcus kept walking, his body getting more and more tired.

When he got to the front door of his house, he put the key in the door without even checking to see if anybody might be watching.

"Marcus, is that you?" called Grandma Maisey.

"Yes, Grandma," he replied. He walked into the living room to find her lying on the couch, her arm draped over her eyes.

"You okay, Grandma?" he asked.

"Yes . . . I just have a headache." Her Jamaican voice sounded quiet and sluggish. "Could you get me some of the painkillers, dear?"

Marcus quickly went to get her the tablet and a glass of water.

"How was your day?" she said, taking the medication.

"Busy." He sat down heavily in the armchair opposite.

"You look tired."

"So tired."

"Why don't you go up and lie down? I'll make dinner in a bit and call you when it's done."

"Nah, it's okay, Grandma. I'll call for takeout. You keep your feet up, and we'll have some breaded chicken for dinner."

"Okay, and make sure you order it from the shop on Evans Road, not the other one. Their chicken is always so oily!"

"Yes, Grandma." He smiled, pecking her on the cheek before he went upstairs.

Within minutes, he'd crashed and fallen asleep on the bed.

Chapter 20

A loud smash startled Marcus out of a dead sleep. Panic signals raced through every nerve.

He sat up, eyes darting around the room, before he realised it must have come from downstairs. He got up quickly and headed towards the staircase.

"Grandma?" he said, moving into the kitchen.

She was on the floor, slumped against the cabinets.

"Grandma!" He rushed to her side.

"Marcus," she said, gripping her chest. "I don't feel so well . . . faint . . ."

"Hold on!" He dashed out of the room to the landline phone and punched in the number for the ambulance. While he gave them the details, he kept peering through the door to check on his grandma.

He rang off as quickly as he could and went to sit with her. "How are you?"

She moaned gently as he held her free hand. What had happened while he was asleep? Had she had a heart attack? Fear rushed through his body as he tried to think about what to do. His phone was upstairs. He could think of only one person who might be able to help.

"I'll be right back," Marcus said before dashing up the stairs. He quickly found Amala's number and called her.

"Amala, I need your help," he blurted out as he made his way back to the kitchen. "It's Grandma. She's holding her chest and lying on the floor. I don't know what to do."

"I'll be right there," Amala said and rang off immediately.

Marcus quickly returned to Grandma Maisey. He started to scroll the internet for heart attacks. Noticing she was beginning to sweat, he grabbed a cloth and dabbed her forehead. She needed to get to the hospital. This was far beyond anything he could cope with. He was finding it hard to breathe.

Within ten minutes, Amala was knocking at the door.

"Don't panic," she said, dashing inside. "The ambulance will be here any minute."

Opening her bag, she yanked out a stethoscope and checked Grandma Maisey's heart rate, pulse, and blood pressure.

"Is that you . . . 'Mala?" his grandma uttered through laboured breathing.

"Yes, my dear friend," Amala said, smiling. Grandma Maisey's eyes closed slightly, and she grimaced.

"I don't have time to do a full diagnostic. I will give her this." Amala pulled out a small vial with light green liquid.

"What is that?" Marcus asked, his voice strained.

"This is a blood thinner. If she is having a heart attack, this will help, and it works faster than aspirin."

"Wait!" Marcus said. "What will happen when she takes it? How do I know I can trust it?"

"It's okay, Marcus." Amala's voice immediately softened. "You can trust me."

Marcus nodded, still reluctant.

CHAPTER 20

Parting Grandma Maisey's lips, Amala poured the liquid in just as there was a knock at the door. She quickly slipped the empty vial into her pocket as Marcus leapt up to let the paramedics in. They surrounded his grandma, hooking her up to beeping monitors and IVs.

"You go with her," said Amala. "I'll take care of things here."

Marcus had hardly noticed the broken glass and liquid sauce all over the floor.

He jumped into the ambulance, and in a matter of minutes, they arrived at the hospital. The next few hours passed in a blur after the doctors' tests showed signs of a heart attack. He sat by his grandma's bedside as she floated in and out of consciousness.

Before he knew it, it was three in the morning, and his head was heavy and throbbing. He needed some painkillers himself. He held on to his grandma, begging any god he'd read about lately to not take the last person he had. The whole evening had been a flurry of doctors and nurses, blood tests and scans. This was the last place he felt at home and welcome.

The doctor came in and checked her chart before glancing over at Marcus. "Would you like us to call anyone?"

His mind flitted to his aunt and cousins. How would they react to this? His aunt would probably think he had caused his grandma too much stress, that he was too troublesome for the family. Maybe she'd even try to put him in care . . . He at least needed more time before he told them.

"There's no one to call," Marcus said flatly.

"How about your guardian?"

"She is my guardian." Marcus didn't take his eyes off of his grandma's sleeping form. "Is she going to be okay?"

"The initial signs look good. We will run some diagnostics

in the morning to determine the damage. If things go well, she should be out in about a week."

A week, thought Marcus. *Anything could happen in that time. She must be pretty sick still. What am I going to do?*

Almost on cue, Amala sent him a text.

Amala: *How is she?*

The doctor slunk away with hardly a sound.

Marcus: *Stable. They will run tests in the morning.*

Amala: *Good, I will come in the morning. Get some rest.*

Marcus put his phone in his pocket. He felt drained. Why could he never catch a break? He laid his head down on the side of the bed, next to his grandma, and allowed himself to succumb to the exhaustion.

When he woke up, he figured the noises behind the door must mean breakfast would be served soon. Stretching his legs and arms, he looked at his grandma. She stirred at his movements.

"You all right, Grandma?"

Her eyes opened, and she looked around. "Ahh . . . so it wasn't a bad dream then." She sighed weakly.

"No, sorry. How are you feeling?"

"Rough. My chest feels so heavy."

"Well, we're at the hospital now. They'll take good care of you."

She rolled her eyes. "We'll see about that."

"I'll make sure they do."

"Are you okay, my boy?"

Marcus had to fight back the tears that threatened to come to his eyes. He swallowed hard. "I'm good. Just want you to get better soon."

She patted his hand. "I'm sorry about this. I wanted you to

have some stability living with me. Now this happens. You must be being prepared for something glorious."

"What do you mean?"

"Those who earn the most respect are the ones who overcome immense suffering and challenges. You will be one of those who will have to fight for everything he has."

Marcus nodded, saying nothing.

"I pray you will be able to see how great you could become, despite what has happened to you."

Marcus smiled at her praise. "This isn't goodbye, Grandma. We don't need a eulogy."

"Maybe not, but I'd rather say this while I still can."

There was a quick knock at the door.

"Breakfast?" called the nurse loudly, breaking the tranquillity and safety of the room.

"What do you have, darling?" Grandma Maisey asked. But after the nurse rattled off what was available, his grandma screwed up her face. "Oh no, none of that."

Marcus managed to persuade her to have some porridge, which she ate a small amount of. Looking at the time, he wanted to go home. He didn't want to be there when Amala arrived. He didn't want to have her breathing down his neck if she'd spoken to Ezra.

"Grandma, I'm going to go and get cleaned up. I'll be back in a couple of hours, yeah?"

"What about school?"

"Don't worry about that." He rolled his eyes. "I'm not going to fail because I missed one day of school."

"I don't want you to get left behind," she said weakly.

I'm always left behind, he thought. "I'll call them, Grandma. I'll be back soon, yeah?"

Giving her a kiss on the cheek, he got himself up and left the hospital room.

He hated the disinfectant smell of hospitals, which hit him hard once he got into the corridor. He walked to the entrance, taking shallow breaths, then inhaled deeply after he got outside. Putting his hood up, he began to walk home. He took his phone out and began to search for his school's number.

The phone started ringing, and he pulled up his jumper around his face, then removed it when someone answered. "Hi, yeah, this is Marcus Edwards? Yeah, I can't come into school today. My grandma is in the hospital."

A familiar black car drove past him slowly as he walked along the pavement.

"St. Anthony's Hospital," he said, watching as the car began to slow down. "Yeah, they think she had a heart attack last night."

The blacked-out windows of the vehicle rolled down, and a head in a black balaclava stuck out of the window.

When guns emerged, Marcus's whole body became cold.

At the sound of the first pop, Marcus dropped his phone and swung his right arm to the left. His hands burned. The car launched into the air, crashing into the shop in front of him.

He spun round as another black car pulled up, their windows already rolled down. The popping of guns rang in his ears as he thrust both hands forward, pushing the car back into traffic.

He began to run like he'd never run in his life. It wasn't until after he'd sprinted a few blocks that he considered he might have stopped the bullets. But there was no way he could have

CHAPTER 20

stopped all of them. Two cars full of gang members could have been ten people.

His legs propelled him forward, his arms hurting as they moved forward and backward. He couldn't think about turning around. That would slow him down. Instead, he bobbed and weaved around cars in the road to make following him difficult. One car came hurtling towards him, and a slight push to the side gave him a hairsbreadth of room to run through.

He couldn't hear any more shots after a few minutes of running at full pelt. He slowed down to a jog and eventually found himself near the park of the Gathering. He hesitated, not wanting to go inside. What if he led the gang to the Gathering? But he was feeling faint and sweaty, and every muscle in his body screamed in pain. He had no choice.

Only then did he look down at his throbbing arm to see his sleeve was soaking wet. Deep red, rich blood dripped from his hand on to the grey pavement.

Gritting his teeth and swallowing rising panic, he cradled his right arm and walked as fast as he could manage to the Gathering house.

"You're lucky you got here when you did," Leonard said, looking down at him as Marcus lay on a medical bed.

Marcus grimaced as Leonard applied pressure to his wound. The man had already taken the bullet out. "One of my many talents," he'd said.

"How come you know how to treat a bullet wound?" Marcus asked. "You don't look the type. Were you a doctor?"

"I've had medical training. I used to be in the army a long

time ago."

"No way!"

"Yeah, it was a lifetime ago."

"Where did you serve?" Marcus was curious at this turn of events.

"A few places . . . Kosovo being one."

Marcus didn't know anything about Kosovo, but apparently, he'd underestimated Leonard. The man knew what it was to fight and earn respect. "Do you miss it?"

"Now and then," Leonard said, handing him a goblet. "Here, drink this."

Marcus peered inside to see a thick purple solution. He wrinkled his nose.

"It'll take the edge off the pain." Leonard smiled, sitting opposite Marcus. "Look, I think we need to start again. I trust you, Marcus. You've had it hard, and trouble seems to follow you. But we need to find a way to rise above that."

"I don't go looking for it," Marcus blurted out. "It just seems to find me."

"Why do you think that is?" Leonard asked.

"There's too much chaos in my life, so I do what needs to be done to keep myself safe and organise other people. No one else can lead the way I do. I make the tough calls to keep everyone safe."

Leonard sighed. "Pushing people away won't help you, Marcus."

"I'm not pushing anyone away." Marcus was puzzled.

"So where's Natalie? Hmm? She told me she doesn't want to come back as long as you're here."

Marcus was silent and kept his eyes on the ground.

"Said you're reckless, that you're going to get someone hurt,"

CHAPTER 20

Leonard tried again.

"She thinks I'm an idiot and that I don't know what I'm doing." Marcus dared to look at Leonard as he said that.

"You've become irritable."

"I'm not sleeping well."

"Marcus, you're under a lot of stress. Two of your clubmates have become possessed by an evil spirit, your grandma had a heart attack, and now you just got shot by some gang members. Look, let us help you. We'll deal with one thing at a time. You stay here while your grandma recuperates."

"With Cassius? Nah." Marcus scoffed.

"It's a big place. You won't have to see him. Plus, Amala stays here if someone is living here, so you wouldn't be alone. She'll take good care of you. She and your grandma go way back."

"I'll think about it." There was no way he'd consider it.

"We need to deal with Charlene." Leonard's tone became sad. "The more time that goes by, the more powerful she will become. We need to fix this today, no more delays."

"But I thought I'd ruined your plans?" Marcus couldn't stop the feeling of hope springing up within him.

"We'll adjust," Leonard said, his voice clipped. "We'll get the others on board."

"How?" Marcus feared he'd done too much damage.

"Leave that to me. Your diplomacy skills still need work."

Marcus smiled to himself. Who would've thought his diplomacy skills would need work? He'd brought gangs together before. Lately, nothing had worked, and he'd been getting deeper and deeper into trouble.

His head suddenly felt heavy, and he bobbed forward as he started to fall asleep.

"That solution is working then." Leonard smiled as he stood up and walked towards the door. "Get some rest. You'll start to feel better in a few hours."

Marcus lay down on the bed and closed his eyes, submitting to overwhelming sleep.

Chapter 21

An abrupt knock at the door shocked Marcus out of his deep slumber. His eyes flew open, his body rigid as his gaze darted around the room.

"Come in," he croaked. Gripping his metal keys in one hand, he rubbed his eyes with the other.

Sean poked his head round the corner.

Marcus sighed, releasing his grip on the metal. "Hey, big man." He tried to lift himself up on the bed. "What are you doing here?"

"Came to see you." Sean smiled and walked in. "You okay? Leonard told me you had an accident."

"Yeah." Marcus nodded. "But don't worry about me. How's your face?"

"It's feeling a bit better. Leonard gave me this purple drink, and it's starting to tingle."

"Now it just looks like someone threw mud in your eye."

Sean laughed. "Bruises look ugly while they're healing, at least that's what Leonard told me."

"Look, Sean," Marcus said seriously. "I meant what I said about looking out for you."

"Yeah . . ." Sean nodded, avoiding his eyes. "Leonard said

he'd take care of that. You should've seen the look on his face when he saw me . . . I just don't want to go into care, you know? End up like Cassius."

Marcus put his hand on Sean's shoulder. "You're nothing like him. Don't even worry about it." Fear gripped his chest as the memory of his grandma pierced his thoughts. "Can you pass me my phone?" His shoulder felt like lead, but it wasn't hurting at least.

Sean grabbed his phone from the other side of the room and handed it to him. Marcus was shocked to see he'd been asleep for hours and not minutes.

"I've got to go." He sat up straight and swung his legs over the side of the bed. His head was swimming.

"Where are you going?"

"My grandma's in the hospital. I need to go and see her." Marcus stood up and waited for his head to clear. "I promised . . . She's there all by herself."

Almost on cue, Leonard knocked on the door and came in.

"You're standing up." Leonard looked pleased. "How's that arm feeling?"

"Better, thanks."

"Good. Now, where are you going?"

"I've got to go back to the hospital."

"You've got to stay and rest." Leonard shook his head, trying to usher Marcus back to bed. "You need to be well for tonight."

"Tonight?" Sean asked.

"We're going to sort out Charlene's problem."

Sean looked back at Leonard and nodded. "Whatever I can do to help."

"I need to go and see my grandma," Marcus persisted. "I'm all she has left." *She's all I have left*, he thought.

CHAPTER 21

Leonard paused, looking at him for a while. "Here's what we'll do," he said, unfolding his arms. "I'll take you there myself in my car. But first, I want you to wait for the others to get here. That way you're safe off the streets. If anything goes wrong, you'll have them with you. Deal?"

"Deal," Marcus said. "What time are the others getting here?"

"In about an hour. But, Marcus, if we're going to pull this off tonight, I need you to listen carefully. We are still going to use the hex gem. I'm not sure who's going to hold it, but whatever the case, you need to be an integral part of this. Amala and I are going to see how much the spirit can be reasoned with and how much she knows about this upcoming war. Once we've gotten all the information we can get, we will place hexes around the house. That way, anyone outside the house won't be influenced by Charlene's ability. Sean and Natalie will be there, as well as Neil. If anything goes wrong, Neil will see it, and Natalie can run in and tell us."

A thought gnawed away at Marcus's confidence. He knew he had to voice it now. "Leonard, one thing I don't get." He struggled to find the words. "Is . . . why is that thing in Charlene? Is it just sitting there? What does it want with her?"

"This creature doesn't have its own body." Leonard sat on the bed next to Marcus. "In order for it to have influence in the world, it needs to work through her."

"Yeah, but that doesn't explain what she's actually doing," Marcus said.

"She's gathering her own army of Ebuns."

Marcus's blood went cold. "What? But how?

"We think she made contact with at least one other

Ebun—an animal shifter—while she inhabited Cassius."

Sean and Marcus looked at each other, stunned.

"What kind of animal?" Marcus asked.

Leonard sighed. "A werewolf."

"Of course," laughed Marcus. As if the scenario wasn't crazy enough already.

"Chances are he is going to be there tonight. We're going to need your fighting skills, Marcus. Make sure you have metal at your disposal. She is going to be very hard to beat, but we're going to need your protection if she sets him on us."

"What makes you think I can fight?" Marcus asked.

"Your grandma has mentioned to Amala you've been involved in a couple of run-ins. I can put two and two together."

Marcus nodded. There was really no comeback to that.

"We're going to run you through everything now," Leonard went on. "Only you will know the full story apart from us."

"What about me?" Sean asked.

"Sean, if that being finds a way to connect to you or your mind, she will know everything. Now, as far as we know, she can't read someone's thoughts unless she's inhabiting that person's body. We're hoping that's the case. We will still need to use that hex, which she has already been exposed to. Unfortunately, she will be expecting that, but it's one of the most powerful things we own here. We would be remiss not to use it."

"But that's not going to be enough," Marcus agreed.

"No, it's not. Sean, when we get to her house, you will be outside with the others. Any errand they need you to do, you must do. If we fail, you alone will have to escape and come back here to find Ezra."

"Is he not coming?" Marcus asked.

CHAPTER 21

"His strengths lie elsewhere. But the point is, one of us has to survive in order to find other Ebuns."

"You mean I could be the last one?" Sean asked, his eyes wide with concern.

"Don't let this scare you," Marcus said. "I'm going to make sure we all get out of this."

Sean smiled nervously.

"Sean, while I give Marcus some more details, I need you to go and find Ezra," Leonard said. "He's got something important to give you."

Sean nodded, looked back at Marcus with a smile, and left the room.

When the door clicked shut, Leonard turned back to Marcus. "She will be expecting us. Maybe not tonight but soon. That spirit knows something about this war between the Orisha that we do not, and she is trying to place herself in a desirable position. Make no mistake, she is a smart being. She is playing with a lot more knowledge than we have at the moment. We are on the back foot."

"Why don't we delay it?" Marcus swallowed, unable to believe he was really saying these words. How could they defeat something like this? "Maybe with more time we could get more information about what's really going on?"

Leonard sighed, seemingly unperturbed by what Marcus had just said. "We . . . deliberated that. Some believed it would be more useful."

Marcus could guess which of them he was referring to.

"Ultimately, we all realised that the psychological damage this could do to Charlene in the long run would be insurmountable. Cassius will probably never quite be the same as he was."

"You mean he was nice and stable beforehand?"

Leonard smirked before becoming sombre. "This being is dangerous, Marcus. She's already gathering her own army. She's found at least one, and a pretty deadly one at that."

Marcus nodded. "I'm surprised Abeo went back and left us. We could have used his experience."

"Amala will be sufficient. I trust her and her judgment. Neil will be waiting outside to foretell the future. He will inform us right up until we enter the house what will happen in the next twenty minutes. Natalie will be outside with him. If anything changes, she will run through the house to tell us."

"Is the future already written?" Marcus asked, trying to take the edge off his fear. "Will he be able to tell us what to do and what not to do?"

"In a way. The future can change. Unlikely things do happen, and all he can see is what is likely to happen judging by the current trajectory of those he is with. He has a very special skill, but it's not infallible."

Marcus sat up straight. "So why do I get to know everything? Why not Natalie? You've known her longer. Isn't she more trustworthy?"

Leonard's voice became quiet. "You claim Ogun came to you."

"He did," Marcus said, holding his voice steady. "At least . . . that's who he said he was. Why didn't he berate Natalie since you guys knew her longer?"

"It's because you bear his gifts, of steel and leadership. Yes, you've been a bit conniving since you got here. I'm not going to deny that. But those are leadership skills. You're able to corral people around you and give others confidence."

"Some might see that as manipulation."

CHAPTER 21

"Sometimes it is. Look, some people are more likely than others to rise to the top. Natalie is a good counterbalance. Every good leader needs that. She will always hold you accountable and up to a high standard. Otherwise, you'd become a dictator."

They both chuckled, a welcome reprieve from the growing tension in the room.

"Me, the dictator . . ." Marcus sighed. The stab of pain he suddenly felt in his stomach was not physical. He knew he had a controlling nature bubbling beneath the surface.

"Or a force of strength and stability," Leonard said. "Cassius and hopefully Charlene will pull through this, but they're going to bear the scars of tonight. They may never be the same. You will need to find a way to pull all of this together."

"Why is this down to me?" Frustration built up inside of Marcus. "What are you adults doing?"

"We don't have the capabilities you do. We will never be fully accepted by some of you, which is understandable. I think our only role in this is to bring you all together."

Marcus knew Leonard was right. The more Ebuns that joined, the more conflict would ensue once Amala's and Leonard's limits were reached. He was needed to keep balance and to set the example.

This was where he was meant to be and who he was meant to lead.

Leonard stood up. "Putting hexes around the house will prevent Charlene from using her magic, and it will stop the being within her from leaving the house. Once she is confined, we will perform the banishment spell. It will thrust the spirit back to where she came from."

"Where did she come from?"

"Because we're not sure who she is, it's hard to know."

"She said she's one of us."

Leonard stiffened, and time seemed to stand still. Marcus swallowed, unease creeping in.

"What do you mean 'one of us'?" Leonard asked.

"An Ebun," Marcus responded. "At least, that's what she told Cassius."

"Hmm . . . we'll need to find out more about that."

"Don't you know who all the Ebun were?"

"It's been a long time since the last generation of Ebun appeared, over twenty years."

"Where are they?"

"We only know where two of them are. We aren't sure where the last one is."

"Will they come to see us? Do they know what's going on?"

"That's why Abeo went back today. He knows one of them, and they live in his village in Nigeria. The other is in Brazil."

"What happened to the last one?"

"All I know is that there was some kind of accident and she disappeared. This was before I came along."

"So Amala and Ezra knew her."

"Yes. The Ebun are like guardian angels to the communities they are in. So you see, the fact that so many have been born here, in such a short space of time, is . . . worrying. It means a lot of guardians will be needed. Something bad is going to happen."

Charlene had already found a rogue spirit by herself. What if there were other evil spirits out there? What if they weren't evil spirits but malicious gods influencing half of the youth in London? It would be anarchy on the streets; there would be nothing but chaos. What would happen to those who didn't have powers?

"What's going to happen to Cassius? Who's going to keep an eye on him while we're gone?"

"He's coming with us," Leonard said quickly.

"Are you mad?" Marcus burst out, swinging to face Leonard fully, his arm twinging in pain. "The guy's crazy. That demon spirit has already been in his head. What if she uses him again?"

"He wants to help us," Leonard argued. "It was traumatic for him being manipulated by that being. He did things he would never have done otherwise. If he wants to help us, we should let him."

"This is a mistake." Marcus stood up, shaking his head. There was no way he was going to work with Cassius. "What good could he possibly do? We only have one hex gem, so she could easily get into his weak mind."

"We're going to enhance his powers with a gem separate from the protective ones around the house. That's how we'll hold Charlene's mind still long enough for us to do the incantation. Any other distractions you will have to take care of."

"This is utter madness." Marcus's insides boiled. They were resting this all on Cassius's stability—which he had shown very little of since Marcus had known him. "What happens if he turns on us, hmm? What then? What if he starts commanding you and Amala and getting into your head?"

"Then you will have to do what is necessary to stop it," Leonard said abruptly. "Knock us all out if you have to. Whatever it takes. We need to have a multiple-angles approach to this situation. She already knows what our most powerful instrument is, thanks to you. The only thing we have left is to try many different approaches simultaneously."

Leonard rubbed his chin, suddenly lost in his thoughts.

"Look, I know how this seems," he said once he emerged from his mind. "Trust me, if there was any other way, I would do it, but we have no other choice. It's either all of us involved or nothing."

Marcus paced the room, desperately trying to think of alternatives. But with his limited knowledge of this new world he was in, he came up blank.

"Neil and Natalie will be here any moment now," Leonard went on. "Get some rest. I'll get you the words of the banishment incantation we'll be using on her tonight. Do not say it out loud under any circumstances. It's a way of removing a spirit from someone's body. It's possible to remove the wrong one . . ."

He disappeared out of the door, leaving Marcus angry and confused. Who would have thought the fate of this night, of his newfound group, would be left in the hands of a crazy person?

Leonard's car pulled up to the entrance of the hospital. It had been several hours since Marcus left Grandma Maisey, and he felt a new desperation to see her. What would happen if they failed tonight? Who would look after her?

She would never know what happened to him, and she would blame herself for failing to keep him safe and give him a fresh start.

They'd all driven in frosty silence to the hospital. Natalie hadn't wanted to go, and Neil seemed unsure of what to say to anyone.

CHAPTER 21

As Marcus slipped out of the car, his eyes darted around, as did everyone else's in the vehicle. Neil had said the coast was clear, but after Leonard's comments on his abilities, Marcus no longer felt so confident in him.

He walked quickly through the doors and the cold, clinical lobby, grateful he'd at least been able to have a quick shower at home and change his clothes. He'd thrown his blood-soaked shirt and jeans in a plastic bag and chucked them in a bin outside. He never wanted to be reminded of that incident.

As he opened the door, he saw Amala sitting in his place.

"Good afternoon, Marcus." Amala beamed at him. Did she know he'd been shot earlier that day? He hoped she hadn't mentioned anything to his grandma.

"Hi." He smiled slightly. "Hello, Grandma, how are you?"

As he walked to the other side of Grandma Maisey's bed, she lifted her hand to hold his. Without her usual powdered face, her skin looked as delicate as tissue paper.

"All the better for seeing you, my dear." She held his hand lightly. "I was just saying to Amala that I can't believe this happened to me. To me? I'm slim and eat well, and there's been no history in our family of heart disease, as far as I can tell."

"It's okay, Grandma. Sometimes these things just happen." He gently squeezed her hand.

Amala's face caught his eye; it was deadly serious, her brow furrowed. The realisation slowly dawned: this might have been intentional.

Heat began to rage inside him. Who could've done this? Why her?

"That's what Amala said, but I'm not having it," Grandma Maisey said dismissively. "I'm going to be back on my feet before you know it. Oh, Marcus, your hands are so hot."

"Sorry, Grandma." Marcus whipped his hands away.

They sat in her room making small talk for a while. About her younger days in Jamaica, playing in the hot green fields. How she missed her brother, who had passed a few years prior. How she had always wanted better for her children, but somehow that plan had been scuppered.

"I want things to be different for you, Marcus," she said, looking him in the eye. Her own were beginning to droop from weariness. "Your life can be different. You have a strength that none of my other children had. Maybe you can show them how to do it. I know you won't settle for a mediocre life."

It was true. Marcus had never wanted to blend in. He had always stood out even when he didn't mean to. Others would gravitate towards him, even when he wasn't trying to make it happen. As some people would say, a born leader—or tyrant.

"Don't worry about me. I'll make you proud." He sighed then, a sadness descending when he looked at his watch. His time was up. "I need to get going, Grandma."

"So soon? No, I mustn't be selfish. You go on home. Maybe even go to Amala's group tonight? I'm sure she could use the help, and it'll take your mind off things."

Marcus glanced at Amala, who looked away from them both.

"Yes, I'm sure they could do with the help." He smiled sadly to himself. "I'll be back tomorrow."

He only hoped he could fulfil his end of the promise.

Amala's countenance remained solemn as they walked to the

CHAPTER 21

exit. Marcus was confused. His grandma looked so much better than she had last night. She had more colour in her cheeks, and her eyes had that familiar spark in them. Why did Amala look as though she'd received bad news?

"Well, she looks much better," Marcus said, trying to lighten the mood. "She looked so bad yesterday."

"Yes . . . she does," Amala replied. "I'm just wondering how she got sick in the first place."

"It's just one of those things, innit? We all get old. Maybe it's just that." Marcus wanted her to come out and say what she meant. He still hoped, despite the sinking feeling in his chest, that his grandma hadn't been targeted because of him.

"She is one of the healthiest people I know. I looked at her medical notes. Her last test results before this heart attack were perfect, especially for a woman of her age."

"So this was intentional."

"It's possible, Marcus. I've had experience with other entities before, but nothing as disruptive as this." She stopped walking and looked at him seriously for a moment. "I've dealt with possession before, but it only involved one person and one spirit. We already knew how to contain it, make sure it didn't transfer to anyone else. But this . . . it appears it transferred to Charlene without us even knowing it happened."

"I think Charlene knows what happened."

"What did she tell you?" Amala asked, her eyes wide with concern.

"Not much," Marcus said. "But what I've been able to piece together is this. She and Cassius spent a lot of time together before, and I don't think it was just dating. She told me they both started having nightmares around the same time, about this woman visiting. She said she was able to resist it, but he was finding it harder. I think they were both messing around. She found something about enhancing powers and asking for help through spirits. I reckon they both got in too deep."

"Did she tell you what she did? Where she got this information from?"

"No . . . but it's obvious they were doing something they shouldn't. They were really cagey about details, both of them. Even Natalie mentioned they were always together a few months ago. Why would they do that unless they were dating? Or had something to hide?"

"Hmmm." Amala continued towards the exit.

"Did Cassius mention anything to you?" Marcus asked, walking alongside her.

"He gave me a pretty good description of what this woman was like, even what she looked like. I'm afraid I might know who this person is, and she may even have something to do with your grandma."

Marcus's whole body went cold. "What do you mean?"

"I'll tell you more later. It may not be safe here," she said as they emerged from the hospital.

Leonard and the others were waiting for them in the parked car.

"Everything okay?" Leonard asked, watching through the rear-view mirror as Marcus sat down.

"Yeah, she's looking much better, thanks."

"Are you okay?" Leonard asked, tenderly putting his hand on Amala's own. The whole car went quiet as Marcus, Neil, and Natalie exchanged glances. Were they an item and no one had noticed?

"Yeah," Amala answered. "I need to talk to you all when we

get back. We have some things to work out."

"Bandha? But that's impossible!" Ezra exclaimed. He was pacing the floor in the Gathering's main room while Leonard, Amala, and Marcus looked on.

"Is it?" Amala queried. "I mean, we never actually found out what happened to her."

"But we thought she was . . . I mean, we saw her . . ."

"Disappear, yes, but evidently not die."

"But we were there. We saw her . . ." Ezra shook his head in disbelief.

"What did we see exactly? Can we even be sure of what it is we saw?"

"I don't understand," Leonard interrupted. "How can she be both dead and not dead?"

"Because we didn't actually see her die," Amala said, exasperated.

"But if you saw what we did . . . she just disintegrated before our very eyes!" Ezra spluttered, his voice high pitched. "People don't survive that!"

"You disintegrated her?" Marcus shot back, his eyes wide with shock.

"No, no!" Ezra was getting more and more flustered. He took an exaggerated deep breath.

"The spell we cast was not supposed to do that," Amala interjected. "We were simply trying to separate her abilities from her, return them to the gods. But she started to counter it—by what means, we don't know. She uttered another spell, one that stopped ours from working the way it should have, and she disappeared, as did her powers."

Marcus shook his head. They'd tried to force this girl's hand, and now nobody knew what could happen next.

"But what does this mean?" Leonard asked, visibly confused. "She's not really dead? Is this going to happen to Charlene?"

"Why would you try to take her magic?" Marcus asked, unable to control himself.

"This won't happen to Charlene," Amala said firmly. "We are not trying to dispel her powers, just a host that doesn't belong there."

"Bandha had become very dangerous," Ezra said quietly. "She stopped listening to us. She became turbulent, unruly. She was hurting others."

Sounds familiar, Marcus thought, his mind flitting to Cassius.

"It was the only thing we could think of doing," Amala explained. "Nobody else knew how to handle this. By Abeo's guidance, we decided it was the safest option."

"Who gave you the right to do that?" Marcus demanded, his anger now bubbling over. "To just take our powers away? They're part of us! Nice or not, shouldn't you have talked her down or something? You've got no idea what it would be like to have that ripped from us."

He couldn't believe it. Charlene was right. When they became too dangerous, the Ebun would be dealt with.

"You think I don't know what that would've been like?" Ezra seethed. "I was once like you, although not quite so arrogant. I had abilities. No one could touch me with the path I was on. I was on course for complete self-mastery. It was becoming like breathing to me. Everything was easier—my ability to recall events, memorise anything. I was even learning how to control my surroundings. Objects were moving at my mere thoughts."

Marcus stared at him, filled with both horror and amazement.

"But I had to give that up," Ezra continued. "One cannot simply banish another's abilities without one's own being affected. When we did what we did that night, we not only lost a fellow Ebun. I lost my own abilities."

This cranky old man now made sense. Ezra would've been greater than everyone standing in the room. Yet he'd given it up trying to save others, and the plan hadn't even worked.

"We had no choice," Amala said quietly. "She would have become a power in and of herself if we'd left it any longer. She would have become even more difficult to stop."

Ezra rolled his shoulders, as if trying to brush off a bad memory. "I don't pretend to be anything more than I am now. But I haven't given up. I've played my part. Now you all will have to execute it."

"Ezra, I'm sorry, man," Marcus apologised. "I didn't know."

"I don't want your pity. I just want you to complete the job at hand. She is an extremely powerful entity. Even back then, there were the seeds of destruction."

"What incantation did she say? What will happen if she does it again?" Leonard queried.

"It was spoken in a language we'd never encountered before," Amala said. "It was ancient."

"How would she even come across something like that?" Leonard's arms spread out wide. "This is a teenager before the internet!"

"Exactly. Someone told her. Or like Charlene and Cassius, her inquisitive nature led her to texts that had these writings."

"But where would she have gotten these texts from?"

Leonard's voice rose along with his confusion. "You can't just walk into a bookstore and pick them up. She must have gone searching for them. That, or someone told her exactly what to do."

"The question is, who?" Amala's voice rose now. "Ezra and I know of many Orisha. I am not entirely sure this is the one we originally thought. I thought it was Eshu . . . but now . . . This is dangerous."

"You told me you both have been keeping an eye on all the witch doctors and Orisha worshipers," Leonard said, looking at Amala and Ezra. "Are you saying you always come up with blanks?"

"We will have to worry about this another time," Ezra said dismissively. "It is clear that something is fuelling her, powering her along. Unless we deal with this threat tonight, she will have her own army and will become impossible to defeat. We will have two war fronts."

"Which side will she be on? For the gods?" Marcus asked.

"The winner," Ezra said. "She wants to be aligned with whoever comes out on top. She has no real loyalties."

"This is a fight between the Orisha," Amala pointed out. "We shouldn't get involved until it's absolutely necessary."

"But we don't even know what they're fighting about. Maybe it *is* worth getting involved," Marcus said.

"We are getting side-tracked," Ezra interrupted. "Let's stick to the job at hand. Once this is done, then we can consider where we will draw the line."

"I'm just saying, if Bandha ends up on the same side as us, she might be worth keeping around."

"You don't know who she is, boy," Ezra snapped. "You have no idea who you're aligning with."

CHAPTER 21

Every muscle in Marcus's body tensed. *Boy?* Who did he think he was calling a boy? He'd earned more than that by now.

Leonard stood up from his spot. "We need to go and prepare Cassius," he said, blowing air out heavily. "He will need to practise before tonight."

Chapter 22

Fear was thick in the air.

The car felt suffocating.

Marcus's thoughts were consumed by the zombified look of Charlene's parents, their eyes vacant, unseeing. He wondered if they still went to work, if this state only came over them once they got in the house with their daughter. Did they have any recollection of what was going on? He remembered the night he had woken up in his bed with no idea how he got there.

"You all right?" Marcus asked Natalie, trying to make small talk and relax.

Natalie slowly turned towards him. "I've been better. I'm just hoping *this* plan works."

Marcus nodded, catching Leonard's eyes in the rear-view mirror. It was just the two of them, Neil, and Natalie in the car. Amala, Cassius, and Sean travelled in a car a few seconds ahead of them.

"There's more of us now," Neil responded from the other side of Marcus. "Lots of angles to take her down. We'll be okay."

Marcus noted his eyes hadn't turned white. He hadn't

CHAPTER 22

looked into the future to check for certain if this was true.

"Look, Amala knows what she's doing." Marcus tried to soothe them. "She's dealt with possession before. If anyone knows what to do, it's her."

"If it was really that easy, we wouldn't all be going," Natalie remarked. "It's precisely because this is so hard we're all having to go."

"Natalie," Leonard said from the driver's seat. "Don't worry. You just need to focus and keep watchful. Be ready to run to us if Neil senses anything, and run as fast as you can to get out. We'll deal with the rest."

Marcus didn't know how that would be possible. Leonard didn't have any powers. How would he be protected unless he held the precious gem?

Suddenly the car was hit so hard from the left that it spun around. Their bodies slammed to the right. Their seatbelts strained to keep them in place.

"What was that?" Natalie cried, staring out of the windows.

"Hold on!" Leonard said as he straightened out the vehicle.

As soon as the car stopped, the right passenger door flew open. A gloved black arm reached in and grabbed at Marcus's clothes.

"Get out of the car!" the stranger growled as Marcus tried to push him off.

Another stranger grabbed Natalie, and she disappeared through the door. Neil punched more hands away, only to get dragged out the opposite side. Marcus scrambled after Neil but was quickly tackled. Something black was draped over his head.

He wriggled and writhed, trying to escape, but his hands were locked behind his back.

"Get off him!" Leonard's voice rang out. Marcus heard grunts and heavy breathing, but someone shoved him hard before he could sense where they were coming from.

"Move!" a gruff voice said close by.

"Stand back! Or I'll shoot!" one of the men said.

Marcus stopped dead, desperately searching for the source of the voice. A sharp kick in his back made his knees buckle, and he stumbled forward. He couldn't get a sense of where he was. He ignored the pain and started walking. He knew there was metal around, but he couldn't discern where, so he slowed his pace.

"Keep it moving," the person said to him.

"Keep the gun away from him. If he feels it, he'll move it!" a different voice shouted.

They suspect I'm powerful, Marcus thought. He knew his time was short. He had to be nearly at the other car. He could move it if he could see it properly, but if he tried, someone would get shot. His mind was racing.

Hands grabbed him by the shoulders and bungled him into the vehicle.

"Let's move, let's move!" said a familiar voice.

Carnell.

All thoughts fled Marcus's mind. Fear gripped his throat and threatened to overtake him.

The feel of the car launching forward shocked Marcus back to his senses. Taking a deep breath, he focused on the vehicle, willing every piece and particle to lift off the ground. His hands were on fire, his face damp with the effort and the heat of the bag on his head.

The car slowed down and began to sway, as if it were on the sea.

CHAPTER 22

"What's going on? What are you doing?" Carnell bellowed.

Marcus gritted his teeth.

"It's not me, bruv. It's the car!"

"Are we off the floor?" Carnell screeched. He kissed his teeth loudly. "Man, I'm putting a bullet through this boy's head!"

Marcus braced himself, his heart racing, his mind a scattered mess as he tried to feel for the gun with his senses.

He heard the door open.

"What the—argghh!" Carnell gurgled.

"What's going on?"

"Get out of the car!"

"He's got Carnell!"

Marcus was fully sweating now. As soon as the car hit the ground, it would be over. Carnell and his men would get their bearings and take him out.

But someone was helping him. Leonard?

Suddenly, he felt tousling on his right-hand side, and someone jabbed him in the ribs. Natalie! He could feel fighting over him. Natalie was taking on the other guy.

The door was flung open on his left, and the other man screamed as he fell out.

A gunshot rang through the streets. The shock cracked his concentration, and the car dropped. They all fell for what felt like an eternity before their heads hit the ceiling as the car hit the road. His head covering was quickly whipped off, and he turned to face Natalie.

"Thanks," he whispered as she unbound his hands, and they crawled out of the car.

Leonard was hunched over with a gun in his hand, but it wasn't aimed anywhere, and he was clutching his chest. On the ground was Carnell, his gun pointed straight at Marcus.

All Marcus could see was red. In the blink of an eye, he thrust his hand forward before Carnell could pull the trigger. The gun flew into Marcus's hand, and he quickly turned it on Carnell.

"Think you're a big man? Think you're going to be the boss of me?" screamed Carnell as he tried to stand up. "You'll never be top of these streets!"

Marcus shot him in the chest, and Carnell flew backwards.

Marcus shot again and again.

He stood over him as the deep red-black blood spread out underneath the man's body. Carnell's life ebbed slowly away. His eyes glazed over.

Marcus finally breathed out; his head was wet with sweat.

"Marcus, look out!" Neil shouted as the other masked men began to run clear.

With clean, cold precision, Marcus shot each one in the back.

He began to shake, his breathing becoming loud in his ears.

"It's Leonard. We've got to get him to the hospital!" Natalie cried.

Marcus turned to see her holding Leonard's crumpled form. He ran over. Blood was all over the man's stomach. The sight made Marcus feel weak with sickness.

"I'm calling the ambulance." Neil grabbed his phone from his pocket, then quickly said to Marcus, "Bro, you need to get out of here."

"What do you mean?" Marcus asked, confused.

"If you're caught . . . too many questions." Leonard's raspy voice carried from the floor.

Marcus dropped to his side.

CHAPTER 22

"I need an ambulance." Neil turned away with his phone.

"What about you guys?" Marcus said, grasping Leonard's other hand. "It'll be the same for you!"

"We need to stop Charlene . . . ," Leonard strained to answer. "You must go."

"I can't leave you!" Marcus's voice cracked.

"Ogun came to you . . . Defend us . . . defend this world . . ."

"But . . ." Marcus could barely whisper.

"We'll catch up," Neil interjected. "Amala? There's been an accident. York Road. Leonard's been shot."

"Go now, Marcus!" shouted Natalie.

With one last look at Leonard's ashy face, Marcus turned to run, but he paused when he saw Sean racing down the street towards him. The younger boy slowed down at the stricken Leonard, all hope draining from his face.

"You coming?" Marcus asked, barely able to speak.

"Absolutely," Sean whispered back.

The two of them ran off, leaving carnage and a river of blood.

Chapter 23

"Come with me," Sean said as they turned down a street.

"Where are we going?" asked Marcus. He felt like the walking dead, completely drained of every life force.

"No one will find you here."

They climbed up some stairs, and Marcus suddenly realised where they were. "Your house?" He glanced around. "You sure this is a good idea?"

"Yeah, my old man's not home."

Relief spread through Marcus's body. His head was a mess—Sean's dad was liable to get hurt. He didn't deserve that.

Sean unlocked his front door, and Marcus stumbled in. His breathing was hard, his heart nearly banging out of his chest. He rubbed his face and head in an effort to calm down, but there was too much adrenaline pumping through him. Instead he began to walk around, tried to think of his grandma and cousins, anything to stop his thoughts and feelings from spilling all over the house.

"You all right?" asked Sean.

"No," Marcus said. His thoughts raced.

CHAPTER 23

He couldn't believe he'd been ambushed.

He couldn't believe he'd shot them all.

He couldn't believe Leonard had gotten hurt because of him.

He'd made such a mess of everything. How could he possibly lead anyone now?

Nothing else would've stopped Carnell—he knew that. There had been nothing but hatred in the man's eyes. But maybe Marcus could've let the others go.

No, this was better. At least now there would be no more looking over his shoulder. No more asking Neil to watch his back. Unless there was someone behind Carnell . . .

"That man just tried to end me," Marcus whispered, still in disbelief. "I need a drink. Can I have a drink?" His mouth was suddenly unbearably dry. He thought he was going to start coughing. His throat ached.

"Yeah, let me get you something." Sean got up quickly and dashed to the kitchen.

When Sean passed a glass to Marcus, he drained it and asked for more. His eyes squeezed shut, and his hands pressed into hard fists. He felt as if he was going to explode as he kept pacing. He took a long drink and rested against the wall.

"He really tried to end me," Marcus said, staring at the ceiling. "You know, I lived with that man, practically for four years. And he was just going to end me . . . just like that?" He shook his head.

"Sorry, man," Sean said, leaning next to him. "If it makes you feel any better, my dad is always trying to kill me, and he's my actual dad. Been with him my whole life."

Marcus rubbed Sean's head affectionately. "I'm sorry about that, man."

Sean nodded. "We're both in messed-up families."

"Got that right." Marcus looked at the floor and took a deep breath. "Thanks for helping me out. I don't know where I'd be right now if you weren't here."

"You'd do the same for me," Sean said. "What are we going to do now? We still going to sort out Charlene?"

"We have to. The more time that passes, the more Ebuns she's going to find."

"What is she going to do with all those people?"

"Build an army."

Sean swallowed. "For which side?"

Marcus paused for a moment, trying to scrub his mind to think clearly. "Whichever god wins."

"Yeah, but why is she getting us involved in that?" Sean asked, puzzled. "No one has told us anything, or even asked for help. Unless the war is going to be down here . . ."

Marcus wasn't in the right mindset to put two and two together.

"What I'm saying is," Sean persisted, "why is that thing trying to alienate us from Amala and the Elders? Why hasn't she gone to them?"

"She doesn't trust them. They tried to take her powers from her."

"What?" Sean's eyes widened.

"She's one of us, at least she was until she went rogue."

"Wow," Sean said, looking around the room. "So really she wants a battle with them?"

"What?" Marcus asked, curious.

"I mean, this is a war between them. It's Amala, Leonard, and Ezra she's after."

Leonard's name felt like a punch through Marcus's being.

CHAPTER 23

He hunched over slightly. He'd been too slow to save him. It was only after Marcus heard that gunshot that he'd somehow been spurred into action.

"Do you think . . . he's going to make it?" Sean asked quietly.

"I dunno . . . We're screwed if he doesn't," Marcus replied.

The phone buzzed in Marcus's pocket. His body broke out in a sweat. He looked at the screen, his heart in his throat. It was Leonard.

"Hello?" he choked out.

"Marcus, it's Ezra."

Marcus sighed heavily. "How is he?"

"Just gone in the ambulance. Only time will tell."

Marcus pressed his lips together and rubbed his head with his free hand.

"Listen carefully, Marcus. We still need to pay a visit to Charlene. Doing it today would be the best thing for her. We need to get that thing out of her. No more unnecessary casualties. The sooner the better." Ezra sounded rattled.

Marcus strained to get his next words out. "Where are we going to meet?"

"Two hours, at Savers Supermarket. I'll drive us the rest of the way. You understand?"

"Yeah, I'm good." Marcus nodded to no one in particular.

Ezra rang off.

Marcus breathed in and out deeply. He felt as if his insides were being shredded. At least he had a couple of hours to try to sort out his mind. He sank to the floor, covered his head, and tried to hide his uncontrollable sobs.

Two hours later Marcus and Sean were waiting outside of

the supermarket. Marcus was still pacing, his mind spinning with what had happened. He pulled his hoodie down farther over his face.

"Marcus, can you stop pacing? You look like a user," Sean said timidly.

Marcus stopped and glared at him, but he went to stand next to him. "My mind feels like it's racing, man. Moving just helps it calm down a bit."

"Do you want anything from the shop?"

"Yeah, go get me some Coke." He put some cash in his hand, and Sean went into the shop. Marcus was sweating and nervous and would have probably made the customers uncomfortable.

He wasn't supposed to be in this position. He'd promised Grandma Maisey he was going to be different, not like all the other troubled boys on the street mixed up in gangs and hurting others. Yet here he was. Just like everyone else, just a different kind of gang. Everyone wanted to escape the street life, but the street life never escaped them. He'd just shot four people.

Sean came back just as bile began to rise up Marcus's throat.

"Thanks," Marcus said as he opened the can and took a large gulp.

A grey van suddenly pulled up next to them. He tried to peer through its tinted windows and instantly imagined flipping it over. His hands burned with anticipation.

The window rolled down, and Ezra leaned his head out. "Glad you're on time," he quipped. "Now get in."

Both boys climbed into the back, Sean sitting with Neil and Natalie. The only space left was next to Cassius. Marcus forced his hands to cool down by thinking of his grandma

CHAPTER 23

Maisey. She was waiting for him to get out of this.

Cassius nodded slightly as Marcus sat heavily next to him. Marcus turned away.

"What's up with you?" Cassius asked.

Marcus waited for someone else to tell Cassius to leave him alone. He'd been through enough. But nobody intervened.

Then he realised the voice was in his head.

"You allowed to do that?" Marcus said quietly, still turned away.

"Don't worry," Cassius said smoothly. "I'm playing ball today. Believe it or not, I'd like to have my friend back too."

Marcus snorted. "What's your job when we get there then?"

"Stay close to you, wait for things to go wrong. Then I'll try and persuade her to keep still so we can complete the freeing. What's your job?"

"To make sure nothing goes wrong."

Cassius sniggered. "You sure you can do that?"

Marcus faltered. He could barely think straight. "I'll do what I've got to do."

Even if it meant he'd go over the edge.

Chapter 24

Ezra parked round the corner from Charlene's house. The tension was so thick it could be split with a knife. Things would've been easier with Leonard here. Marcus had been afraid to ask about his condition in the car, and no one had mentioned it. He hoped with all he had Leonard was alive, rooting for them to succeed.

"Are we ready?" Ezra said, his voice eerily calm.

Amala finally spoke. "Ezra, I really think you should stay here."

"I'm coming. You all were supposed to face this with Leonard. It's the least I can do."

"I'm not sure if that's a good idea . . ."

"It's settled. Now, everybody, let's go."

Everyone piled out of the car. Night was descending fast, and for the first time, it made Marcus nervous. Normally the dark offered freedom from the responsibilities of the day, comfort and camouflage. But now he felt exposed and vulnerable. The dying light made him worried about what lay ahead.

"Neil, are we clear for the next twenty minutes?" Ezra asked, straightening out his jacket.

CHAPTER 24

As everyone searched the streets to ensure no one else was watching, Neil turned to face them, away from the road. His eyes twitched slightly, his mouth pulling to the side, before he relaxed and his eyes normalised.

"I can't get a clear picture, man," he said, his forehead wrinkling.

"Well . . . that's it," Ezra said with a sigh. "We possibly walk to our doom, or to victory. Marcus, I will ask you to go inside with Amala. I will stay outside with Neil, Natalie, and Sean."

"What are you going to do?" Natalie asked, turning to Cassius. She looked angry.

"Perhaps he should go in at the last minute, if it is necessary."

Cassius looked surprised.

"Of course it will be necessary," Natalie shot back. "Leonard's not here. How is Marcus supposed to defend Amala from everything Charlene could possibly throw at her?"

"She's right," Cassius said.

"I don't need your support," she snapped at Cassius.

"Look, I know you all hate me. I see how you all look at me. Give me the chance to make things better."

They all looked back at him in silence.

"If I start to struggle, I'll just leave," he said, trying to reassure them.

Cassius looked pale and avoided the eyes that bore down on him. Maybe he was telling the truth. Maybe he wanted to turn things around. Marcus would never trust him under normal circumstances, but what choice did they have right now? He nodded at Ezra.

"Very well," Ezra said. "If you're sure you want him with you."

Marcus wasn't sure about anything in that moment.

"I suggest you take some extra precautions." Ezra walked around the car. "Have a look in the back."

Marcus followed and opened the back of the van. There were four long metal poles.

"Small coins and a knife might not be enough," Ezra said.

Marcus lifted the poles, and an electric energy passed through his hands. The metal vibrated under his skin, and for a split second he thought he could hear it hum, as if it were alive.

Renewed strength rose within him. His thoughts became clear for the first time in hours.

"Where did you get these from?" Marcus asked.

"The scrapyard. They're nothing special," Ezra said as they turned to walk towards Charlene's road.

Marcus held the poles tight. When he turned to encourage the others, he noticed Cassius had halted. "You all right, bruv?" he asked, confused.

Cassius looked at him for a moment before licking his lips, his head beaded with sweat. "Yeah, I'm just psyching myself up . . . you know?"

He's afraid, Marcus realised. *This might be a mistake. He's clearly still fragile.*

"Look, man," Marcus said, getting closer. "You have the chance to make this right, yeah? We're here for you. Anything goes wrong and we'll get you out. Now, let's step up."

Marcus's voice was calm and smooth, despite his own fears. Cassius said nothing but followed closely behind him.

They caught up with Ezra, who stopped a few paces from Charlene's house. He sifted through a satchel on his shoulder and pulled out a box.

CHAPTER 24

"Now, Neil and Sean, take these crystals and put them around the house. Sean, you go round the back. Don't get caught, and do it as quickly as you can!"

Neil placed three stones around the front of the house. Sean took a deep breath and looked at his surroundings before putting the crystals in his pockets, then climbed up Charlene's house with ease. He disappeared over the roof. Marcus swallowed his nerves, putting his trust in the metal in his hands.

After a couple of minutes, Sean's head poked over the top of the roof. He glanced around before climbing down the house, out of sight of the windows.

"Are you ready?" Amala asked Marcus.

"Let's do this," he replied, moving his jaw around to relieve some tension.

They walked up the steps to the front door, the gem in Marcus's pocket between the two of them.

Amala rang the doorbell. "Leonard is really proud of you, you know?" she said in a low voice.

"What?"

"He knew you'd have to be brave and take his place. He wanted you to know he's grateful, and you'll get this right."

The door opened, and a tall, pale, skinny teenager stood in the entrance. A dark mop of hair obscured his eyes.

Marcus did a double take. Were they at the right house?

"Yes?" the boy said.

"Oh, I'm sorry. I thought this was Charlene's house," Amala said sweetly. "I must have got it wrong. My mistake. Let's go, Marcus."

She was turning to leave when Charlene appeared right behind the other teenager.

"It's okay, Nick. I know these people." Charlene smiled sweetly at the boy.

Marcus's heart and hands burned equally hot. Was this guy his replacement? The boy didn't have purple eyes. He was here by choice.

Nick stepped to the side so Charlene could walk forward. She was just as beautiful as ever. Her brown skin glowed in the sunset; her lips were cherry red and full. Marcus had forgotten what an effect she could have on people. Even without her powers, she was captivating. He could see the purple tinge to her eyes.

"It's so good to see you both. What have I done to deserve your company today?" She folded her arms.

"We just wanted to talk," Amala said. Her features were soft. Only a line of concern creasing her forehead betrayed their true intentions.

Charlene bobbed her head before gesturing for them to come in. "Just a few minutes," she said dismissively.

Amala stepped in first. As Marcus tried to follow, Nick blocked his way.

"You need to leave those outside."

Marcus looked down at the metal in his hands. "Can I just leave them inside the front door?" He smiled. "I don't want them to get wet." There was no way he wanted to leave them out of the house when he might need them.

Nick paused for a moment. "All right."

Marcus placed them inside, propped against the wall, as Nick slammed the door behind them. Without those poles, he felt vulnerable and alone.

The house was deadly quiet.

"It's good to see where you live, finally," Amala said, absorbing her surroundings. "It's a beautiful home. Are your parents in?"

"No, they've gone to visit family." Charlene sat down heavily on one of the sofas.

"You're here by yourself?"

"Only for tonight." She avoided Amala's gaze. "Anyway, I have Nick here. He's a friend from school."

"Nice to meet you, Nick." Amala smiled. "We won't stay long."

Nick came and sat beside Charlene. A twinge of anger pulled at Marcus as Charlene laced her fingers in the back of Nick's long black hair.

"If we could have a word, privately," Amala said, looking at Nick.

"Anything you want to say to me, he can hear. He's one of us, you know, Amala."

Amala nodded. "Very well. We haven't seen you in a while, Charlene. You haven't responded to any of us. Is everything okay?"

"What do you mean?" Charlene said, absently twirling her fingers around Nick's strands.

Marcus wanted to punch Nick through the face, but instead he fixed his eyes on the floor.

"We know you're having the same issue as Cassius," Amala went on.

"Which is?"

"Possession."

Charlene's purple eyes flicked towards Amala. "Is that how you see it?" her deep voice drawled. "I think it's merely . . . borrowing."

"So you asked for permission?" Amala asked, a firmness in

her voice.

"She knew what she was getting into when she allowed me in."

Marcus's whole body froze. Hearing the creature through Charlene, fully acknowledging what she was doing, chilled him to the core.

"Maybe she did," Amala interjected. "But the question is, why would she let you do that?"

"I had knowledge she wanted," Charlene said, smiling, "that they *both* wanted. They wanted to know more about their powers, its origins, what the Orisha were really like. They even wanted more power, if you can believe that. Of course, that's what got the young boy into trouble."

No wonder Cassius was so cagey, Marcus thought bitterly. He and Charlene had invited this being into their lives. They'd wanted extra power and knowledge, and they'd found a shortcut to access it.

"I bet I know what you're thinking," Charlene purred, her eyes boring into Marcus. "How stupid of them, wanting more than they already have. But you would do just the same. You're just like them, attracted to power and control. You just pretend not to be."

"Let's leave him out of this," Amala said abruptly. "What do you want? Why are you putting others like yourself in harm's way? What are you not telling us?"

"Why should I tell you?" Charlene's eyes narrowed.

"You're trying to resolve something. Many spirits have things they still want to rectify. Maybe if we could help you do that, you could pass on to the other side and leave the kids in peace?"

"Peace to do what exactly?" Charlene said. "You realise that they found me? I didn't just colonise them. You didn't give them enough, offer them enough opportunities. They were hungry for more. You all did the same to me, of course. Cut me down when all I wanted was to understand what I could do and where I stood in the world."

Amala said nothing.

"That's it." Charlene's lips curled. "You know who I am. Say my name."

Amala sat very still, her eyes never leaving Charlene.

"Say my name!" Charlene said, shooting forward on the sofa, glaring at Amala.

"Bandha," Amala said finally.

"Yes." Charlene reclined backwards slightly. "You've been neglectful of your duties again, losing two other students."

"I didn't lose them. They chose their own path, as did you. But I'm here to give them another chance. Just as I offered you."

Charlene scoffed. "What you offered me was passivity. I felt nothing, like I was dead inside, despite the marvellous gift I had."

"Bandha," Amala said, her voice rising. "You chose to operate outside the bounds of acceptable society. You used your powers as an excuse to hurt others."

"I never tried to hurt them . . . at least not long term. I wanted to see what was possible! Even great scientists do that!"

"But even scientists have ethics—rules by which to abide to prevent them from going too far!"

"I overcame death, you know, Amala. I'm still here. I didn't die. If you had let me be, who knows what I would be able to cure now? I could have cured every disease going!"

"Wait, you could cure sick people?" Marcus said in disbelief.

"What she hasn't told you is that she also had the power to impose sickness," Amala interrupted, her eyes never leaving Charlene's form.

"Still have," Charlene corrected.

"And she also hasn't mentioned what happened to those she made sick." Amala's voice had turned cold. Marcus glanced at her for a moment; she was staring straight at Charlene's eyes.

There was an uncomfortable silence.

"You want to make me the monster," Charlene said, "but you, dear Amala, neglected your duties. And I can see you haven't learned. It was easy for me to infiltrate these young ones' minds, because you had not taught them the darker side of their powers. You seem to think that everyone wants the same thing. The same hum-drum life in the background. But Charlene was born to shine. She will have great influence in this world, not just with her grace and beauty but her sharp and observant mind. She is the perfect host."

"And what about Cassius?" Amala said through her teeth. "Was he simply a test run?"

"He had great potential. What power he had! I can't say I didn't enjoy his power. But he was too fractured. He couldn't hold a thought. On one hand he wanted to help, serve me, but on the other he was conflicted, doubtful, unruly."

Marcus's eyebrows shot up. Cassius had tried to resist her; he just hadn't been very good at it. But Charlene, could she be embracing this entity? This Bandha person seemed to be enjoying her host rather too much, almost as if they were working together.

This might be much more difficult than he'd feared. He had thought he would be freeing Charlene from this possessor,

CHAPTER 24

but maybe she wanted Bandha there. Liked her there. After all, this being had promised her greater powers, a further reach, *the world*. How do you free someone who doesn't want to be freed?

What made Marcus feel even worse was that he knew he wouldn't have been able to resist such a promise of power either. He would've taken over the Q Block crew as well as the Gathering. His spirit sank.

"Bandha, I'm asking you to go back to where you came from. There's not a day that goes by that I don't think about you." The edges of Amala's mouth had softened from their previous hard line. "You could have been one of the greatest scientists this world has ever seen. Your abilities would have moved this world further by decades. But you were impatient. You wanted it all now.

"What you say about Charlene is true. You should give her the chance to do this the right way. You should be in the land of the ancestors, with your family, navigating your way through the metaphysical plane with the gods. Why haven't you done that?"

Charlene was silent for a moment. "I made a deal with the wrong person on the other side."

The whole room seemed to freeze. Charlene stopped playing with Nick's hair.

"Who was that?" Amala asked.

Charlene was silent, her eyes fixed on the floor.

"Was it Eshu?" Amala probed. "I could speak to a priest I know. Eshu usually just delivers messages. He is not always the author of misfortune—"

"It wasn't him."

"Was it Ogun?" Marcus asked.

"Ogun?" Charlene threw her head back and laughed. "That drunk? What has he got to do with anything?"

Amala shot Marcus a warning glance, and he quickly shut his mouth. His mind started to race. Ogun was a drunk? Was he not trustworthy?

"We can't keep having this conversation, Bandha." Amala had an edge to her voice now. "Can you at least tell us what's going on with the Orisha?"

"Why should I?"

"I assume we're on the same side. Neither one of us wants to see all-out war on earth."

"See, this is where you always misunderstood me, Amala. I want to have a better life, the life I deserved. Charlene can give me that, and she'll enjoy the ride. I have no allegiance to any of the gods. I want to keep my options open."

She's dodging the question, Marcus thought. "Why wouldn't you just want to be on the right side? And help us?"

"What makes you think there is a right side?" Charlene's eyes locked with his. "If I offer either side allegiance now, with no leverage, I will not get what I want."

"Which is what?" Amala interrupted.

"The life I was denied. Now, enough of your questions. Leave." She stood up.

"Can you at least tell us who is fighting?" Marcus pushed.

Charlene stiffened. Her lips moved as if she was murmuring. Marcus leaned forward to see if he could hear anything, but then she shuddered suddenly, as if coming to herself.

"Nick will see you out," she said, turning to leave as he rose.

"I think not," Amala said quietly. Putting her glasses on, she pulled out a bag of powder and deftly threw the white contents on Charlene, who instantly froze.

CHAPTER 24

"What are you doing?" she said, as if seized by some terror. "Nick!"

Nick whipped around and crouched down, preparing to pounce on Amala, who rose and moved to put Charlene between them. Charlene lunged for her, but Amala stepped out of the way. Marcus caught Charlene and held her back. Nick remained still as Amala started to speak words Marcus couldn't decipher.

He didn't have his metal bars. Somehow he would have to manoeuvre his way to the front door.

"Don't make me hurt you, Marcus," Charlene seethed as she tried to fish the gem from his pocket. He released her and slipped away, circling around the room as Amala continued to chant.

Nick's body began to shudder, almost as if he were a dog flicking off water. It suddenly dawned on Marcus what was happening.

He was turning.

Black fur sprouted all over Nick's skin and tore through his clothes. A guttural growl escaped his mouth as his face contorted into a snout. His body began to ripple and elongate, his frame bulging upwards—just as Natalie came barrelling round the corner holding two of Marcus's metal bars.

Nick's black dog eyes looked up at Marcus. With his pointed canine teeth bared, he sprang forward at the same time Natalie swung one of the bars. It struck Nick's side, but the blow only slightly veered him off course, and the werewolf's body still clipped Marcus as he tried to dive out of the way.

Amala paused her chant to move away from the tussle. Charlene was now on the floor, clasping her head as if she were holding it together, an unearthly cry emanating from her mouth.

Marcus held out his hand, searching for the vibrations of the metal poles. His fingers tingled as one flew towards his grip. One remained in Natalie's grasp.

Nick rose up, towering over Marcus, his shoulders hunched to prevent his head from hitting the ceiling. Hate rippled from his eyes, and he howled so loudly everybody clutched their ears.

Marcus barely had a chance to recover his hearing before Nick's massive black claws swiped at him. Marcus jumped back and threw one of the metal bars towards him. It wasn't long enough to wrap around the werewolf's torso, but it snaked around Nick's arm and pulled him to the wall.

Marcus quickly scanned the room for any other metal to pin Nick's free arm. His eyes fell on Natalie grabbing Charlene and pulling her out of the room.

Natalie's eyes were purple.

Amala followed them, loudly shouting, "I can't stop this, Marcus!"

He quickly slipped the gem into her pocket. "You've got the gem. Don't stop the incantation!"

A sharp scratch stung Marcus's chest as Nick swiped him hard. He stumbled backwards, out of Nick's reach, and looked down at the large scrape. His shirt was already turning crimson, but the wound didn't feel too deep, despite the pain.

He spotted Natalie's dropped bar and lifted up his tingling arm. As he circled his hands, the bar circled around Nick's flailing paw and pinned his arms together behind his back. Marcus desperately tried to fuse the metal together, but he didn't know how.

Nick thrashed back and forth, making it increasingly

CHAPTER 24

difficult to keep him restrained. Marcus was desperate for backup, though he knew it would put more people in danger. He just needed a distraction.

The fusion wasn't working.

Amala still wasn't chanting.

Adrenaline and fear kicked in. Using a nearby metal vase, Marcus swung his right arm hard at Nick's head. The metal followed his movement and hit Nick between the eyes.

Nick blinked wildly and stumbled backwards, and Marcus struck again, this time taking the knife from the back of his jeans and swiping between Nick's thighs. The werewolf bent over, crying out in pain. Hopefully the knife hadn't pierced him too deep,

Marcus dashed up the stairs towards Amala. She was walking slowly behind Natalie, who was dragging Charlene away. At first, Marcus wondered why Charlene couldn't just instruct Natalie to attack Amala, but then he saw Charlene was only semiconscious. A weak moan came from her mouth.

Marcus started to pull Natalie away from Charlene and down the stairs.

Amala resumed her chant, saying the words much more quickly, her hands outstretched in the air.

Suddenly, the looming figure of Nick appeared out of the corner of Marcus's eye, but he saw him too late. A metal-enclosed paw swiped at him again.

For a split second there was darkness. Marcus couldn't see or hear.

He finally came to when he hit the bottom of the stairs. Blinding pain on his right cheek made his eyes start streaming. He clasped his face, checking for blood, and tried to figure out how to stand up and escape.

The werewolf grabbed him by the legs, but Marcus used his powers to make Nick punch himself in his own face with a metal-bound claw. Nick tried to grab him again, but Marcus didn't let up with the punching, even when he began to feel lightheaded. Blood ran down his neck and face from the gash in his chest.

Natalie was going back up the stairs to help Charlene.

Marcus saw some metal coat hooks by the door and reached for them. They strained against the wall as he battled to bring them towards him, his sight beginning to dim.

A crash through the front door fired up his senses.

There stood Cassius and Sean. Sean took one look at Marcus and the hulking Nick, and his confidence seemed to melt into the floor.

Everyone hesitated for a moment before Cassius darted forward, looking for something to grab. Sean had climbed up onto the door frame and was scurrying across the ceiling. Nick flung Marcus across the room, and he careened straight into Cassius.

"Upstairs!" Marcus tried to shout to Sean.

Sean nodded and crawled towards the stairs.

Cassius rolled Marcus off him with a grunt, grabbed a nearby umbrella, then charged at Nick from behind and rammed it into his back. Nick howled so loudly it pierced Marcus's very being.

Marcus scrambled to his knees as Cassius went barrelling up the stairs. Hopefully the guy would hold his nerve. Amala limped after him; she had stopped talking.

Marcus glanced back at his chest. He was becoming colder, and the realisation made his blood become ice. He turned back to the stairs to see Natalie and Sean standing on either

CHAPTER 24

side of Charlene.

Cassius was holding Amala by the throat.

Terror filled Marcus, his whole body turning limp.

They'd failed.

Cassius didn't have the hex. It was in Amala's pocket, but Charlene's power shouldn't have been able to affect him when he was so close to the gem.

He'd chosen this.

He'd chosen Bandha.

Marcus felt as if he'd been stabbed in the gut.

He did the only thing he could think of. He lifted up his hands in defeat.

Charlene smiled.

"It's not as bad as it looks," she said, white powder covering half of her pretty face. "I just need to know what you want to do now, Marcus? You can side with me, willingly. I know you would never serve me—you're much too proud for that. If you're going to be with me, I want your mind, not just your metal talents. Or you could decide to be my enemy, and it ends right now."

"I don't want any more bloodshed. Just let Amala go."

"That's not what I'm offering. This is about you. Amala's fate is already decided."

Marcus swallowed. "All right, what do you need me to do?"

"Look in Amala's bag. There's a spell I want you to do for me."

Marcus slowly moved over towards Amala's bag.

"Marcus, don't do this. There's too much at stake here!" Amala pleaded.

He ignored her and pulled out a worn old brown leather notebook.

Charlene nodded. "The spell I need you to find regards inhabiting a body . . . permanently."

Marcus's throat tightened up as he flicked through the pages, looking at each spell. He found the one Amala had been doing and somehow understood the words on that page, as if it had brought a long-forgotten memory to the surface.

He looked up at Cassius.

The other boy's mouth moved inaudibly. "Hurry up."

Cassius was buying him time.

"Have you found it yet?" Charlene asked impatiently.

"Yes," Marcus said as he flipped to the right page, holding his thumb in the place of Amala's spell.

"Show me," she demanded.

He turned the book round to show her, and she grinned.

"Good. Friends, I want you all to pin her down."

Cassius laid Amala down as she kicked and fought. Sean pinned her legs while Natalie stood guard.

Shocked that Sean was helping her, Marcus looked down at the page and noticed something glowing just on the floor. Moving the book slightly, he saw the gem in between his feet. It must have fallen from Amala's pocket during the scuffle. With one swift move, he shoved it out of sight, just behind his heel. The sound of his heart hammered his ears like a beat from a music track.

"The knowledge I will have when I get access to your body, Amala!" Charlene laughed. "It would've taken me years to accumulate! Now, prove yourself to me, Marcus. You will do the spell."

Marcus swallowed a shaky breath. He began to say the incantation, the one Amala had done. Luckily, the beginnings of both were very similar.

CHAPTER 24

Suddenly, a dark shadow appeared in the room, cold and pulling. It began to spread into a dark hole. Charlene looked up, her eyes and mouth wide with horror.

"What is that? What have you done!" She tried to stand up, but her feet had become unstable. Still, Marcus continued. He was over halfway through now. A language he didn't understand flowed out of his mouth. A sharp coldness began to seep into his being.

Charlene looked around frantically, then fixed her eyes on Sean. Marcus tried to speed up.

Sean blinked and glanced between him and Charlene. He got off Amala, rubbing his head as if the spell on him had been broken. Natalie did the same, both spotting the black vortex forming in the room. Charlene was staggering away from it, but Marcus blocked her path.

"Fine!" she screamed, lunging at Sean and holding on to him. "Stop! Or I'll kill him."

Marcus's eyes left the book for just a moment. He was nearly done. Just two more sentences to go.

He took a deep breath, dropped the book, and ran straight at Charlene, knocking her over and forcing her to let go of Sean.

"Sean, quickly! Last two sentences!" Marcus said, pinning Charlene to the floor with all his strength.

"You'll pay for this," she said through gritted teeth. She grabbed his head, her long fingers pressing on his temples.

Sean was saying something, somewhere, but Marcus could barely discern it. His hearing suddenly vanished, and all he could feel was pain—blinding pain. He scrunched his eyes as his body seemed to be set alight. Fire burned through his clothes, his muscles, his bones. Charlene screamed, and his voice joined hers, both cries of agony. She began to rise up, trying to slide him off. His limbs felt dead, as if all strength had left him.

Suddenly, a voice from deep within came to him, clear and strong: "Be the leader you were meant to be. Don't disappoint me!"

Using everything he had left, Marcus pressed Charlene down. He held her as firmly as he could as her body began to shudder as if she were having a seizure. Marcus tried to open his eyes, but they were burning too.

A sudden grip closed around Marcus's arms, prying them open and pulling him off the convulsing body. Someone began to drag him away. Through dimming vision, he looked up to see Cassius's face.

"It's all right," Cassius said. "You've done it."

"We've got you, Marcus," Amala said, her form coming into focus. "Don't give in to the fire!"

Marcus turned away from them, his skin ablaze. Charlene's body lay on the other side of the room, and a grey form was seeping out of her, funnelling into the black hole.

I did it, thought Marcus as he too faded into the darkness.

Chapter 25

"He's coming round," a man's voice said from the void.
Marcus opened his heavy lids.
"Let's get him to my house. We will not get him to the Gathering without being noticed by the park attendants."

Marcus was able to make out Ezra's outline and glasses as Amala's figure bustled around him.

"Boys, can you help him up?" Amala's comforting voice soothed.

Marcus felt his lead-like body being lifted up on both sides. He wondered if he was disabled, his legs barely able to support his frame. He rested heavily on his aiders.

"It's all right, bruv. I've got you."

Marcus turned his face to see Neil's blurred outline. When he looked to his other shoulder, he saw Cassius, his head down, avoiding Marcus's gaze. For the first time, Marcus felt nothing but gratitude towards him.

The fatigue in his body was overwhelming. Every ounce of energy had been drained from him. He made his way gingerly down the stairs with the help of the two other boys. He could barely see what was going on. Was this beautiful house completely destroyed? How would they explain this to

Charlene's parents?

Marcus was carried gently into the car, and his head fell back in exhaustion. He looked out of the window at Natalie, Amala, and Ezra bringing Charlene down. They laid her in the back of the van.

"Natalie, you stay at the back with her," Amala said, taking the gem out of her pocket and giving it to her. "Just in case. Neil and Sean? Stay here with me. We will need to get some things sorted."

Marcus turned his head slightly to look at Charlene. She seemed as if she were asleep. Despite her perfect angelic features, her soft lips and long eyelashes, Marcus felt dread as he watched her.

She had befriended him merely to seek gain.

Maybe most of those actions at the end weren't her, but as Bandha had known, what she really wanted was power.

Marcus felt nauseated. The truth was that power had been his driving force too. He was no different from Charlene. His only saving grace was that he hadn't encountered Bandha first.

His mind flitted to Eshu. Eshu must have known this would happen, which was why he'd interfered in Marcus's plans to become the new head boy in the Q Block crew. He knew Marcus would've become a tyrant. Instead, he had redirected him to use his abilities properly with the Ebun and protect them instead.

An all-encompassing heat began to consume his body, as if he had been set alight. He checked his hands. He was completely blemish free. He closed his eyes and rested his head back as Ezra and Cassius slammed their doors shut and the car started.

CHAPTER 25

The burning intensified, but he had no energy to cry out for help. Oblivion beckoned. He heard no voices, no sounds, and soon he was back in the void, in too much pain and too tired to be afraid. He would welcome whatever was on the other side.

***

Marcus's eyes flew open in an unfamiliar dark room. He sat up quickly, his gaze darting around. All tiredness fled him, and even his upper body felt as if he had some strength returning. The small room smelled as though it was from a distant past of old books. He could see heavy dark green curtains and an old patterned carpet that reminded him of his grandma's house.

He felt an ache inside for home and family. He wanted to see his grandma.

He carefully put his feet on the ground, stood up, and slowly made his way to the door. Down the short hallway, he could hear the sizzling and popping of what could only be bacon. The smell that accompanied it made his stomach growl.

His legs felt a little heavy as he made his way to what he hoped would be a delicious breakfast. The hallway brought him to a large room, the kitchen on his left and the living room on his right.

He froze. Sitting on the sofa in the living room was Charlene, the purple gone from her eyes. She patted the seat next to her, inviting him to join.

He didn't want to be anywhere near her.

"Ahh! Finally awake, I see," Ezra said. "Bacon? Eggs?"

Marcus stopped staring at Charlene long enough to nod slowly. "Thanks."

"I tell myself I only have these foods here for when I have guests, but it's a lie," Ezra said to himself. "Bad for my cholesterol and all that."

He plated up as Marcus looked at Charlene. She held a giant mug in between her delicate hands.

"How are you?" she asked. A softness he hadn't remembered was present in her tone.

Marcus just stared. He was afraid to say anything. Her brown eyes watched him intently. Begging.

"He'll be fine in a couple of days," Ezra answered for him. "Now, both of you come and sit down before it gets cold." He put two plates full of bacon, eggs, and tomatoes down at the small breakfast bar. "Marcus, how are your legs?"

Marcus sat down on one of the stools, shifting slightly away from the other stool as Charlene took her seat. "They're fine."

"No numbness?" Ezra enquired.

"No," Marcus lied. His legs were feeling pretty heavy now he was out of bed.

"Good! Now, you must take your healing tonic four times a day for the next week. Any residual issues will be gone by then."

What had happened to him? Why couldn't he even talk before? His body had felt as if it were on fire. "What did she do to me?" he asked quietly.

"*Bandha*," Ezra said pointedly, "tried to curse you with a sickness. We're not entirely sure what kind exactly. We didn't really have time to ask you questions. Because she'd lost most of her hold on Charlene at that point, it wasn't as effective as she wanted it to be. I doubt we would've been able to save you if it had been."

Marcus shifted in his seat, chewing the food that had now lost its flavour. He wanted nothing to do with Charlene now. Just being next to her made him feel physically sick. He didn't even want her looking at him.

"It is done now, Marcus," Ezra said. "You are safe and, in the next couple of days, will be back to full health. Now, eat up. It's been a couple of days since you last saw your grandma, and I'm sure she will be getting suspicious."

A couple of days?

"Okay, I'll see her later today."

"That's not advisable," Ezra said, placing a hot mug of coffee in front of him. "Because we didn't know what was wrong with you, we had to keep you in a deep sleep while we tried to determine what Bandha had done."

Marcus couldn't stand it any longer and stood up swiftly. Shaking his head, he tried to walk around, but his legs felt much weaker now, and he suddenly felt the need to sit down.

"Come, let me take you back to your room." Ezra walked round the counter and put his shoulder underneath Marcus's. He was much shorter than Marcus, and the ratio worked out perfectly.

When they reached the end of the hallway, Ezra pushed the door to Marcus's room open, helped him over to the bed, and shut the door.

"Marcus, you have to understand," he said. "The girl that sits out there is not the one who cursed you and put all our lives in jeopardy."

"Yeah? How do we know that?" Marcus muttered.

"We vanquished her, Marcus. Maybe you were too unwell to see Bandha's form leave Charlene's body."

"No, I saw that," Marcus said flatly. "What I'm saying is . . . how do we know it was all Bandha? She invited her in! What person does that? Invites somebody into their body?"

"Do you really think she knew what she was doing when she did that?"

Marcus looked away from Ezra. "I don't believe she's truly innocent."

"Is anyone truly innocent?" Ezra's voice softened. "People make mistakes. People do things, oblivious to what might happen, to the truth behind their actions. What Charlene did is no different to what other youths her age do when they play with Ouija boards. The only difference is she found a real spirit and Charlene has powers."

"She's going to be a liability," Marcus said. "Look at Cassius. He's so shifty now. His mind is all over the place after what that thing did to him, and she'll be just the same."

"We don't take you all in because we are concerned about liabilities. We take you in to try and help. Some could argue you were our biggest liability! Yet Leonard and Amala were eager to have you join, to show you a better way. It seems your previous actions still follow you, and now Leonard is gone."

Marcus felt lightheaded, his stomach disappearing into a pit. He looked up at Ezra. "When?"

"Not long after he arrived at the hospital."

Marcus hung his head between his hands, fighting and fighting for the engulfing despair to leave him.

But he caved in.

CHAPTER 25

Ezra left him alone after that.

Marcus spent the rest of the day in the dark bedroom. It should have been obvious this would happen. Everyone he ever got close to left. What was the point in even trying anymore?

That evening, there was a gentle tap at the door. He said nothing, but the slight click of the latch and the stream of light flooding the bedroom informed him someone had entered.

He didn't care if it was death itself. It might give him some reprieve.

The bed compressed as someone sat down.

Make it quick, he begged.

"Marcus," Amala's gentle voice called.

He didn't turn round. He didn't deserve her friendship or care.

"Ezra told me he informed you about Leonard's death. He should never have told you that way."

"He was being honest," Marcus replied hoarsely.

"Ezra is not a tactful man. He should've seen you were hurting and held back for once in his life."

Clearly there was history between them, but Marcus didn't even know if he cared. "You told me Leonard wanted me to be brave and step up, just before we entered Charlene's house. Was that a lie?"

Amala paused. "He did say it, just a few days earlier."

Clever woman, thought Marcus, shaking his head. "He died because of my idiocy. I shoulda killed Carnell the first time I shot him."

"You wouldn't be here if you had. In fact, I don't know if we would've defeated Bandha without you. You didn't kill Carnell the first time because it was self-defence. Carnell was a monster before you came along. You stopped him and his crew from doing any more harm."

"Was the cost too high?" Marcus asked, his eyes burning.

"Leonard would say no. He knew what he was doing when he took on Carnell. That wasn't his first brush with gangsters."

"It's always me though." A tear ran down Marcus's cheek, but he tried to keep his voice steady. "People always leave *me.* My parents, my cousins, my grandma, and now Leonard." Even Charlene, who he thought understood him and cared. "What's wrong with me?"

"It's lonely at the top," Amala whispered. "Ogun appeared to you for a reason, Marcus. He is known as the god who never sleeps. He works tirelessly to ensure the safety of others. He is not just the god of steel and metal. He is a defender. When all is lost, you will be the one who will have to make it possible to move forward. That is why he was so hard on you. You cannot give up."

Calm washed over Marcus as Amala put her hand on his shoulder.

"And your grandma is still here. A little fragile, but still here. I'm sure she'd like to see you tomorrow, and don't worry, I covered for you. I said you'd gotten a bad cold and stayed home from school. I told the school the same thing and that I was looking after you while your grandma recovered."

"Thank you," whispered Marcus. He refused to look at her, but her words offered him a slim chance of escaping the hell he was in.

The next morning, the sunshine blinded his eyes, and he scrunched them up tight. Next to him on the bedside table,

CHAPTER 25

his tonic waited for him. He left it alone as he went to freshen up.

When he wandered into the kitchen to hunt for some food, he saw Charlene with her backpack on, making herself some tea.

"You leaving then?" he asked without looking at her.

"Yep." She sighed as he continued to hunt through the cupboards for some cereal.

"Well, take care of yourself," he said dismissively.

"You too." She shuffled towards the door, but he didn't hear it open. "I didn't mean for this to happen. Any of this," she said, almost pleading.

He turned around slowly and tried to flatten his voice. "What are you telling me for?"

"I just want you to know. To understand."

"Understand what?"

Charlene looked around the room, as if the right words would appear on the walls. "I just . . . wanted more, you know? I'm here in my boring life, unable to try new things, only allowed to read or do what I'm told to read or do."

Marcus said nothing. He folded his arms and rested against the countertop.

"I wanted more than I was being allowed to do." She shrugged. "I can't practise my powers, Marcus. Not normally. I kept hearing it's dangerous to mess around with people's feelings."

"It is," Marcus said.

Charlene squinted at him. "I'm trying to help you see that my powers are considered unacceptable. I'm seen as a liability, dangerous, manipulative."

"That's how you used them." Marcus's voice rose, but he

quickly caught himself.

"I know! And I'm sorry. I'm sorry that you guys got hurt and that I turned everyone against each other." She paused and looked at the door. "But for the first time, I felt free. Bandha was the one who controlled me, but I didn't fight it as much as I could have. It felt like a release to allow someone to take the reins and use my abilities in a way I never imagined."

Marcus felt as if he were turning into a statue. He knew exactly what she was saying. "This can't ever happen again, Charlene. If you're going to be part of this group, you're going to have to keep yourself in check."

"I know that," she said, almost exasperated. "I'm just trying to help you see I'm not a monster. I want to be seen as equal and not a threat."

"That's not what your powers do though, is it? And now you know how to force people into doing things."

"Just stop. I don't know why I'm even having this conversation with you. I thought you would understand."

"What? Understand what it's like to manipulate people?"

"Yes! I saw you do it all the time! You think you're better than me, that you have more self-control. Well, I bet if Bandha ever came across you, you'd take her up as soon as she offered."

"No, I wouldn't."

"Yes, you would! Because despite your pretence of knowing how things work and having everyone's best interest at heart, I know that what you really want is power. You want people on your side. That's exactly what she offered me and Cassius. And I was unafraid of my abilities because of her! Not Amala or Ezra or . . ." She faltered. "Or Leonard . . . as nice as he was. I was afraid of what I could do because of them. But not anymore."

CHAPTER 25

"What are you saying, Charlene? You're just projecting now."

It was a weak defence, and he knew it.

Charlene started to head towards the door.

"Was any of it real?" Marcus said as he stared at the kitchen counter.

"Any of what?"

Marcus exhaled heavily. "Us. Or did you manipulate me too?" He forced himself to look at her, though every part of his body ached with pain.

Charlene turned to face him, her bottom lip trembling, eyes shining. "It was real to me," she whispered.

Marcus nodded, looking away. "Well, that's a shame."

Charlene turned slowly back to the door. "I'm not going to be afraid of who I am anymore," she said, her voice thick with emotion. "I suggest you do the same."

She opened the door and walked out.

* * *

Marcus stepped into the hospital with Amala after being dropped off by Ezra. He didn't want to mention it, but he was feeling much better, enjoying the sensation of being pain free and burden free. For the first time in a long time, he didn't feel tied down. Carnell was gone, despite the terrible cost. Crazy B had thrown him out of the Q Block crew. He wondered what Leonard was doing now on the other side with the spirits and ancestors. Was he part of the coming war?

Would he protect them or guide them somehow?

Amala put her arm around him and looked into his eyes. She was shorter than him, so it was a strain.

"We'll be all right, Marcus. We're going to continue his work." She smiled as tears glistened in her eyes. "I knew Leonard for a long time, and he was so impressed when you turned up."

Marcus nodded but said nothing.

"He was a loner like you. Parents died when he was young. Grew up in foster care, not too different from Cassius. That's why he was so protective of him—of all of you, really. Him joining the army was what helped him take charge of his life. He had a wife once too. They ultimately drifted apart when he was on duty and met someone else."

"How did you meet him?" Marcus said as they walked through the corridors of the hospital.

"We used to work together. We both worked closely in social care with children. I needed something less physically taxing than the nursing I had been doing before. He was charming, and we both had a love for the historical origins of our ancestors. Of course, he didn't know I'd been on the periphery for years. My mother was a healer, and my dad had the gift of foresight, although nothing as pointed as Neil. More of a prophet, speaking in symbols and allegory. Even in the diaspora these things are found, although they're less common than in Nigeria."

"Have you ever been married?" Marcus realised how little he knew about this mysterious lady next to him.

"Almost, once, but it didn't work out."

"What happened?"

"He changed. He wasn't the man I had first met. The life

CHAPTER 25

and vitality he once had . . . just left after a while. Anyway, we're here at your grandma's door. Do you remember the story?"

Marcus nodded, thinking on her words. He wondered how Charlene would change after this day.

They opened the door to see his grandma sitting upright, reading a book.

"Aah, Marcus, so glad you're here." She reached out to hug her grandson.

Marcus embraced her warmly, feeling at home in her arms. His muscles instantly relaxed.

"Amala told me you weren't feeling well," she said, intently looking into his eyes. Her skin felt soft and paper-like as she held his hand.

"I'm all right. Just a cold."

"Have you been eating enough? Staying warm?"

"Amala's been helping me out."

"Well, I'll be out tomorrow, gods willing, so I'll make sure to feed you up well."

"Don't worry about it, Grandma. I'll be looking after you!" He grinned.

They stayed with her for a couple of hours. Despite her cheery demeanour, Marcus could tell some of her vitality had been lost. She seemed frailer, her smile less firm, her eyes tired and slightly strained. It was as if she'd aged years in just under a week. Marcus couldn't wait to get her home, in her domain, with everything just the way she liked it.

That evening, they all sat in the Gathering's spacious main room, eating pizza and fizzy drinks with the promise of ice cream after. Everyone had finally relaxed and was enjoying one another's company. Marcus looked at their faces; Neil, Natalie, and Sean chatted with relative ease. Even Cassius sat with them and seemed more comfortable than he had in weeks. The only one missing was Charlene.

"You seen her recently?" Cassius asked Marcus casually after glancing at Ezra and Amala, who were farther off.

"Charlene? No."

"Don't be too hard on her, man. She's kind of weird that way. It's like she's promising you the world. But you can tell something's wrong, you know?"

Marcus shrugged.

"Messes with your head. You can't think straight. Anyway, it might be different for you. She actually likes you."

"It's never going to happen."

Cassius shot him a look before taking a bite of his pizza. "Don't be like that."

"Like what?"

"Self-righteous."

A phone started ringing just behind them. Everyone paused and watched as Ezra waved his hand to dismiss their looks, then disappeared from the room with his phone.

"I'm not being self-righteous, bruv," Marcus said, keeping his voice low. "But she's trouble. I've had enough of that. You know I nearly got killed the other day, and instead, it was Leonard who paid."

"Yeah, but that wasn't your fault."

"So everyone keeps saying." A familiar ache lingered in his stomach. "But I'm not putting anyone or anything at risk now. We all just got to walk the line. Keep our noses clean. From now on, I'm just focusing on these guys here and keeping

CHAPTER 25

them safe."

Cassius shrugged. "If you say so," he said, turning away. "As long as you don't think you can walk around telling us what to do, everything will be fine."

"Stick by the rules, and I won't have to."

"What rules?"

"Ezra and Amala are going to sit down and discuss some rules and guidance so we all don't get into trouble. Since Charlene will be coming back and Nick might be joining, we need to make sure these things don't happen again."

Cassius gave Marcus a curious look as he chewed his food. "You think you're going to be able to stop what's coming?"

"What do you mean?" Marcus asked, confused.

"I'm saying this can't work. Charlene and I know too much, have done too much. We'll never be accepted like you lot. Amala and Ezra will never trust us again, no matter what we do, and neither will you."

"Shut up, man. What are you saying? Are you saying you want to walk?"

"No, I'm just saying we need a voice. It can't just be about you, or them. It's got to be about all of us."

Marcus didn't want to have this conversation. Even now he questioned if Cassius was still in full control. Was he being manipulated? What kind of residues would be left on him and Charlene from the possession? Didn't Marcus have a duty to protect everyone else from them? Could he really do that? It was stupid to expect Charlene to go back to how things were before, given what she'd said to him in their last meeting.

Ezra walked into the centre of the room and cleared his throat. "I've just come off the phone with Abeo. He has had some contact with many of the other priests in Nigeria. What

I can confirm is that the rumours of their being a rift among the Orisha is true."

Everyone stopped eating.

"It seems Olorun is displeased with another Orisha. Which one, we cannot be sure," Ezra said.

Marcus couldn't help but wonder if it was Eshu for interfering. Ogun had mentioned him making things worse.

"But he's the head Orisha. Can't he just sort them out?" Natalie asked.

"You'd think so, but something is stopping him, or at least, he is reluctant to do so."

"What do we do now?" Natalie asked, her eyes wide and scared.

"I need you all to pay attention. Any unusual activities need to be reported back to us. Somehow, I think Bandha was part of this."

"How?" Cassius asked. His voice sounded strained.

"It's not clear right now. Right from the very beginning, she had knowledge she shouldn't have."

"So it's definitely another spirit?" Marcus asked. "An Orisha that's instructing her?"

"Yes." Ezra's eyes flicked towards Amala.

"The bigger question," Ezra said quickly, "is why. Keep your eyes open and ears to the ground. Any strange activity, friends or family acting out of character, talk of portals, or random explosions must be reported. The sooner we figure out what's going on, the sooner we will know what we must do. That will be it for now." He nodded as he walked off, and Amala got up swiftly and followed him out of the hall.

"They have no idea what they're doing," Cassius said.

"What do you mean?"

"They want us to act like spies? Skulking round the place? I'm not doing that, man."

"Why not?" Marcus asked, increasingly frustrated with Cassius's lack of commitment to the group.

"You still don't get it, do you? They are making all the rules here." Cassius pointed an accusing finger after the two adults. "They are controlling us! They're not asking us to get involved. They're *demanding* it. You want to live like this? Being told what to do constantly? Grow a pair, bro!"

Marcus clenched his jaw. "You need to sort yourself out," he said through gritted teeth. "Otherwise, I'm going to make you leave."

Cassius smirked and lay back in his chair. "*They* won't let you do that. *They* make the rules."

The End

Thank you so much for reading Rising Warrior: The Ebun Chronicles. I hope you enjoyed it!

It would mean so much to me if you could leave a review on Amazon. Just a few words really help small indie authors like myself. You can do that here.

If you want to discover more about the Orisha's involvement then you can read the exclusive short story: Orisha: Fate of the Gods, by signing up for my newsletter here, and you will be the first to read it. You will also be notified of more upcoming books in this series coming very soon.

About the Author

You can connect with me on:
- https://www.kmhamiltonauthor.com
- https://www.instagram.com/authorkhamilton
- https://www.tiktok.com/@kmhamiltonauthor

Also by K M Hamilton

Printed in Great Britain
by Amazon